FATKINI

THE FATKINI CHRONICLES
BOOK 1

MONICA ROSS

This is a work of fiction. The names, characters, places, and incidents are either the product of the author's imagination or are used fictitiously and are not to be construed as real. Any resemblance to persons, living or dead, actual events, locales or organizations is entirely coincidental. The author and publisher do not have any control over third party websites or their content.

Copyright © 2023 by Monica Ross (aka Monica Enderle Pierce)

Editor: Mel Sanders

Proofreader: Lea Vickery

Print ISBN-13: 978-1-7342440-2-1

Alt ISBN: 979-8-2236049-8-3

All rights are reserved to the author. No part of this book may be used or reproduced in any manner whatsoever without written permission except in the case of brief quotations embodied in critical articles and reviews.

For all the curvy ladies.
Know what you want and ask for it.
You deserve no less.

1

WHALES DON'T BELONG ON THE BEACH

GOOD GODDAMN, I thought, *sex should not be boring.*

At least not according to the books I narrated for a living. But I lay staring at the ceiling while Tristan screwed me with as much gusto as an eighth grader taking an algebra test, and I was B-O-R-E-D bored.

Anemic morning light filtered past the room's dark-blue, floor-length curtains. Early October rain drummed on the townhouse roof and pinged off the gutters. Across the driveway, a garage door rattled open, a car engine revved, then the garage door clattered and thudded shut as one of my neighbors left for work.

Seattle was waking up and starting its day.

I was flat on my back, legs spread, getting nothing.

I sighed. *It really shouldn't be like this.*

My boyfriend of two years was what dreams were made of — six-two with green eyes, an angular jaw, and a body like Thor, the Motherfucking God of Thunder. But Tristan proved looks weren't everything. Turns out giving a shit counted for a whole helluva lot more than a pretty face did.

Tris came with a grunt, rolled off me, and sat up. It was his day off, and hoping to interest him in getting me off too, I caressed the hills and valleys of his wide, pale back. He was a personal trainer and it showed on every inch of his lean, muscular body.

"What's your hurry?" I murmured, hoping I sounded alluring.

He glanced over his shoulder at me, then stood. "Going for a run."

Okaaay, looked like Zelda's orgasm was off the Monday morning schedule.

I threw back the covers. "I'll come with you."

"No." He tugged up his boxers.

His curt tone stung. "Why not?"

"Because I don't want to run with you today."

He never wanted to do anything outside the house with me anymore. "Sometimes I think you don't want to be seen with me." The bitter words slipped out before I could stop them.

He pulled his shirt down then leaned over the bed, fists planted on the mattress. "Zel, I work out with people all fucking week. Sometimes I just want to set my own pace and run without dead weight."

I pressed my lips together. He didn't look so handsome when he was being an asshole.

Tristan grabbed his red hoodie from the foot of the bed and headed for the door. "Everything isn't about you, Zaftig."

I collapsed back into the bedding and wrapped the yellow comforter around me. It was warm and cushy, but it didn't keep out the chill of his cold shoulder. Nor could it cushion the blow of the nasty nickname.

Zaftig Zel.

I didn't know who started it, but in fourth grade one of the kids learned the word meant plump and juicy. Of course they pinned it to the school's only chubby girl.

Me.

It stuck. And Zelda Claudette Gordon got to be Zaftig Zel for eight long years.

"Fuck-nut." I gnawed my thumbnail. He was perfectly happy to eat my cooking and stick his dick in me, but God forbid I should expect anything in return.

With a delicate trilling meow, Lulu, my little calico kitty, hopped onto the bed and made her way across the mountain of covers to head-butt me. Right behind her and twice her size, Frank launched all fifteen pounds of his furry self onto my stomach.

"Oof! Frank, you're killing me!" He was a tuxedo kitty with white whiskers and white paws that somehow managed to feel like they were crushing my ribs with each step.

The cats smashed their fuzzy faces against my fingers. "It wasn't always like this, right, guys?" They purred in response and Lulu chewed my thumb like a kitten.

No, it wasn't. The first six months were fun. Tristan had reveled in my body. We'd had sex in the shower, on the couch, in the kitchen — all the time. He'd said I was the sexiest woman he'd ever known. That he'd had a crush on me since the day in first grade when I punched Greta Smalls for teasing him.

He'd said being with me was the happiest time of his life. Considering we'd known each other for eighteen years, and I knew what a shitty childhood he'd had, those words meant a helluva lot.

But things had slowly changed. He stopped seeing his therapist and taking his meds. His phone became more interesting than talking or screwing or doing anything with me. Slowly he reverted to the angry guy I remembered from school. The guy who didn't want to love or be loved.

Frank interrupted my dark thoughts with an insistent meow. I glanced at my cellphone. October seventh. Seven forty-five a.m. New day, but same time I always woke. Or rather, same time the little fink got my ass out of bed to feed him and Lulu every morning.

Some things never changed.

Flinging off the covers again, I said, "Okay, okay. I hear ya." I peed then grabbed a heavy, curved hair clip and, with a few deft twists, had my long chestnut hair secured in a bun atop my head. It was wavy and wild, but I liked it long. People always remarked on how lovely my hair was, and my voice, and my face.

What no one talked about was my figure. Except the weird pervy guys — you know, the ones you *don't* want noticing you? I was insanely careful about my eating and ran daily, but genetics made me tall and curvy. I had big tits, full hips, and hadn't had a thigh gap since *ever*.

The fashion industry called me plus size.

My mom called me voluptuous.

And Tristan had just called me Zaftig.

"What a dick."

Was I obese? For my height, not really. But I definitely wasn't what society called slender.

I dragged on a pair of burgundy sleep pants and a black T-shirt, shoved my feet into old shearling boots, and followed the cats downstairs to the kitchen.

Three stories and less than ten years old, the townhouse was my sanctuary. I'd bought it with my own hard-earned money, proof of my success after only a few years in the audiobook business. The wood trim, cabinets, and carpet were shades of gray, and the kitchen, living room, and dining room floors were hand-scraped hickory planks. Color popped in the artwork on the crisp, white walls and on my bedding and throws. I especially loved my blue sofa and loveseat.

After breakfast, I showered and dressed then went down to the office, powered up my computer, and opened my current job file. If I wasn't going to get off, I could at least enjoy telling the story of someone who would.

With headphones on, I lounged on the loveseat and listened to what I'd recorded the previous day. Four chapters awaited editing. I ran the files through proofing software, then listened to the problems it flagged. Most were pickups I needed to edit, but one section had too much mouth noise, so I decided to rerecord it.

If the townhouse was my sanctuary, the ventilated vocal booth in my office was my pride and joy. Covered in dark-gray fabric, it measured six feet by four feet and stood almost to the ceiling. A small table with an adjustable stand for my tablet reader and a comfortable office chair took up most of the interior. Blue pyramid-shaped acoustic foam covered the inside — sound-dampening material to deaden ambient noise. Headphones and a selection of mics hung from wall pegs, and strip lights illuminated the space. I used a separate monitor and mouse to control my computer, which remained outside the booth to prevent fan noise from ruining my audio files.

Inside the booth, silence reigned. The real world slipped away, replaced by the fictional world of Juno Galore, heroine of the fourteenth novel in a reverse harem science fiction series by Drew Katterman. He was prolific and campy and his characters were a hell of a lot of fun to narrate. *Stars and Strippers* was the latest title of his bestselling *Starship Steam* series.

Drew's books had introduced me to reverse harem, and I'd fallen in love with the genre's feisty female characters. These women had multiple lovers and said, "Why the fuck should I choose one man over the rest? If a man can have a harem, so can I." Drew's Juno Galore expected her guys to put her first. If they didn't, she kicked them to the curb.

I closed the vocal booth door and sat at the table. Donning headphones, I pulled up the passage to rerecord on my tablet and turned on the monitor. My digital audio workstation appeared on it. I adjusted my mic, pressed the RECORD button, and returned to Juno's world.

"If Neutron Jon thinks one good shagging will send me head-over-heels, he's a dip-shit." Juno crouched as blaster bolts hit the walls around her, sizzling the wallpaper and frying the green plasteen carpet. Smoke obscured the hallway, but that didn't stop the morons from firing at her. Apparently, seeing what they were shooting at didn't matter. *"Quality over quantity, bitches."* Juno blinked her viz implants over to infrared. Spying a dozen heat signatures, she grinned, aimed, and picked off her enemies.

No, Jon needed to fuck her a lot harder than that if he wanted to keep his place in her harem. She holstered the blaster and made a run for the exit.

Of course, she might just fry the fucker and move on. After all, he'd screwed her over after he'd screwed her this morning. That was just plain rude.

"At least buy a girl dinner." Juno exited the Solaris Science Center into a half-circle of blasters pointing right at her heaving chest.

"Well, fuck me." She started shooting again.

Four hours later, I saved the edited audio files and sent them to Drew for approval, then quit the application and took off my headphones. Only two chapters remained to finish the book. Stretching, I looked through the glass slider to the patio. Seattle remained under dark-gray clouds, but the rain had stopped. Water dripped from red and gold autumn leaves and drops shimmered on the screen door.

I stowed my computer, then went outside for the mail. Orange and purple Halloween lights glowed in the front window of the townhouse opposite mine. A black wreath with white skulls and orange bows adorned another neighbor's front door. Wind whooshed between the two rows of facing townhomes, making me shiver.

A package waited on my front doormat. Picking it up, I smiled when I saw the return address. I'd waited a week for this. The rest of the mail was junk and got tossed in the office recycling bin, then I headed for the master bedroom.

Plastic crinkled as I pulled two items from the package and unwrapped them.

One was a pink wiggle dress with a flared skirt — flirty and a little risqué.

The other was a bigger risk. I laid it across the unmade bed: a purple bikini. Faceted, oval pins embellished its shoulder straps and the bottom, catching the bedroom light and winking at me like diamonds. Definitely sexy. Definitely posh. And definitely scary for a woman called chubby, thick, and big-boned all her life. A woman taught not to wear a bikini. Ever.

But, dammit, Zaftig Zel wanted to live a little and shut up the voices in her head, so I'd planned a vacation with Tristan. Puerto Vallarta was a warm paradise in December, and I needed a swimsuit.

"If this and a few margaritas don't warm his willy, nothing will." I laughed.

The front door slammed.

"Speaking of dicks, mine has returned."

I glanced at the skimpy pieces of purple fabric. Maybe that orgasm wasn't a complete write-off yet. I shed my shirt and pants, and put on the bikini. Pulling and tugging and adjusting and, hmmm, there was a lot less coverage than a bra and panties offered. I chewed my lower lip. Maybe a sneak peek at my PV wardrobe might not be such a good idea. Looking around for my robe, I glimpsed myself in the full-length mirror and stared.

Full breasts, tiny waist, wide hips, and long legs. I took the clip out of my hair and let the reddish-brown waves cascade over my shoulders. I turned and looked at my ass.

Whoa.

"Well, you fill it out, Zel," I mumbled, "that's for sure." *In a good way or bad?* I wasn't sure.

With a deep breath, I screwed up my courage, retrieved my robe from the foot of the bed, and headed down the stairs, lower lip still firmly lodged between my teeth.

Tristan slouched on the blue sofa, texting someone on his phone. He didn't even glance up when I padded into the living room, my bare feet slapping the wood floor.

"Sooo, I got some new things to wear in Puerto Vallarta."

He grunted and stared at the screen, blond hair falling across his face.

"What d'ya think?" I dropped the robe.

He still didn't look at me.

"Tristan?"

I wanted him to grin lasciviously. Hell, let's be honest, I wanted him to pop a boner and give me a preview of the festivities *he* planned for Mexico.

Instead, he dragged his gaze away from the phone and frowned at me. "What is that?"

My brows arched. "A bikini." He wasn't *this* dumb. The smooth fabric felt cool under my fingers. "I haven't had the nerve to wear one since I was a kid." Like pre-Zaftig Zel, to be exact. "But, I dunno, I'm feeling daring. It's our second anniversary and this'll be my first winter vacation." I shimmied my hips, hoping to get a rise from him. "Sunshine and hot sandy beaches while Seattle sits under rainy skies. Aren't you excited?"

He gave me a slow once-over, his green eyes finally stopping on my face. "You bought a fatkini?"

Fuck. Wrong kinda rise.

"A bikini. It's a bikini … to wear in Mexico …." My voice trailed off and my face heated. I folded my arms across my body.

"Zel, it's a fatkini. A bikini chunky girls wear." He shook his head. "Did you get a coverup? Tell me you did."

"What? No." A lump clogged my throat.

His lip curled. "You can't wear that thing. Whales don't belong on the beach. You want everyone to see your body?"

My heart felt like it was being crushed by my ribcage. Blinking back tears I looked down and dragged in a slow breath. "You didn't buy the plane tickets yet, did you." It wasn't a question. He had only one thing to do for our vacation. *One. Fucking. Thing.*

"Eh. No."

Humiliation and rage were having a meeting in my brain to decide which would take the lead on this shit. "Why not?" Oh, yeah, the sudden pounding in my ears and that twitchiness spreading through my body said rage had shoved humiliation aside. For now.

He shrugged and returned his attention to the phone. "Don't know if I want to go."

I grabbed my robe and jammed my arms into its sleeves. "Yeah, I don't want you to fucking go either." I snatched a book off the breakfast bar and threw it across the room. It hit the wall behind him with a satisfying thud. "In fact, I don't want *you*, Tristan. At. All."

That got his attention. "Huh?" He looked up, stupid and confused.

"Whale? *Zaftig?* You have no fucking idea how cruel that is. You clueless dick! If you're embarrassed to be seen with me, at least have the balls to admit it!"

"Why are you so pissed? I was just being honest." He stood. "Some chicks are dolphins and some are whales. Dolphins are tiny and can play in the surf. Whales are big and can't. That's all I'm saying."

I couldn't believe my ears. "Cripes, Tristan. Try a little harder not to be such an unmitigated moron."

He threw up his hands. "Fucking hell. I can't even be honest without you freaking out. How the fuck do you expect this relationship to work, if you get hysterical over a little comment about your body?"

"Honesty shouldn't feel like a kick in the tits!"

"Oh, c'mon, Zel. You're tall, but you're not a *model*. You know that."

"And I appreciate you throwing it in my face."

He shoved his phone into his pocket. "You're way too fucking sensitive."

"No. I'm way too fucking lenient. I'm *done*. We're *done*. Get the fuck outta my house."

"Fine. Whatever. Shit, you're a bitch on your period."

"I'm pissed. That doesn't automatically mean I'm menstruating, you ignorant prick!"

He grabbed his jacket and headed for the stairs. "So glad I didn't move in."

"Me, too!"

The front door slammed.

2

THE UNDISPUTED CHAMPION OF DICKISHNESS

I DON'T KNOW how long I sat on the couch, arms folded, seeing nothing and feeling even less. Long enough for the world to grow dark outside and for my neighbors to return from work. Should I have felt sad or something? After all Tristan and I were together for almost two years.

But, no, I felt *nothing*.

Beside me, Frank yawned and stretched. Lulu looked up with bleary eyes and started purring. "Hello, kitty-kitties," I said and they climbed onto my lap, their little motors buzzing.

I gently tapped Lulu's nose. She slowly closed her eyes, mesmerized. What a weirdo. "You guys always make me smile."

Frank jumped down and trotted into the kitchen. Lulu climbed onto my shoulder and smashed her face against mine.

"Why the hell did I put up with the undisputed champion of dickishness for so long, Lu? It's not like he was nice to me when we were in school. I mean, he was hard to ignore 'cause he was so freakin' good looking, but we had nothing in common. I was into books. He was into vandalism."

Tristan and I ran into each other two years ago when I was house hunting in Seattle. I didn't even know he'd moved south from Bellingham. I stopped for tea at a coffeehouse across from Blue Water Fitness where he worked. He recognized me and bought my drink. We chatted briefly and exchanged numbers, two childhood acquaintances catching up awkwardly. I went off to meet with my realtor, not really thinking anything would come of our encounter. But he texted a few days later with an address; one of his clients was selling her townhouse. It was perfect. I bought it and invited Tristan over for dinner to thank him for the referral. For some reason we just kept seeing each other until we ended up the unlikeliest couple.

Honestly though? I was never friends with Tristan Blaylock. Not in elementary, middle, or high school. And, apparently, not as an adult either.

I'd stuck it out because we had history. Plus, I liked knowing Zaftig Zel was fucking the hottest guy from my high school class. Never mind that we'd graduated six years ago and I rarely saw anyone from school anymore. Yes, it was petty, but can't a girl gloat every once in a while?

I also wasn't a do-shit-halfway kinda person. I'd committed to the relationship. If I walked away from everything that got tough, I wouldn't have a six-figure income.

What can I say? I relish a challenge.

And Tristan Blaylock was definitely a motherfucking challenge.

"But sometimes, you gotta walk away, Lu, for your own sanity." I stood and carried her into the kitchen. "Not all wars are winnable."

While the cats chowed down on kibble and canned food, I raided the freezer. Two heaping spoonfuls of chocolate ice cream later — Tristan's junk food — I didn't feel any happier or sadder. So I made some tea and returned to my recording booth.

When I was nineteen, I'd met a woman who made her living as a narrator. She did commercial narration and was trying to break into audiobooks. I'd never considered being an audiobook narrator but was intrigued. After all, I'd been in chorus and drama all through high school, so why not try this? I'd signed up for a class, which led to a couple more classes. I put together a demo reel and was booking gigs within weeks.

Turned out, I was pretty fucking good at it. Now, five years later, I had a handful of awards for my work, an agent, and contracts with multiple bestselling authors and New York publishers.

I checked my email. Drew had approved the four new chapters, just like he'd signed off on the rest of the novel. I sent him the chapters as I finished them so he could give me immediate feedback before I got in too deep. I didn't do that with all my authors, but Drew was unique … in more ways than one.

I sat in the booth, put my headphones on, and started recording again.

"A busty brunette with stars in her eyes and endless thighs," Neutron Jon said to the man behind the bar at the Cobalt-Five Dive. "She's unforgettable."

"I know just the woman." The craggy bartender jerked his chin toward the end of the bar.

Jon's gaze followed and there she was, Juno Galore, in a tight red dress with blue hair and a smirk twisting her lips. She raised her glass and her middle finger in his direction.

An hour later the rough file was finished. I wasn't entirely happy with the performance. It felt flat. But I didn't want to rerecord the whole thing just yet. Sometimes when I thought my narration was shitty, if I sat on it for a day then listened back, it turned out to be fine. So I saved the file, planning to come back in the morning and clean it up or rerecord if it really sucked that badly.

When I stepped out of the booth, I noticed Tristan's Seahawks scarf and his anorak hanging on the coat pegs in my hallway. "You know what?" I muttered. "Fuck you. You're outta here."

While fetching empty boxes from the attached garage, I spied his goddamned bike still hanging on the wall.

"Idiot," I muttered, "why the hell didn't you take that when you left?"

I hauled the flattened boxes into the house. It took a little searching to find tape, but soon I was packing everything that asshole had brought into my home.

The first thing to go was the nasty-ass protein powder and bulk-up bullshit powder he kept in the pantry. How many fucking flavors and varieties of that crap did one man need? Hell if I knew or cared. Into the box all of it went. So did his sugary cereal and a box of sandwich cookies, a shit-ton of vitamins and minerals that, I swear, he didn't actually take. He just bought them to make himself feel like he was being healthy.

"Fucking hypocrite." He had some frozen and refrigerated crap. I wanted to get rid of everything, but I was too nice to chuck it in the trash. I organized it onto one shelf in the fridge and one in the freezer, figuring I'd pack that last. Next, I pulled all his dirty clothes out of the hamper in my bedroom, threw that in a box and added his razors, shampoo, soap and deodorant. I made another trip downstairs to the garage for two more boxes, dropping the filled ones on the second-floor landing.

Only the family room remained. The TV was his, and he could have it. I didn't watch television that much and he'd fight me for it. He had a bunch of fucking fitness magazines, and those went in a box with a couple more caps, two pairs of shoes and his hiking boots, his iPad, and his Ultimate discs.

FATKINI

Once I was done, I checked every room for anything I'd missed. When I was sure I had it all, I sat on the couch. I should text him to come get his shit, but I really didn't want to see him again. Maybe I could put it in front of the garage when I knew he was coming and he could pick it up. "Yup," I said, chewing my lip, "that's what I'll do."

But I stared at the phone. I just didn't have the energy to talk to Tristan tonight.

Instead, I texted my mom.

> Hey. I just kicked Tristan out.

Her reply came almost immediately.

> What? Why? What happened, honey?

> He was a dick. Didn't get the vacay tix & called me Zaftig.

> Oh, honey, I'm sorry. Are you okay? Do you want to come up here for a few days?

> No, I'm good. Just wish I figured out what an a-hole he is sooner.

> Well, you always want to think the best of people. You know that about yourself. You're trusting and generous. I don't know who you get that from. *wink wink*

> Ha! True, Mom. It's all your fault.

> Moms always get blamed. I guess that's just part of being a mom.

> I guess. Anyway, just wanted you to know PV is off & I'm gonna eat a ton of junk food tonight.

> Please don't. You know that'll make you sick.

> *sigh* I know. I won't. I ate two scoops of ice cream & feel gross. That's all the pity eating I can stomach.

> Are you sure you're OK?

> Yeah. Bummed but fine. Better to figure it out now, right?

> Right. Listen, your sister will be in Seattle at the end of the month. I'm sure she'd come sooner if you want her company.

"Greer? Oh, hell, no," I muttered. My overbearing half-sister was the last thing I needed.

> No, Mom, I'm good. There's no need for that.

> Are you sure?

> 100%

> Well, if you're sure. Call me tomorrow?

> OK. Love you. Gnight.

> Love you too, hon. Goodnight.

I tossed the phone on the couch. Add that to the list of shit to do tomorrow:

- Fix Drew's book
- Call Mom
- Text a dick about his crap

Frank and Lulu charged across the room, tails high and puffy. Frank stopped in the middle of the rug. Lu tackled him. They rolled around hissing and growling, then sat up on their haunches and played rock 'em sock 'em catbots before charging up the stairs.

I laughed. "Thanks, guys. I needed that."

The book I'd thrown at Tristan lay on the floor by the balcony door. It was a travel guide to Mexico and the cover depicted a sexy, young smiling couple in bathing suits on a white sand beach.

"Fatkini." How could one word fuck up everything and take my confidence from eight to zero in a heartbeat? "Mexico's too sexy for your fat ass," I mocked as I retrieved the book. I wandered into the kitchen and stared at the dishes piled in the sink. Sighing, I decided it was better to do something than nothing. Doing nothing meant letting myself think. And that just led down the drain. If there was one thing I'd perfected as a tall, chubby kid, it was pretending to be tough and happy while actually hating myself and believing I was a freak.

"You gonna let that dick ruin you?"

Silverware rattled in the drawer as I sorted knives, forks, and spoons into their slots.

"Cripes, You wear a size twenty, Zelda. That doesn't mean anything." I guess it was pep talk time. "It's just a number. Like five-eleven. Does that mean you're worthless?"

I didn't have an answer. Maybe because I didn't know a lot of women to compare myself to. There just weren't that many women like me, so I always felt like an elephant in every crowd.

Lulu wandered into the kitchen and looked at me like I was nuts.

"Does being tall and curvy mean ugly and unloveable, Lu?"

She flicked her tail then twined around my legs. I picked her up. "You don't care how fat my ass is, do you." She purred and I scratched.

"Well, maybe my confidence is slightly more than zero. I

did kick that prick to the curb." Guess I'd learned something from narrating all those Juno Galore books.

Frank peered around the corner into the kitchen and meowed.

"You agree?" I put Lulu down. "Good."

She and Frank charged up the stairs again and started a knock-down-drag-out in the hallway.

"And now you're abandoning me?" I called after them. Tristan's stuff would get out of my house soon, then I could move on. No point letting it linger. That was one thing everyone always said about me. I knew how to keep going, even when life got really shitty.

My phone buzzed with a text message from my dad.

> Your mom said you dumped that jackass.

I laughed. Dad's bluntness was rarely charming, but sometimes I could appreciate it.

> Yeah. You were right about him.

> Good. Did you get all his shit out of your house?

Mom said I got my stubbornness from him.

> Not yet. But it's packed into boxes.

> Bet that feels great.

> Yeah. It kinda does.

> That's my warrior princess.

I rolled my eyes at that, but dads ….

> Don't lose your nerve, Punky.

> I won't. You know me, as obstinate as my dad.

> So your mom says. When is he getting his crap?

> Dunno. Need to text him.

> Do it. I'll wait.

> Dad ...

> Now.

The man was fucking pigheaded, but it's what made him a successful intellectual property attorney.

> OK. Hold on.

I texted Tristan:

> Come get your stuff tomorrow. Your bike and TV are here & 6 boxes of crap.

The message was delivered but remained unread while I stared at it, so I went back to my dad.

> No response yet.

> Alright. Give him one week to remove his property. If he doesn't respond, give him 24-hours' notice that you'll donate everything. If he has a problem with that, give him my number.

> Dad ...

> Don't Dad me.

> OK. You're right.

> Of course I am. I'm your father. Get some rest and get your locks rekeyed. If you're feeling down, come stay with us for a few days. Okay? Don't be alone.

> I will and I won't. Mom already offered.

> I love you, Punky.

> Love you too. Thx.

It was only eight o'clock, but I changed into my pajamas and got ready for bed anyway. I put clean sheets on the bed, because I didn't want to smell Tristan, then snuggled under the covers and opened Drew's newest book. I already had the contract to record it.

My phone buzzed.

Tristan.

> Are you kidding, Z?! You threw me away that quickly?

> Why not? You're embarrassed to be with me. Why should I pretend there's anything worth keeping?

> You're one cold bitch.

> And you're a dick. We already covered that.

There was no response for a moment, then he texted:

> You really think you can manage without me?

My jaw dropped. That self-important son of a bitch.

> Yes, since I've been doing exactly that for most of this lousy relationship!

> Whatever. How the hell am I supposed to carry all my stuff on the bus?

> Not my problem.

> Can't you drive it to my place?

I rolled my eyes at his pity party.

> Repeat: Not. My. Problem. Pretty sure u know someone else with a car. Ask one of your gym buddies. Text me when you're coming over. I'll leave your shit in the garage with the door open. Don't come in the house. I don't wanna see u. Leave your key on the hot water heater. I want your crap gone in 7 days or I'll donate it to the Goodwill.

I hit the home button, changed the settings so I would only get notifications from family during the night, then started reading about a woman getting a good, hard fuck from four men and enjoying every minute of it.

3

THE MOST GODLIKE MAN

FRANK MEOWED in my face louder than a freight train. Seven forty-five a.m. I could set the time by him. "Frank, it's Saturday. Why can't you sleep in for once?" I scratched his squishy face and sat up. Stretching, I glanced at my phone. Tristan had finally texted five days after I told him to get his crap outta my house.

> Aithan has an SUV. He'll get my stuff this morning.

Aithan was Aithan Mazur, his boss at Blue Water Fitness. I'd never met the guy.

> I gave him your key & your contact info. He'll be there at 8.

"Are you fucking kidding me?" I muttered then texted:

> WTF? U gave my house key to some dude I don't know?

It took a minute then he replied.

> He's my boss, not a stranger.

> He's a stranger to ME 'cause u never let me go to BWF. Now I know why. Didn't want the guys to see your chubby gf.

> Whatever, Z.

> Srsly? Do u have shit for brains?

> Fuck u.

> No thanks. I'm texting my dad to tell him it's your fault if I end up dead in a ditch.

> Whatevs.

"Fuck." I had fifteen minutes to get dressed and haul all the boxes downstairs.

The doorbell rang.

Aithan Mazur was early.

"Fuckity-fuck-fuck-fuck!"

I yanked on a pair of sweats and shoved my feet into my shearling boots then ran downstairs. I went out on the second-floor balcony. A white Lexus SUV was parked in front of my garage.

"Aithan?"

The most godlike man I'd ever seen stepped back from my porch and looked up at the balcony. "Good morning. You must be Zelda."

With that deep voice he even sounded heavenly. All my nerves sat up like hungry dogs and begged for more.

"Yeah, I just got Tristan's text that you were coming here. Gimme a minute?"

"Sure. No rush. I'm running errands all morning, and my first client isn't until one-thirty."

"Thanks. I just rolled out of bed. Gotta text my dad to let him know who's to blame if I end up dead because my jackass ex gave my house key to a stranger."

He laughed. "Fair enough. Text Dad. Then let me know if you need help hauling boxes."

I smiled. "Thanks. Be out in a few minutes."

He saluted me with a blue travel mug.

I texted my dad, 'cause I wasn't stupid, but I *was* paranoid. Then I put on a bra and a clean shirt and pulled my hair into a ponytail. It wasn't the sexy look I would've chosen if I'd had fair warning that one of the Spartans from *300* would be at my front door, but I couldn't leave Aithan waiting while I got gussied up.

"Fucking Tristan." I descended to the first floor, opened the garage door, and carried out one of the lighter boxes.

Up close, Aithan was even more beautiful. He had the kind of thick dark hair women in romance novels always wanted to comb their fingers through – short on the sides, longer on top, and …. Yeah, okay, that trope was real.

He was taller than me by about six inches and chiseled, but not so bulked up that he couldn't reach his own ass. He had fair skin and the kind of full lips that a girl could sink her teeth into. Five o'clock shadow defined his strong jaw, and thick eyelashes framed his sky-blue eyes.

He had a quiet, confident masculinity that was really fucking appealing after Tristan's aggression and insecurity.

"Thanks for doing this. I hope Tristan is cleaning toilets to repay you."

He put down his coffee and offered an easy smile as he opened the SUV's hatch. "Nah. I just wanted him to stop moping."

I bit my lip. "Sorry about that. Hopefully, he'll get over this quickly."

"Eh, he's allowed to whine a little." His grin was charmingly lopsided and formed a dimple on the right side of his cheek. The man was playing with a loaded deck, I swear. He added, "It helps that he's a good group instructor, or I'd smack him and tell him to snap out of it." He dug into his pocket. "Here's your key. I swear I didn't make a copy."

I took it, trying to ignore the little thrill I got when his fingers brushed mine. "Thanks. I really did text my dad."

"Good. If I was a dad, I'd want to know some strange guy had access to my daughter's house. Dunno how Tristan let such a smart lady escape." He pulled a face. "Wow, that sounded creepy."

I laughed again then pointed at the bike in the garage. "That's his. I'll get the other boxes. The only thing I can't carry down easily is the TV."

"I can get that. No problem."

We loaded everything then went upstairs. While I threw Tristan's cold food in a grocery bag, Aithan crouched to give Frank and Lulu belly rubs and got purrs and head-butts in return.

"Aw, man, you guys are cute." He stood. "I love cats, but one of my roommates is allergic. Otherwise, I'd have three or four or eight."

"You wanna be a crazy cat lady?"

"Totally." He sniffed. "It smells great in here."

"It does?" I inhaled. "Oh, grilled onions. I made pot roast last night."

"Beautiful *and* she cooks? Can't believe Tristan messed this up."

Blushing, I busied myself with the paper bag and watched him from the corner of my eye. Good goddamn, the man was a visual feast. I'd thought Tristan was hot, but next to Aithan Mazur, my ex was chopped liver.

That was the one thing I'd liked about Tristan; he was a good-looking guy. Too bad he was ugly on the inside.

After another appreciative whiff, Aithan hefted the TV and headed for the stairs. I followed, enjoying the view. The man's physique was a marvel, corded muscles flexing under a tight, long-sleeved T-shirt. Hell, he probably had an eight pack that I definitely didn't need to be thinking about.

He loaded the last two items, then closed the back of the SUV and offered his hand. "It was really nice meeting you, Zelda."

I returned his handshake, relieved when he didn't crush my fingers. (Fuck, the guy was a gentleman, too? Not fair.) "Thanks for taking all this stuff and for not being a creeper."

He shrugged. "I'm pretty wholesome."

I laughed. "Wholesome? I can't remember the last time I heard someone called that."

He grinned. His whole face lit up with it, and I think I ovulated. "That's what my littlest sister calls me. She's fourteen."

"Well, I like wholesome. Don't have enough of that in my life."

His smile widened. "Good to know."

"That sounded idiotic, right?"

"Nope, it sounded *wholesome*."

We laughed. He climbed into the SUV and started the engine. I headed into the garage but stopped when I heard his window roll down.

"Zelda?"

I went back outside. "Yeah?"

"You wanna get coffee some time? My treat."

"Coffee?"

"Yeah. You know," he raised his blue mug, "this stuff. Popular in Seattle."

This walking man-god was asking *me* out? Was this a joke? Or did he just smell an opportunity to get some easy tail? "Maybe." I chewed my lower lip. "I mean, it's been less than a week since I split with Tristan." I looked down and kicked a stone across the driveway. "Wouldn't it be kinda bitchy to dump him, then go out for coffee with his boss a week later?"

He smirked and it was so friggin' cute. "That's probably true. And I don't want you to feel pressured, so take your time." He pulled out his phone. "I'll text you so you have my number. The offer doesn't expire."

My phone buzzed in my pocket. "Okay. Thanks, Aithan. For that and for schlepping Tristan's shit. And for being wholesome."

"No worries. See you soon." He rolled up the window and pulled out of the driveway. I closed the garage door and fanned myself.

"Cool off, Zelda. You don't need anymore manly hassle."

The cats assaulted me, meowing and running toward the kitchen when I reached the top of the stairs.

"Oh, shit, you guys. I'm sorry! I forgot to feed you." I opened a can of tilapia and split it between them. Lulu made the little num-num noises she always did when she liked what she was eating. "Aithan is right, you guys are stinkin' cute. And so is he, in a ridiculously sexy and wholesome kinda way." Unless that was an act meant to impress me and get into my pants. "Don't be paranoid," I muttered. "A guy who looks like that doesn't need to lie to get laid."

I shook my head and looked around. Not much had changed without Tristan and his crap. Except the spot on the mantel where the TV once stood. Leaning against the kitchen counter, I downed a glass of water. "Guess I need to get a new TV." But that could wait for a sale.

I glanced at the time. Nine o'clock. Time for a run. I changed, laced up my shoes, and headed for Green Lake. Fall in Seattle was my favorite time of year. The air was crisp but not freezing and the trees morphed from green to brilliant golds, vibrant reds, and deep purples. It was a five-mile run from my townhouse on Phinney Ridge, through Woodland Park, around the Green Lake Loop, and back. I tried to get out every day, even when the weather sucked. I didn't mind running on rainy days, however today was perfect. Cool and gray but not wet.

My phone buzzed a few times while I ran the lake's outer, unpaved trail. I ignored it, figuring it was my parents making sure I was still alive or Tristan bitching. Sunshine and blue sky peeped through breaks in the gray clouds. A breeze made the fall leaves dance and raised small waves on the lake. Ducks glided through the shallows. Dogs barked and people jogged by. Some regulars I nodded to as we passed, people I saw daily but never spoke with. The air smelled sweet and fresh.

When I got home, I peeled off my sweaty sports bras — two of 'em to keep my tits strapped down tight so I didn't get a concussion from boob rebound. I draped the bras and my damp shirt over the open washing machine door.

Boob sweat ranked among the top ten worst things that no one mentioned about having big tits. Sure, guys worshiped a full rack, but they didn't know the downsides of double-Ds. The sweat, the rashes, the painful pendulum effect if those bitches weren't tied down during exercise. Ugh.

I took a long, hot shower, then ate leftover pot roast for breakfast while playing a word game with my family — Mom was winning, Dad was barely ahead, Greer was losing. After making all my moves, I remembered the text that came in while I was running.

It was from Drew Katterman.

> Hey, Brick! I'm in Seattle. Let's get together, babe.

Brick was his nickname for me, short for Brick House. Yes, like the Commodores' song.

"No way."

I quickly typed a response.

> Dude! I'd love to see u. I need some of your I don't give a fuckery right now. Everything's gone to shit with Tristan.

> What? Oh, no, babe. Lunch? Where can u safely eat?

Aww. Drew always remembered that I adhered to an autoimmune diet.

> Are u staying downtown?

> Nope. I'm at a little hotel in Ballard. Got a book signing around here tmrrw.

> Nice! There's a great place on Market Street by the movie theater. Hippy Eats. You'll love it & they know me. Should I pick you up?

> Nah. I'll meet u there. I'm a few blocks from Market. 12:30?

> Perfect!

After we finished texting, I went upstairs to change, because leggings and an old T-shirt wouldn't cut it for a client lunch, even if that client was a laidback friend like Drew. I opted for one of the few outfits I felt really good wearing — skinny jeans tucked into over-the-knee boots, a burgundy sweater, and my favorite leopard-print coat.

Standing before the mirror, I considered my reflection and chewed my lip. As a teen, I used to squeeze into size twelve jeans, look in the mirror, and see an obese girl staring back. In a *twelve*, for fuck's sake! It was still hard not to see myself that way. The internet said I should weigh one hundred forty-nine pounds. What a joke. I think I weighed more than that at birth.

"You look fine, Zelda," I said. "Put away your fat eyes."

That's what my mom said back then: *"Put away your fat eyes, Zelda Claudette. You're not seeing straight."*

I nodded and turned away from the mirror. "You're right, Mom."

I had some time to kill, so I went down to my office and pulled up the book files from yesterday. Listening back, they didn't sound too bad, so I ran them through editing software, cleaned them up, and uploaded them for Drew to listen to.

> Just uploaded the last 2 chapters of Stars and Strippers. Gimme feedback when I see u?

> Done. Thanks! See u soon.

As I shut down my computer and closed up the office, my phone rang. I answered it without checking the caller ID and was greeted by the distinctly imperious — and annoying — voice of Greer, my older half-sister.

"Zel, it's Greer. I'm coming to Seattle at the end of the month. I'll stay with you and we'll work through this mess you've made of your relationship."

"What mess?"

"Mom told me everything. Don't worry. I'm sure I can help."

"Greer, Mom doesn't know everything or you misunderstood her." I rolled my eyes. *Obviously.* "There's no mess to fix. I'm fine and I have a friend visiting. You don't need to fly in."

"I'm flying in for a convention, idiot. But I'll come to your place rather than stay at the hotel."

Jeez-us. Why was she like this?

"You're worse than Mom. I don't need to be babied. I'm fine. I dumped Tristan, not the other way around. And, I told you, I have a friend in town. Stay at the hotel and we can get together for tea."

"Mm. So, I'll see you Friday, October twenty-fifth. Don't worry. We'll fix everything. Bye." She hung up.

I stared at the phone. "*Fix?*" Typical Greer. She never listened to the words coming out of anyone's mouth. On the one hand, she was right about my relationship being a mess. On the other hand, she didn't seem to understand that ending it was the only way to fix it.

My half-sister was five years my senior. Her dad was my mom's second husband. (My dad was Mom's third.) Mom was preggers with me when she and Prentice — Greer's dad — got divorced. I got an overbearing sister who thought my business was hers and was convinced from Day One that I couldn't take care of myself. Seriously. She even talked for me when I was a toddler, which slowed my language development. I had to go to speech therapy because my sister wanted to play mommy.

I tolerated Greer only because I didn't have a choice in who got to be my sister. Fortunately, she lived in the Bay Area, so I only saw her a few times a year.

I sighed and glanced at the time. "Better go." It'd take half-an-hour just to find parking in Ballard at this time of day. I rubbed Frank's and Lulu's bellies then clattered down the stairs to the garage.

At least I had Drew to look forward to.

4

HIS QUINTESSENTIAL WOMAN

DREW GRINNED, though he knew he shouldn't.

Everything's gone to shit with Tristan.

Those words meant pain for Zelda, but they answered his prayers. Not that he prayed much, but he'd been begging his guides, angels, gods, lucky fucking stars — whatever people wanted to call the mojo that kept lining up good shit in his life — to make Brick single while he was still young enough to seduce her.

Drew owned every audiobook Zelda Gordon and her pseudonym, Fannie Gordon, had ever recorded. He couldn't get enough of her sultry voice. The first time he'd heard her — reading an incredibly shitty paranormal romance about gecko shifters, of all things — he'd creamed his jeans and known immediately that she *had* to narrate his novels. No one else would do. No one else had a voice like hers, like velvet and steel.

They'd met in person at an audiobook conference in Los Angeles. Statuesque and curvaceous, Zelda was his quintessential woman. And the fact that the audiobook industry loved her, yet she remained humble and professional, only made her sexier. Her voice was icing on the feminine confection that Zelda Claudette Gordon was in Drew Katterman's mind.

Drew wasn't just smitten. He was head-over-heels, tongue-lolling, eye-popping infatuated with her.

But Zel had a boyfriend. Some douchebag named Tristan. And, despite what people believed about Drew, he wasn't a home wrecker. And Zel? She was faithful to that undeserving fucker, faithful to a T.

Drew hired her to narrate all his books. He kept her very busy. He wrote faster and better because he wanted to hear her voice wrapped around his words. He wanted her working and well paid. He'd determined to be Zel's employer and her friend, and to remain steadfast and stable until that boyfriend screwed up. Then, he'd move in and romance the ever-loving shit out of her.

He listened to Zelda's chapters while he shaved, but stopped the recording halfway into the first chapter. What he heard wasn't Zel's usual fire. The read felt as flat and dry as Texas roadkill in July. He scowled. "Shit, babe, what'd that ass-hat do to you?"

Wearing only his pajama pants, Drew opened his travel bag and pulled out all his clothes. He laid them across the bed. Considering the tee shirts and pants he'd brought, he frowned. These were fine for meeting readers, but not good enough for impressing Zelda Gordon. The whiskey-brown wool car coat, dark wash jeans, and black monk strap shoes would work, but he needed a better shirt.

He glanced at his watch. Just enough time. Drew threw on everything, opting for his vintage Clash tee, and headed for a small men's haberdasher a few blocks away.

Leon's carried a limited but fine selection of clothing and smelled like a manly orange grove wearing new leather shoes. Ignoring the racks of neatly folded sweaters and the color-blocked shirts on hangers against the walls, Drew approached the gentleman behind the counter. "I'm a man with a purpose."

The gent considered him over his horn rims. "Which is?"

"Romance. I've got a lunch date in forty-five minutes and I need something more impressive than the Clash." He tugged on the hem of his tour shirt.

"Price point?"

"Doesn't matter."

The man nodded, his bald pate so clean it caught the light. "Cashmere."

"I like how you think." Drew followed him to a display of sweaters.

The man introduced himself, not ironically, as Leon and suggested a pale-gray or burgundy V-neck with a white or pale-blue dress shirt underneath. "Tie?" he asked.

"No tie."

"Very well."

Drew bought all of Leon's suggestions and left the store wearing gray and white. He had just enough time to drop off his purchases at the hotel before sauntering into Hippy Eats and lucking out with an open table by one of the front windows.

Seattle strolled by — middle-aged millionaires surprised by their good fortune, silver-spoon-sucking twenty-somethings taking money for granted, the muttering homeless losing arguments with themselves. It was a town filled with dichotomies, made rich and unaffordable by billionaires desperate to fix the problems they'd inadvertently created with their own success.

Drew glanced at his phone. Twelve twenty-three. He sipped the coffee the waiter set down in front of him. Its warm, acrid aroma mingled with the restaurant's scents — grilled veggies, lentil stew, and fresh bread.

He frowned and returned to scanning the sidewalk, not really noticing anyone because none of them were Zelda. He knew her face, her figure, and her voice, could pick her out in a crowd.

His girlfriend, Livi, resented his infatuation. She more or less ignored the infrequent lovers he took, but something about Zelda stuck in her craw.

"What the hell bothers you so much about her?" he'd asked a few nights ago.

Livi shrugged, her straight platinum hair swinging across her back. "It's not her that bugs me. It's you."

"Me?"

"You're always different when you talk about her."

"Different how?" He knew the answer, but he wanted to know if she did.

Livi had sat up and pulled her silk robe around her thin shoulders. "She's all you think about after you've talked to her. You're not like that with other lovers, and she's not even your lover!" She'd thrown up her hands and slipped from his bed, gone to the window and stared out at a rainy day as she lit a cigarette.

"Don't smoke in the apartment. You know it violates my lease."

She flipped him off, but stubbed it out anyway and opened the window. The noise of Manhattan rolled in — cars, horns, people — a ceaseless cacophony. The noise irritated him more and more lately.

So did Livi.

She crossed her arms and leaned against the sill, facing him. "Why don't you just fuck her already?"

"She has a boyfriend."

"So?"

"So she doesn't sleep with other people. She's devoted to just him."

Livi's lip curled. "Old-fashioned. She sounds boring. Why do you obsess over someone who's so fucking dull?"

He fell back into the pillows and put his hands behind his head. "Zel's not boring or old-fashioned. She's ... perfect."

"Ugh. You sound like a middle schooler with a crush. Fuck her mouth. Eat her pussy. Tell her it's not sex, so she wasn't cheating, and get over your stupid infatuation with her. It's been going on for too fucking long and I'm sick of it."

She'd left to meet up with her Norwegian boyfriend, and Drew had flown to Seattle.

Now he sipped a dirty coffee and scanned the sidewalk.

And there was Zel, striding past a young couple who were walking two chihuahuas dressed in matching striped dog sweaters.

Skinny blue jeans hugged her curves. Brown leather boots rose up her impossibly long legs to cover her knees. A wine-red, V-neck wrap sweater accentuated her perfect breasts. And a leopard print swing coat gave her sass. She usually wore her chestnut curls long and today they cascaded loosely around her shoulders.

Zelda Gordon was exquisitely fuckable, and Drew couldn't imagine anything more glorious than being balls-deep in her, lips on her skin, and hands wrapped in all that gorgeous hair.

He couldn't stop the shit-eating grin that spread across his face as she stepped into the restaurant and looked around. She spied him and returned his smile.

"Brick." He stood and opened his arms. She slipped into the hug and he resisted grabbing two handfuls of luscious ass. Still, he held her close, loving the feel of her ample breasts against his chest, the cashmere against his skin. He inhaled. Like always, she smelled like vanilla and cinnamon. "You smell like a fucking bakery."

Zel ran her fingers across his sweater. "And you feel expensive."

Yep, cashmere had been the right call. "Pet me all you like, babe."

She laughed. "Tempting."

Reluctantly, he let her go, and they sat.

The waiter greeted Zel by name and set a white teapot before her. She returned his pleasantries and filled a teacup, adding a spoonful of honey.

"What's good?" Drew asked her.

"Everything. Want me to order for you?"

He closed his menu. "Do it." While she chose their lunch, he studied her face. She was even more beautiful than he remembered. Ivory skin and bow lips; perfect, high cheekbones; and eyes as turquoise as the waters of the Caribbean. He wondered, fleetingly, what he'd do about Livi. She wanted to have her lovers without giving him any say. Which was fine, as long as it went both ways, but she felt threatened by his friendship with Zelda and made little effort to hide it.

Drew was losing patience with his girlfriend.

Zel finished ordering, handed the menus to the waiter, and smiled at Drew. "How's writing going? And sales? You on track to break eight?"

She meant an eight-figure salary. They joked about it all the time. How he was a rich bitch but owed it all to her. Considering he consistently ranked among the top five audiobook authors worldwide, he wouldn't argue with her.

"Getting there, babe. Probably has nothing to do with my sultry narrator, though."

Her eyes gleamed over the rim of her teacup as she sipped hot tea. She lowered the cup. "You lying little bitch. I should raise my hourly rate just for putting up with your bullshit."

Drew laughed. "Probably." He savored more of the dirty coffee, enjoying the sensation of espresso combining with whole milk in his mouth. The drink was hot, cold, bitter, sweet. Perfect.

The waiter brought an appetizer. Sliced pears wrapped with arugula and prosciutto.

"This is some good shit," Drew said after eating two.

"I know, right?" Zel finished one and licked her fingers.

While he loved that she didn't act demure around him, didn't she know what she was doing to him? He shifted in his seat, aware of the growing tightness in his jeans.

But Drew didn't miss the tension in her jaw and the way she tried so hard to act relaxed. Whatever her dick-wad ex had done, it had rattled her. It came through in the last two chapters she'd sent him. They were far below her usual standards. Anyone unaccustomed to Zelda Gordon's narration would've thought they were fine, but he knew her and he knew better.

This it was something he'd never heard before from his narrator, and judging by the way she avoided his gaze and kept her arms crossed protectively, Zel remained rattled.

Their food arrived and they dug in. She'd gotten him the Kobe burger and he was not disappointed. She was tucking into a salad with grilled chicken and artichoke hearts. They ate for a few minutes, only pausing to remark about how good the food was.

He'd have to bring up the chapters and her lackluster performance, but he hated upsetting her. Still, if there was one thing he knew about Zel, it was how much professional pride she took in her work. She'd be pissed if he let her half-assed narration slide.

So he downed the rest of his coffee and sat back.

Time to rip off the bandage.

5
___

TENDERNESS

AFTER CHITCHATTING about the industry and Drew's sales, which continued to line his pockets with fat stacks of cash, he finished his dirty coffee and sat back in his seat. "I listened to the last two chapters. Honestly, they suck, Zel. You completely lost your mojo and they're flat as fuck. What happened?"

The salad and grilled chicken I was motoring through lost all flavor when that bit of criticism bellyflopped into my lap.

To be fair, he was right.

But *ouch*.

I put down my fork. "Fucking Tristan happened."

"Tell me," he said around a mouthful of burger. Drew rarely worried about being couth. It wasn't like he needed to impress me or anyone else.

He stood an inch taller than me and had fair skin covered in tattoos. His eyes were the soft green of sea glass, and his hair was dirty blond and cut like Aithan's fade, only shorter all around. He usually sported a beard of some kind. Today, he'd trimmed it close to his jawline. Wearing a gray cashmere sweater over a white dress shirt, he looked expensive. Of course, the man could fill out a three-piece suit like God made him and it for sin.

Drew was very easy on the eyes. Not beautiful like Aithan Mazur. Rougher. More raw-edged, I guess. He had this wild, anything-goes vibe, and a grin that could melt a woman's ovaries. He was impish and sexy at the same time, and being around him raised my spirits.

"We were supposed to go to Puerto Vallarta in December." I tracked a drop of water as it wept down the side of my glass. "I had the whole anniversary trip planned out. All he had to do was buy the plane tickets. Motherfucker couldn't even manage that."

"Too broke?"

"Too embarrassed."

Drew's face screwed up. "Huh?"

"I bought a bikini for Mexico. I modeled it for him, thinking it would get him more excited about the trip. You know what he said?" He shook his head, and I continued bitterly. "It was a fatkini — a bikini worn by fat chicks — and whales don't belong on the beach." The table got blurry and I grabbed my napkin to blot my eyes. "Fuck," I whispered. Thank God we were in a booth. I hated making a scene, but Drew didn't seem fazed by my sudden waterworks.

"Aw, hell, Brick. You don't deserve to be cut up like this. That sad sack didn't know how good he had it and you're definitely better off without him. Boy's got shit for brains if he can't see how beautiful and amazing you are."

I laugh-cried at that. "Thanks. I don't know why I'm crying. He's not worth it."

"You got invested in the relationship because you never do things halfway." He offered his napkin.

I waved it away. "I'm okay. Not wearing mascara, so the only loss was my eyeliner."

"You don't need makeup, babe. Your face is perfect no matter what."

"Thanks."

"Just calling it like I see it. I've been trying to get in your pants since the day we met."

I laughed. It was true. He was an unbelievable flirt.

He sat back. "Let's finish lunch, then go back to your house and go over those chapters. Let me help you reconnect with your mojo."

"And Juno?" I meant his main character.

"Her, too."

He paid the waiter, against my protests, and we walked back to my car. Drew looped my hand through his arm and kept me close. My boots made me a little taller than him, but he didn't seem to mind as he strolled beside me, chin up, shoulders back, strutting like a motherfucking rooster.

"You're acting like we're together," I remarked.

"'Cause we are."

"No, I mean *together* together."

He grinned. "I'm acting like a man who's proud to have a beautiful woman on his arm, Zel. It's the way a guy *should* act when he's with you."

Then, in typical Drew Katterman fashion, he changed the subject, giving me whiplash. "You finished reading *Meteors and Mistresses*?"

That was his latest title. "I'm halfway. Juno just blew up the spaceport then blew the dude with two cocks."

"Tentacles."

"Tentacles. Cocks. C'mon, admit it. He's a jock with two cocks."

Drew snickered. "Yeah, totally two cocks. Kinda makes you wonder why she needs a harem in this one."

"Not true. She gets different things from all her lovers. Mr. Two Cocks brings extra fun to her bed when no one else is home."

"Better than a dildo."

"I hope so."

He waggled his brows at me. "Trust me, I know so."

I shook my head. "You're a terrible flirt."

Drew pressed his hand to his chest in mock pain. "How can you say that? I'm an excellent flirt. A professional!"

"World class?"

"Abso-frickin-lutely world class."

We got into my blue Mini and I drove home.

"I get the feeling Juno's gonna add Mr. Two Cocks to her harem, even though they don't like him. Am I right?"

Drew rested his hand on my seat, fingers tucked under my right thigh. "You want me to spoil it for you?"

"Yes. Wait ... no."

He chuckled. We came to a red light. He leaned close and whispered, "You like to be teased, Zelda Claudette Gordon."

I shivered as his warm breath brushed my ear. His gaze flicked from my eyes to my mouth and back.

"What are you doing, Drew?"

"Flirting, Brick." His smile was sexy and knowing. He slowly leaned back and nodded toward the windshield just as the car behind me honked. "Green light."

Shit. I accelerated a little too hard. He was being pretty fucking unsubtle about his interest. Of course, this was Drew Katterman. He'd always been a touchy-feely guy and hadn't hidden his attraction to me. But that had never led to anything.

Because you didn't let it, moron, my brain pointed out.

I asked, "Why?"

"Why am I flirting with you now?"

"Yeah."

"Whenever we saw each other before, you were committed to that douchebag, and you know I wasn't gonna get in the middle of that. Plus, you wanted to prove that your success wasn't earned by boinking me. Now, Tristan's out and you're a respected world-class narrator. So I'm making a move I've been wanting to make for years, Zelda."

I pulled the car into my garage and turned off the engine. Resting my hands on the steering wheel, I looked at the white wall for a long moment. "I just broke things off with Tristan a week ago. I'm not looking for a rebound."

"Me neither."

"I don't really know what to think about this."

"Maybe that's your problem. You overthink everything." He got out of the car and came around to open my door.

I climbed out, unsure of what he would do, but Drew just closed the car door behind me and followed me into the house. I felt jumpy and self-conscious, which I'd never felt around him before. But he'd made me suddenly very conscious of my body ... and his.

"Relax," he said as we reached the main floor. "Make some tea. Let's just hang out and talk."

I put the kettle on to boil and pulled out my tea selection while Drew hummed and found the mugs.

"I'm not gonna jump you, Brick."

"You're not?" I wasn't sure if I was relieved or disappointed. I mean, hell, I'd be lying if I said I wasn't attracted to him from the moment we met.

He laughed. "Not yet." He leaned against the counter beside me and elbowed me gently. "Don't get me wrong, I definitely want to. But if and when we fuck are your choices. I won't be another reason for you to hate sex."

"I don't hate sex." I couldn't look him in the eye when I told that lie.

"Ah, but you wouldn't say you love it, right?" When I didn't argue, he continued. "You never learned to love fucking because you've never had a man care enough to put your pleasure first."

"Ouch." I glanced at him.

"Painfully close to the mark?"

I put the teabags into the mugs and nodded. That question shouldn't surprise me. Drew saw things other people missed.

He dug deeper for the truth with his next one. "Is it totally their fault?"

I looked up. "What do you mean?"

"I mean, Zel, did you tell them what you wanted? Did you ask for satisfaction? Or did you think you didn't deserve to feel good because you heard you were fat and ugly so many times that you believed it?"

I swallowed and couldn't meet his eyes again. It was too hard. "How did you know?" I whispered.

Drew reached past me to turn off the flame under the kettle. He took hold of my shoulders and gently turned me to face him. His hands slid up to cup the sides of my neck. "Because I've been there, babe. We've talked about it. I was a scrawny, scared kid who got the crap kicked outta him daily at home. My dad called me all the names. I hid from my misery inside make-believe worlds."

"Yeah." I bit my lip. "I find it hard to think of you that way."

"Me, too, which is why I don't talk about my childhood. It was violent, it sucked, and it's history. Therapy is my favorite hobby. I started writing to purge the monsters from my mind. Turns out my books help other people, too. And the tats?" He touched his inked forearm. "They hide a lot of scars.

"Here's the thing," he continued. "Along the way, I learned I was worthy of love and pleasure. And I realized a lot of the people I met didn't know that about themselves. You're no exception, Brick, but you are exceptional."

I shook my head. "No, I'm not."

"Yeah, babe, you really are. The allure of your voice is only superseded by the sexiness of your body."

He brushed my hair back from my face with a tenderness no man had ever shown me. I just stood there staring at him, unable to come up with a response.

"Now, I'm going to kiss you, Zelda Gordon. Unless you

ask me not to?" He waited, head cocked, brows arched, his fingers resting on my skin, a butterfly's caress.

"I ... don't know what I want."

"That's okay. Let's start with a kiss and go from there. You tell me to stop or go. I'll do whatever you say." His face drifted closer as he spoke until his breath brushed my lips when he added, "I just want to make you feel good." He kissed me gently, lovingly. His mouth wasn't greedy or aggressive, but it held a question: *Do you want more?*

A voice in my head answered, *No. Stop! What are you doing? He'll see your fat body. He'll know Tristan's right.*

As if he heard my vicious thoughts, Drew pulled back just a little and murmured, "It's okay, Zel. Take your time, but tell that voice in your head to shut the fuck up."

I opened my eyes to meet his gaze. Stepping into his touch, I pressed my mouth to his. I wanted this, had wanted it — *him* — for a long time. And I really wanted to silence all those self-doubts once and for all.

Drew pulled me close. His tongue teased my lower lip and slipped past my teeth. Our tongues touched and I sighed.

His hands went to my waist and he lifted me to sit on the counter. Surprised, I squeaked, and he chuckled against my mouth.

"Wrap those long, luscious legs around me. We're moving this to the couch."

I hesitated. "I can walk."

"I know." His lips drifted from my mouth to my jaw and teased their way down my neck. "Don't care. I wanna put my arms around you and get a good handful of ass."

I panicked. "I'm too heavy. You'll hurt yourself."

Drew stopped kissing and eased back. He gave me a slow searching look. "Brick, let me worry about how much I can carry."

"But—"

He slid his thumb over my lips to quiet the next protest.

"That's the voice in your brain. Silence it, babe. It's not doing you any favors."

I chewed my lip. "I don't know if I can."

Sliding his hands under my thighs, he leaned close again and gave me a feral grin. "Then I guess I'll have to do it for you."

With that he lifted me off the counter. I gasped and grabbed hold with my legs and arms. Drew just chuckled again, then crashed his mouth against mine.

He crossed the room with me like I weighed nothing, turned, and sat on the blue leather couch.

"Leather. Niiice." Cupping the nape of my neck, he held my gaze. "Any other worries?"

"Um. Protection?" I had an IUD, but that didn't prevent STDs.

"Got it covered." He pulled a condom from his pants pocket. Did he always carry them or had he planned on us ending up in bed?

Drew dragged his finger to the tip of my chin and tilted my face up until I met his gaze. "Zelda, you doing okay?"

Aside from hyperventilating? I nodded a little too vigorously. "Yeah."

"You wanna keep going? Or should I stop? You're in control of this."

Feeling nervous as fuck, I weighed the options. I hadn't been with very many men before Tristan. A six-month boyfriend in the last year of high school, a handful of one-nighters, and a few make-out sessions that led to nothing. Drew was different. He cared about me, about my comfort and my pleasure. But what if he didn't like what he saw once I was naked? Or realized how vanilla I was in bed if we really got going? Yet every time he touched me, my nerves zinged from my brain to my crotch. He knew how to excite a woman, and I knew what kind of sex he enjoyed — I'd narrated scenes that would make a hooker blush.

And I'd be lying if I said the idea of getting fucked like Juno Galore didn't make my panties wet. They most certainly were.

So, I sucked in a breath, leaned forward, and murmured, "Keep going," before running my tongue across his lower lip.

He groaned and pulled our bodies together. "I'm gonna give you the best fuck you've ever had."

6

TELL ME WHAT YOU LIKE

DREW FOUND the bow holding my sweater closed and pulled it apart, unthreading the length that wrapped around my waist and exposing my nude bra.

"Good God, you're beautiful." He brushed his fingers over my breasts and kissed me. My nipples hardened under his touch and I moaned into his mouth.

He pushed the sweater from my shoulders and arms, then slid his hands around my back, pausing to unhook my bra before continuing their upward slide. He shoved his fingers into my hair and made an appreciative little noise in his throat.

"I've wanted to get a good handful of this glorious hair for way too long." He pressed his face to my curls. "Fuck, you smell amazing, Brick." He tilted my head back, trailed his lips along my jaw, and nipped down my throat, murmuring, "Definitely something I want to eat."

Gooseflesh rose all over my body and I shivered.

Good goddamn, he knew what he was doing. I definitely was not bored.

Now his fingers played along my loose bra straps. He met and held my gaze. "Tell me what you like, Zel."

I licked my lower lip and he growled as his gaze followed the slow trace of my tongue.

"Tell me."

"Giving head."

His eyes closed and he released a slow breath. But when he met my gaze again, he surprised me by saying, "That has to wait."

"Why?"

"I have a rule. No BJs and cock stays wrapped until we've both had our junk tested for STDs. I'll never make anyone sick with my dick, babe."

"Oh." I smiled and bit my lip. "I tested clean last month." My breath hitched on the last word as he eased off my bra. Self-consciousness surged and I fought an overwhelming urge to cover myself with my arms.

He caressed my breasts. "Perfect. You are absolutely perfect." His tongue found my right nipple and I arched against his mouth. Evidently, noticing my brain's confusion, my body took control and responded to Drew's touch on its own.

"What else do you like?" he asked again, his lips drifting up to my jaw, his fingers stroking my hard nipples and sending jolts straight to my crotch.

"Doggie style," I panted, suddenly very much wanting to feel him inside me.

"Oh, yes, that I can do, but your knees deserve a nice soft mattress." He set me on my feet then stood, swept me into his arms like a fucking bride, and headed for the stairs.

I panicked again. "I'm too big," I squeaked.

He just strode across the room and started upward. "Hush, Zelda's brain. No one wants your opinion."

I giggled, wrapped my arms around his shoulders, and trailed the tip of my tongue over his ear.

"Damn, Brick." He slowed and squirmed. "Wait 'til I reach the landing. You're making my knees weak with that tongue."

In my room, Drew set me on my feet beside the bed, then pulled his gray sweater over his head and unbuttoned his dress shirt. Holy crap, I'd never seen all his tattoos. His torso was covered — chest, back, and both arms. Rocket ships, asteroids, goddesses, and dragons. A triquetra atop a golden chrysanthemum on his ribs, and a sweet little angel holding a blue bird on his right shoulder were the only ones sporting color. The rest were black and gray.

Before I could get distracted by all the glorious ink, he hooked his fingers in my waistband and pulled our hips together. There was no missing his erection. The man was as hard as a rock.

"Time to lose these." He unzipped my jeans and worked them and my panties off my hips. He helped me step out of them then slowly stood, his hands running up my bare legs, his lips brushing my skin — knee, thigh, hip, belly. He lingered on my breasts, kissing and sucking and making me sigh.

Drew straightened and cradled my face, his green eyes searching mine with tender intensity. "Do you still want this, Zel?"

Fuck, he was handsome and *kind*. Why had I waited so long to touch this man?

In response to his question, I unbuttoned his jeans, lowered the zipper, and pushed them off his fine, tight ass. His cock tented his boxer briefs and I freed it from its striped cloth cage. Thick and upstanding as a general, with dark short-and-curlies he kept neatly trimmed.

"That's one impressive dick, Mr. Katterman," I murmured.

He smirked. "Thank you." Off went his jeans and boxers. "What's really impressive is what I do with it."

"Oh?" My gaze returned to his as he straightened. "Is that a promise?" I took hold of his cock. Slowly stroking and squeezing, I watched his eyes flutter closed. His skin was silky, but the muscle beneath was hard, his pulse keeping an excited beat beneath my fingers.

"Goddamn, babe, you're doing me in." He cupped the nape of my neck and kissed me, fiercely this time, his tongue stroking mine, his lips demanding more. He walked me backwards until my legs bumped the bed. "Turn around," he said against my mouth.

I let go, faced the bed, and we both climbed atop, our movements in unison, our bodies pressed together. The crinkle of the condom wrapper proved he was a man of his word.

"Wrapped tight and ready to go." He moved me up toward the pillows and guided my hands to the top of the fabric headboard. "I'm gonna worship every beautiful inch of you, Zelda Gordon." His hands caressed my shoulders, my ribs, my back and breasts. "Inside and out." He kissed my spine from nape to tailbone, lingering on the dimples just above my ass. His fingers slipped between my thighs and into my folds. He stroked my clit, sending bolts through my belly and releasing a sigh from me.

Then Drew's cock nestled against my opening and teased me for a hot minute before sliding inside. He took his time, feeling every inch of me, letting me revel in the delicious stretch as he filled me until he was balls deep. Then, languidly, he withdrew and repeated the stroke.

He groaned. "Fuck, you feel amazing."

I couldn't even form a reply. My brain was transfixed by what Drew Katterman's cock was doing to my body. No one had ever made love to me like this. Hell, no one had ever made love to me, *period*. This was what sex was meant to be. This was what Drew wrote about in all his books, what he seemed to know I was missing. Two people connected physically and emotionally, two people enjoying each other's and their own bodies.

I moaned as his lips found my neck and his hands cupped

my breasts. I didn't worry about him seeing my pudgy ass, my jiggling tits, or my thick thighs. I focused only on the growing tension at my core, the clench of my muscles around his cock, the slow, sure stroke of him in and out of my body.

"Drew," I panted.

"Let go, babe," he whispered in my ear. "Let me make you feel good. Cum for me, Brick. You're perfect and kind and beautiful and you deserve this."

"That feels so fucking good."

"God, yes." He shifted his hips and I thought I'd crawl right up the wall. I don't know if he'd found the fabled G-spot or fucking nirvana. Whatever his cock hit, my body bucked against him and a gasp tore from my throat. This was no measly tingle, there and gone again in a blink. No, this was a fucking avalanche of sensation, and Drew noted my reaction. He grabbed my hip with one hand and wrapped the other around my chest, then increased his speed, all languor gone. Long, sure strokes pushed me further into ecstasy and my muscles locked onto his cock. I arched and pushed back against him, fucking him as much as he was fucking me.

His teeth found my neck and the pinch on my skin shoved me over the edge into an abyss of pleasure. My orgasm broke in waves and dragged a cry from deep within me. I reached back and grabbed his thigh as he thrust into me, driving the waves until he, too, crested. With a low groan, he drove deep into my body one last time and came, holding our bodies together, his mouth on my skin, his breath hot and ragged.

When the tremors finally eased, we sank to the bed and Drew pulled out. He wrapped the yellow comforter around us and spooned against me, kissing my shoulder and neck and confessing against my skin.

"I've jerked off so many times while dreaming about doing you, but my imagination conjured a weak story compared to the real thing."

I smiled and rolled over to meet his gaze. Trailing my

fingers down his nose, over his beautiful mouth, and across his scruffy chin, I said, "You're the first man to ever make love to me."

He gifted me with a dazzling smile and a sweet, lingering kiss. "Glad I could show you what all the fuss is about."

I nodded. "Oh, yes. I can learn to love sex if it's gonna be like this every time."

He snuggled me closer. "Sometimes it'll be even better."

"Mmm, nice. I think you're gonna need a lot more condoms."

"My thoughts exactly."

7

SHE'S A REAL BITCH

"*GÓWNO*. WHAT AM I MISSING?" Aithan muttered as he considered the stairs leading up to Tristan's front door. Everything he'd seen of Zelda said she was smart, capable, and stunning. In all the time he'd employed Tristan, the guy had been a reliable worker and an excellent group trainer. So how had their relationship gotten so screwed up that she'd kicked him to the curb with blinding speed?

He stepped from his SUV, opened the back, and pulled out the TV. "Something doesn't make sense," he muttered and headed up the stairs.

Tristan met him at the front door and took the TV. "Thanks for hauling all this, man. I hope Zel didn't hassle you too much."

"Nah, no problems at all. She carried down the boxes. Seems like a nice girl."

"She's not. She's a real bitch when she's not getting things her way. Totally insecure." Tristan trotted down the stairs and headed for the open SUV. Aithan slowly followed. Tristan hefted three stacked boxes. "She's an actress of sorts, so don't let her fool you, man. She's good at playing the perfect, put-together professional chick. But her head's a real fucking shit show."

Aithan pulled out the bike and followed Tristan back up the stairs. His impression of Zelda didn't match the picture the dude was painting of her. "Honestly, she seems really cool. I'd've been ticked off if I only had a few minutes of warning before some strange guy showed up at my house. But your ex just rolled with it."

"She was putting on a show for you." Tristan dropped the boxes in the foyer and headed back down for more.

After they'd unloaded everything, Tristan shouldered his gym duffel bag and they headed to Blue Water Fitness. They drove in silence for a while. Tristan stared out the window and Aithan navigated Seattle's traffic.

Towering construction cranes dotted the port city's evergrowing modern skyline. Glass-and-concrete condos replaced rickety wooden houses along Aurora Avenue. Cars sped past on the narrow Aurora Bridge, crossing high above Lake Union.

As Aithan exited onto Bridge Way and slowed with traffic heading into Fremont, his curiosity got the best of him. "So, you can tell me to keep my nose out of it, but I gotta ask. What happened between you two?"

"Zel doesn't like the truth, especially if it's critical of her. She asked my opinion about something. I gave it, honestly. It wasn't what she wanted to hear and she went ballistic." He looked back at Aithan. "She'd rather I lie than give her an honest answer." He scratched his jaw. "I'm relieved it's over between us. I couldn't keep up the charade anymore."

"What charade?"

Tristan remained silent for a long moment. "That I was attracted to her." He shrugged. "You saw her. Chubby ain't my jam, and Zel's body definitely needs improvement. I mean, her face is pretty enough, but the rest is ...." He shrugged again. "I only stayed because she can't make it alone, and she gives head better than any other woman who's ever sucked my cock."

Aithan schooled his expression and just grunted in response. Granted, Zel wasn't a hard-bodied gym rat, but she was far from obese. She was statuesque and curvy, and she definitely wasn't ugly. She had wild, wavy reddish-brown hair that Aithan wanted to wrap around his fingers. Her smile was broad and bright behind full, sexy lips. And he admired her willingness to kick Tristan out and not waver on that decision. Plus, her voice was out-of-this-world sultry.

"What about her voice?" he asked.

"What?" An edge crept into Tristan's tone. "Her *voice*? Fuck that," he muttered. "Everyone talks about her *amazing* voice." He jabbed his finger at Aithan. "It ain't so sexy when it's bitching at you about every fucking little thing you do wrong."

"Whoa, man, ease off the accelerator."

Tristan blew out a long breath. "Sorry. That shit just annoys me. People only hear half the story and jump to conclusions. Zel's not the angel everyone thinks she is. She can be a real bitch. Trust me and run away. Don't be seduced by that sexy voice. That and her face are the only things going for her. She's pretty fucking insecure and self-centered."

They pulled into Blue Water's employee parking lot. "No worries," Aithan said as the security gate rattled closed behind his SUV. "You got your things, so you can move on, right?"

"Yeah. Right." Tristan got out of the Lexus, slung his duffel bag over his shoulder, and headed for the rear entrance, not bothering to wait for his boss.

Aithan watched the door close between them. Something still didn't sit right. The woman Tristan described was nothing like the woman he'd met that morning. And Tristan's lewd comment about her made Aithan uneasy.

"Leave it." He climbed from the SUV. "If she agrees to coffee, buy her a cup, keep the talk small, and go home. Put the woman out of your head. That's probably best for everyone in this mess. Don't get involved with your employee's ex."

Blue Water Fitness was Aithan's baby. He'd bought the failing gym the year before he graduated from college. It'd been a big risk, but he had degrees in business admin and physical therapy, and a master's in kinesiology. He'd spent more money on hiring great trainers than buying fancy equipment, and word-of-mouth had brought in most of his clients. Now, eight years since opening, BWF was profitable and he was considering expanding into the empty retail space next door.

Blue Water was small. The main room held free weights, pull-up stations, tires and ropes, and six rowing machines. Two additional rooms allowed for private lessons and smaller classes. The walls were white. The mats were blue. Silver lockers took up one wall opposite the management office. Two restrooms were the only spaces for changing.

The first afternoon class was tossing medicine balls high up against the far wall. Catching, resting, and throwing again. "Harder, Better, Faster, Stronger" by Daft Punk thumped throughout the room as the members shouted encouragement to each other. These were the hardcores — the people who came to Blue Water to sweat during their lunch hour, eat a sandwich in the car on their way back to work, and do it all with a smile.

Tristan was already on the floor, assisting with spotting and correcting form. He stopped one of the students as she caught a medicine ball. She was red-faced and breathing hard.

"Slow down, Natalie."

She shook her head and panted. "Five more … to go."

"Not today. I want you doing half your normal reps. If I

can *see* your fatigue, that ain't good. I don't want you hurting yourself."

She peered at him through sweaty bangs and nodded. "Gotcha."

Aithan high-fived the class instructor, Beth, as well as a few of the regulars as he crossed the gym. Watching Tristan take so much time and care with Natalie left him even more puzzled over the guy's attitude toward his ex-girlfriend. Obviously, he and Zelda shared a complicated history.

Aithan's first training session was with a husband and wife. He'd worked with Dennis for over a year, getting the guy into great shape. He was in his mid-sixties and retired from one of Seattle's big tech companies, making up for the pressures of corporate life. Working out regularly had normalized his blood pressure and cured his pre-diabetes. For their anniversary, he'd bought a six-month private training package. His wife, Judy, was tiny and appeared fragile, but she constantly surprised herself with her own strength and stamina. Aithan loved working with them.

"Get Lucky" came on over the sound system as he entered the smallest private classroom. "Who's excited about squats?" he asked.

"Me!" Judy raised her hand like a kid.

Dennis pulled her up from the mat where were stretching. He beamed at her. "Three miles yesterday, Aithan. That's a record for her."

"What?" Aithan bumped fists with her. "Nice work, lady! I said to run just two miles, remember?"

She shrugged. "I still felt strong when we hit that mark, so we kept going."

"Were you sore afterward?"

"Nope." She sounded surprised. "I thought I would be, but you're so right about stretching before *and* after. That makes such a big difference."

"And staying hydrated," Dennis added. "Judy made sure we did that. She's killing this whole exercise thing."

Aithan nodded. "Just like you said she would."

Judy hugged her husband. "He's my cheering squad."

He squeezed her back. "And you keep me alive, wifey."

She laughed. "Only because I want to take out one more life insurance policy on you before I hold a pillow over your face."

Dennis grinned. "She's so romantic."

They all laughed, then Aithan clapped his hands. "Okay, let's do this."

After the session with Dennis and Judy, he put the advanced boxing class through seventy-five minutes of calisthenics and sparring in the main gym before checking in with Juan, Blue Water's office manager.

"Got November's schedule ironed out?"

"Yeah," the man replied. "Holidays are a bitch 'cause everyone wants days off before or after, but Tristan's looking for extra hours, so I gave him Chel's and Paco's shifts. He'll have some OT, but I didn't think that'd be an issue. If it is, lemme know."

Aithan pulled his office laptop from the safe and turned it on. While it booted up, he sat back. "How's he doing?"

"Tristan?" Juan perched on the edge of the small office's only desk and swigged water from a metal BWF bottle. "Okay, I think. Bit quieter than usual, but he's not letting his personal problems impact his classes."

Aithan nodded. "Had a talk with him this morning. He's pretty pissed at his ex, and I don't think he's as golden as he'd like us to believe right now." He watched the man in question correcting a gym rat's form during pushups. "His ego got kicked pretty hard and something tells me he brought this all down on himself."

"Huh. We gonna have trouble?"

Aithan screwed up his mouth, thinking. He shook his head. "I hope not, but it's probably too soon to tell. Keeping him busy through the holidays is a good idea. The OT isn't a problem."

"Okay, boss. I'll keep an eye on the dude."

"Thanks, man."

Juan waved that away and closed the door as he left the office.

Aithan scrolled through the schedule, but he didn't see any of it. His mind wandered through the conversation with Tristan and landed on his memory of the morning with Zelda Gordon.

She was beautiful. Statuesque and shapely, confident enough to boot Tristan from her life with a swift kick.

People assumed Aithan was attracted to the hard-bodied women he saw in the gym all day, but they didn't really do much for him. He liked curves and softness on a woman. Healthy was sexier than hard, in his opinion. When he pulled a woman into his arms, he wanted something to sink into. Maybe he was a bit old-fashioned, but Aithan Mazur liked women who hid their steel spines beneath voluptuous curves.

And instinct told him Zelda Gordon was just such a woman.

A new message buzzed his phone. Tobias, his best friend, wanted to know if he was available for a deposition on November Third. Aithan checked his calendar then texted back.

> Yeah, man, I'll free up the day.

Tobias replied:

> Thx. I'll let u know the time. Fuck, I hope this stops Maeve's BS. U know how much I appreciate u backing me up, right?

> Yeah, I do. And u know I'll do whatever it takes to help u get full custody.

> I do. Thx. See u tmrrw.

> Yup. Gonna make u dragon walk across the gym.

> U suck.

Aithan laughed and returned to the files on his open laptop.

Hours passed as he analyzed the gym's finances and next year's marketing plan. Classes came and went. Afternoon crept toward evening. Finally, he sat back, stretched, and rubbed his eyes.

Aithan picked up his cellphone to check his personal email, then scrolled through his text messages, pausing on his offer of coffee to Zelda. He absolutely should not make her another offer. But he wondered why the woman Tristan described was so utterly at odds with the woman he'd met that morning.

His gaze wandered and he spied Tristan coaching a beginning resistance class on the main mat. The man was a damn good trainer, patient and observant. So why hadn't that translated over into his personal life?

Aithan slowly shook his head. "Whose loss is that?" he murmured to the man, "Yours or hers?"

Returning his gaze to his phone's black screen, he made a decision. Tristan was an adult. So was Zelda and so was he.

> Ready for that cup of coffee?

He hit the send button before he changed his mind.

"It's just coffee," he murmured as his gaze returned to Tristan and the sweaty beginners. No harm in buying her coffee. And maybe she could shed some light on Tristan's behavior. It was smart, as his employer, for Aithan to understand what made the man tick and what might make him snap.

8
SAY YES

"NOTHING freakier than a cat sniffing your ass while you're banging his owner," Drew remarked the next morning. He was snuggled under my down comforter like a tattooed grizzly in a cozy, yellow den.

I laughed. "Sorry about that. Frank's pretty possessive."

"Little cock blocker. He's lucky he's cute or I woulda knocked him back a few feet."

"Oh, I wouldn't pick a fight with him or Lulu. They each carry an arsenal of knives, sharpen them on the furniture and clean them with their tongues."

Drew peered at me. "You hang with a rough crowd."

"That's my posse. Little shits got my back."

"Speaking of. How *is* your back?"

I stretched, arms reaching up, toes pointing down. "Good actually."

Drew growled. "If you do that again, I'll roll you over and bang you like a screen door."

I stroked his jaw, tugging on his bearded chin. "You already did that several times last night."

"Complaining?"

"Only in good ways."

He surged up and kissed me. "Yeah you were. You make some incredibly sexy noises when you're getting fucked."

Then, like the alarm clock he was, Frank popped up onto the bed. He stalked along the edge, got in my face, and meowed, ignoring Drew.

"See?" Drew said. "Cock blocker."

I laughed. "More like hungry, hungry hippo. He's always prompt when it comes to mealtimes." I scratched Frank's ears then sat up as Drew snuggled back into the bedding. Lulu sat in the bedroom doorway. She turned tail and ran down the stairs as I dragged on my robe.

"Nice view."

I turned and considered him. "I think you really mean it when you give me compliments."

"Yeah, Brick, I do."

I leaned over and kissed him. "Thanks."

He grinned. "You're welcome."

I peed then fed the cats and drank my morning water. Two glasses, this time. Drew had taken everything out of me. My cellphone sat on the dining table. I picked it up, but the battery was dead. "Crapola." I plugged in the nearest charger and left the phone on the table.

"I'm going for a run," I said as I returned to the bedroom and started pulling clothes from my dresser.

"Got any sweats I can borrow? I could use a run."

"Uhh." I'd dumped all of Tristan's clothes. "Oh, wait. Yeah. I have a pair of my dad's old sweats. They've got dried paint on them, but if you don't mind, they're free of holes." I dug them out of my "old clothes" drawer, along with one of my dad's burgundy Harvard Law School tee shirts and a gray hoodie. "Here."

He crossed the room, naked as a jaybird and completely unselfconscious. The view was damn nice. His tattoos were amazing. A rocket ship launched on his right forearm and soared over the back of his hand. A paint bucket spilled a starry sky down his chest, sending planets and galaxies across his skin. A black-and-gray scrollwork *M* rested over his heart. A triquetra nestled inside a chrysanthemum on his ribs. So many tats covered his whole torso, front and back. I could stare at Drew's skin for hours and not learn the whole story written upon him.

I touched his arm. "Are all your tats somehow related to your books?"

"Most. Science fiction on my chest," he turned and added, "fantasy on my back. Both on my arms."

I cupped his ass where a grizzly roared. "You've got a bear behind."

He flexed his cheek. "That's a new one. RH bear shifters. Don't have a title for the novel yet. I'm thinking maybe *Grisly*."

"Female MC?"

"Aurelia. She's a badass warrior who cuts down her enemies and boinks three brothers."

"The three bears?"

"Exactly."

"Nice." I grabbed socks. "Oh, wait. What about running shoes?"

"I run barefoot."

"Really? Doesn't that hurt?"

Drew shrugged. "Eh, not anymore. I've got wicked calluses on my feet. Just gotta watch for glass and dog shit."

"Goose poop, in this case. Canadian geese forage all around Green Lake."

He pulled a face. "Oh, fun."

I laughed. "Why no shoes?"

He shrugged. "It's therapeutic, being able to feel the ground under my feet."

We dressed and ran, discussing his bear book as we circled the lake. It was colder than the day before, but the sky was clear and the air smelled fresh and clean. Another beautiful Seattle fall morning. After returning and showering, I trotted downstairs, toweling my hair dry, and found Drew at the dining table with two cups of tea and his computer open.

He tapped my phone. "You should say yes."

"Huh?"

"To Aithan Mazur."

I blinked, a little taken aback. "You read my messages?"

"Just one. It popped up when I moved your phone. He wants to take you out for coffee. Say yes."

That just added to my confusion. "Why?"

"Why not?"

"No, I mean why do you care?"

"Because you like him and he likes you."

"Uhh, how do you know that?" I picked up the phone and opened the messages app.

Aithan's text came up first:

> Ready for that cup of coffee?

"You put his name and number in your contacts. You would've deleted it if he was an asshole. And he's not giving up after one no."

I bit my lip. "I hardly know him, Drew. He's Tristan's boss."

"Is he hot?" My blush answered him. Grinning like the devil, he grabbed my phone and talked as he typed: "Love to. I'll meet you. When and where?"

My jaw fell. "Are you nuts?"

"Yes. And you love me for it. You deserve a date with a sexy beast, Zel."

"How do you know he's sexy?"

He held up a finger. "Number One, you blushed." He raised a second finger. "Number Two, he's your ex's boss. Ergo, he's ripped. He could have a face like a horse's ass —

which he doesn't according to Number One — and he'd still be sexy."

I sat open-mouthed, still trying to wrap my head around Drew's reaction to Aithan. "But you and I just screwed."

"Which was amazing, and I have every intention of doing it again and often. What's that got to do with you seeing Aithan Mazur?"

"Um."

"Nothing. We don't own each other just because we fucked like monkeys, Brick. I won't stop you from seeing other people."

Did that mean I had to share him? I wasn't sure if I wanted to, but I also didn't have the right to keep him to myself. We'd fucked once. Okay, it was more like three or four times, but that was nitpicking. "Okaaay. I guess I have a coffee date." He had me off kilter. Again.

My phone buzzed to confirm it.

> Today? Liquid Mud on Phinney at 10:30am?

> It's a date

Drew grinned. He pulled me up and sent me toward the stairs with a slap on my ass. "You get pretty. I'll pick out something sexy for you to wear."

As I applied a little eyeshadow and lipstick, he shuffled through my wardrobe, complaining. The man was incorrigible.

"Hell and damnation, woman. Don't you own anything sexier than jeans?"

"It's coffee, remember?"

"It's a first date."

"He's already seen me in shlubby morning clothes looking like I just rolled out of bed, because I'd just rolled out of bed. I don't think he's expecting much."

"Which is why you want to wow him." The clatter of

wooden clothes hangers drifted from the closet. "Hello. What's this?" He emerged with the wiggle dress.

I arched a brow. "A bit much for coffee. I don't need to look desperate."

He considered the dress and nodded. "True. Save this for a dinner date. This says, 'Fuck me,' for sure."

I laughed. "You're outrageous. You know that?"

"I do." He waggled his eyebrows at me and dove back into the closet. "No. No. Nooo. Why do you even *own* this? No. Wait. Yes. No. Annnd, yes." Drew returned with a black, pinstriped pencil skirt and a button down denim shirt. "Please tell me you own heels that don't look like a sixty-year-old substitute teacher bought them."

I chewed my lip. He wasn't far from the truth. "I have leopard print wedges."

He nodded. "That'll do. Dress, I'll find them."

Thirty minutes later I was sitting at a two-top in my favorite Phinney Ridge coffeehouse, enjoying the heavenly aroma of freshly ground coffee, when Aithan strode in.

"Sorry to keep you waiting." He took the seat opposite me. "Parking's a nightmare around here."

"Oh, I know. Construction's made a mess of it up and down Phinney."

He nodded. "And there's always construction in Seattle, right?"

I laughed. "Right."

We chatted about Seattle's endless building boom and all the massive cranes dotting the skyline as the line at the counter thinned, then he pushed back his chair.

"What can I get you?"

"Earl Gray with honey, if they have it."

"Food?"

"Nothing. Thanks. I'm good."

"Okay. Be right back."

A few minutes later he settled into the seat opposite me

with my tea and a grande latte. He'd also gotten a pumpkin scone and placed the plate between us.

"Help yourself."

"I wish, but I can't."

He squinted at me. "You're not dieting are you? Or not eating in front of me? Because, honestly, it really bothers me when women do that."

"No, nothing like that. I'd eat that whole fucking thing if I could, but I adhere to the AIP. The Autoimmune Protocol?" I glanced up to see if he followed.

Aithan nodded. "I've heard of it. To control inflammation, right?"

"Exactly. Grain, dairy, and refined sugar never cross these lips."

His gaze lingered on my mouth, then lifted to my eyes. "What autoimmune disorder do you have? If you don't mind me asking ...." He pulled the scone back and shoved a big piece into his mouth.

"I hit the jackpot with Graves' disease."

"Oof. Did you have thyroid ablation?"

I nodded. "Twice. Neither dose worked and I'm still hyperthyroid."

"Oh man. That sucks."

I shrugged. "It's okay. There are worse things. I take my meds, stick to the AIP, get exercise and adequate rest. It's all good."

He nodded. "You handle it well."

"Not like I have a choice." I shrugged. "How do you know about ablation?"

"I've had a few clients dealing with Graves'. When you train people for a living, you have to know about health problems. Autoimmune disorders come up a lot."

"That makes sense." I glanced away from his intense blue gaze. "I thought maybe Tristan mentioned it."

"No. He never talked about you, and now I see why."

Ouch. I bit my lip.

"He didn't want any of us luring you away from him."

I looked back at him, surprised. "Uh, no, I don't think so."

He frowned, a bite of scone halfway to his mouth. "Why not?"

Fuck. Deep breath. "I'm not exactly a hard body, in case you haven't noticed."

"Zelda," he looked up at the ceiling like he was choosing his words carefully then met my gaze and continued, "I definitely noticed your body. And I like what I see." He reached across the table and brushed his fingers over mine. "I'd like to see more of you." He gave me a lopsided grin. "I mean that in the best and worst ways."

He liked me? Like, really *liked* me? This beautiful man? Why?

I stared at his hand beside mine long enough to make him ask, "Is that okay? Or did I just freak you out?"

I touched his fingers. "You're fine. I'm just not used to compliments, sooo I tend to doubt them."

"What?" He sounded genuinely shocked. He leaned forward and I could see him putting two and two together. "Are you saying Tristan insulted you about your appearance?"

I bit my lip again and looked down.

"That's unacceptable." He shook his head and muttered, "Damn, I may have to let him go."

I grabbed his hand. "Don't. Please don't, Aithan. I don't want him to lose his job because of our past. That's not fair."

His blue eyes pinned me as his fingers gripped mine. "But it's fair for him to destroy your self-confidence?" He pressed his lips together. "Think about what you just said. He made you feel bad about your body but should keep his job training people to appreciate and strengthen theirs? That's a double standard and it's not what Blue Water is about."

Oh my God, this man was as decent as they came.

"I understand where you're coming from. And I appreciate it. But he shouldn't lose his job because of our personal shit. Tristan and I have a lot of history. Yes, he was a dick to his ex-girlfriend. That doesn't mean he isn't a good trainer."

Aithan released my hand and scratched the back of his head. He sat back and exhaled a slow breath. "Okay. I won't can him, but we *will* have a long and ugly conversation. He better get his head on straight. If he crosses the line in any way, I'll kick him off my crew. Personal trainers are supposed to lift people up, not put them down, Zelda."

I sat back, too, relieved. I'd had more than enough drama with Tristan and I really didn't think he deserved to lose his job. "Thanks."

He eyed me. Leaning forward again, he lowered his voice and asked, "Did he ever hit you?"

"What? No. He was never like that. Tristan is a dick, but he's not a monster." I sipped my tea, taking a moment to get centered, before continuing. "He wasn't very physical at all with me, to be honest."

Aithan shook his head and took a drink. "That would not be our problem," he murmured into his cup. I was about to respond when his phone chimed. "Tobias. Right. Damn. And now the best part of my day comes to an end way too soon. I gotta get back to the gym for a session."

"Tobias?"

"My client and my best friend."

"Oh. Bummer. This wasn't enough time."

"I agree. How about dinner this week? Wednesday or Thursday?"

"Sure. Wednesday," I said before I lost my nerve. "But let me cook."

He looked surprised, then nodded. "Right. AIP. Okay, what can I bring?"

"Just yourself. That's more than enough." I couldn't stop the blush that warmed my cheeks.

Aithan smiled slowly. "You're even more beautiful when you blush."

I pressed my hands to my cheeks and giggled like a goddamn little girl. Fuck. But he didn't seem to mind. "Is six p.m. okay?"

He pulled up his calendar on his phone. "Six thirty?"

"Yeah, that works."

He sorted our trash and recycling into the right bins then held the door for me. "Where are you parked?"

"Halfway down the block."

He walked with me, his hand lightly touching my lower back. At my car, he held the door while I slid in, then came around to the passenger side and tapped on the window. I lowered it. Aithan rested his arm on the frame. "I'm looking forward to seeing you again, Zelda. You look amazing today."

I tucked my hair behind my ears and smiled. "Thanks, Aithan. You always look amazing."

He smiled and stepped back. "Bye, beautiful," he said then strode down the block, hands in his jacket pockets.

I couldn't stop a shit-eating grin from splitting my face. "Fuck, that's hot." I watched him go. "Wonder what it's like to see him cum." I shook my head at my own horniness. But some urges just couldn't be helped, and Aithan Mazur triggered all my naughtiest ones.

9

ALL THE NEGATIVE VOICES

A TEXT from my mom chimed my phone as I got home.

> How are you holding up?

>> Fine. Drew's in town & we've been hanging out.

> Your father told me you got Tristan's stuff out of your house. That was fast. Maybe too fast, honey?

>> No. Not too fast. He was a dick. Don't start thinking like Greer.

> What do you mean?

>> Like I've made a mistake. I didn't. I don't need a man in my life if he's just gonna treat me like dirt.

I'd thought about what Aithan had said and he was right, Tristan should know better than to tear me down.

> Well, if you're sure you're making the right decision, I'll support you. You know I love you.

> I know, Mom. Thx. I'll talk to u later.

Drew was at his book signing, so I had the place to myself. I thought about rerecording the two chapters of his book, but decided to listen to them again instead. I got my computer and flopped down on the couch in the living room. Opening the file I cued up the last five chapters and hit play. He was right, everything was fine until those last two. They had no spark. It was as if Juno Galore had deflated under the weight of my emotions.

Even as I listened to the chapters I heard the bitterness in my voice. Why had Tristan been such a turd?

"And why was I so damn patient and stupid?"

Lulu jumped on my lap and started making bread with her front paws. I ran my fingers through her fur. "You don't know either do you?"

I'd gained so much confidence with the success of my business, but obviously that self-assurance hadn't extended into my personal life or my self-image. If I truly had confidence in myself I wouldn't have put up with Tristan's bullshit for so long. He never took me to any of the events at Blue Water. He didn't take me to his Ultimate games or invite me to cheer him on at his ultras. He always said he didn't like being watched when he was competing, that he found it distracting. But that was a lie.

"He kept me away because I didn't look like the sexy, fit girlfriend he thought a trainer should date, Lu."

There were other problems I'd ignored. He stopped complimenting me. He never bought me gifts, not even for my birthday or Christmas. He didn't know when our anniversary was and never seemed to care either.

Quite frankly, Tristan was a shitty boyfriend.

Okay. Fine. But why did I tolerate him?

"Drew was right," I said. "I thought I didn't deserve love because I believed the people who said I'm fat and ugly."

The room blurred as tears filled my eyes and spilled down my cheeks. "Fuck," I muttered and wiped them away.

Lulu captured my wrist and smashed her face against my hand then sniffed my fingers and licked the tears.

I uttered a sad, little laugh. "Weirdo."

But Drew and Aithan insisted I was attractive. No, more than that: They said I was sexy. Yet no matter how many times they repeated it, I couldn't help but doubt their words. There were just too many snide remarks from Tristan, and years of nastiness from schoolmates, and a lifetime of comparisons I made between myself and Greer. I couldn't overcome those feelings of inadequacy so easily. I wasn't obese; I knew that, but when I looked in the mirror, I saw fat and flaws.

Worst of all, I couldn't shake the feeling that people were just being nice when they gave me compliments, that they didn't *really* mean the kind words they said. I felt like they were pitying me and thought they were making my life better by lying.

"My head is so fucked up."

I'd even started thinking that Drew had left me behind while he went to the book signing because he was embarrassed to be seen in public with me. It didn't matter that yesterday he'd proudly strolled beside me down the street, my arm tucked through his as he smiled and complimented me. The negative voice in my head was always louder than the positive voices in my ears.

But I needed confidence, whether or not I was hearing encouragement or criticism from other people. I needed to feel beautiful. I needed to look in the mirror and like what I saw.

I needed to love myself.

Of course Drew hadn't left me behind. I had a date with Aithan. He told me to go to coffee because he wanted me to find someone who would make me happy. But did that mean the happiness I had with Drew, as sudden and brief as it had been, was a passing thing? I didn't want it to be a meaningless fling. I liked Drew. I'd *always* liked Drew. And I didn't want our relationship to be a flash in the pan.

I scratched Lulu's chin. "I want more, Lu." He knew that didn't he? I thought so, but …. "I should say it. I need the confidence to stand up and say that I want more than a couple of good fucks."

It was scary to say aloud, but also exhilarating. I was assertive in my work because I believed in my abilities, but I hadn't ever been that way in my personal life. That was obvious from all the bullshit I'd taken from Tristan.

"Dammit, Zelda, get your head out of your ass," I said. "Ask for what you want."

Drew said I was in charge and it made sense coming from him. He wrote reverse harem, after all. The women in his books were assertive and strong, they surrounded themselves with men who respected and admired them, and they got what they wanted by asking for it. No, by demanding it. That was the kind of woman Drew liked. He didn't want a wilted flower. I had a feeling Aithan wasn't interested in a damsel in distress either.

The question was, could I be that assertive woman? Could I see myself the way they did?

"You can, if you just get out of your own goddamn way," I answered.

Frank appeared at the top of the stairs. Lulu spied him, meowed, and charged him. Both cats wrestled, then raced down the stairs.

The rah-rah speech was good, but I still needed to put it into action, and that was easier said than done. I had a lifetime of self-doubt to overcome. That wasn't going to go away overnight.

I got up and went to the kitchen. The dishes needed doing, so I tackled them, then went downstairs to clean the cat box. Feeling motivated I kept going and cleaned all the bathrooms, dusted my office, and took out the trash.

I was running the vacuum on the third floor when Drew returned. I didn't hear him come in, so I came out of the guest bedroom and nearly jumped out of my skin to find him standing at the top of the stairs wearing a shit-eating grin.

I gasped. "Jesus H. Christ, you scared the hell out of me!"

He looked contrite. "Sorry, babe. I called you, but I guess you couldn't hear me over the vacuum, then I got to the top of the stairs and was enjoying watching you wiggle while you worked." He cradled my face in his hands and tilted my head back giving me a long, sweet kiss. He wore jeans and a tight, black T-shirt, and his body felt way too sexy under my hands.

"How was the signing? Good turnout?" He looked terrific, and I was grubby and sweaty.

Drew leaned against the half wall that capped the stairs. "Line was out the door and my hand is cramped as fuck, so I'd say it was a success. But I missed having you around." Frank and Lulu arrived to hiss at the vacuum, the evil monstrosity that terrorized them on a weekly basis. They charged past Drew into the bedroom. He laughed. "I screwed myself when I told you to go have coffee this morning. Honestly, Zel, I'm jealous of Mister Fitness."

"Why?" Hearing him say it was exciting. It meant there was more to our relationship than fucking in every room of my townhouse.

"Because I'm a possessive motherfucker when it comes to you." No one could miss the seriousness on his face and in his voice.

"So all of that stuff about us not controlling each other was lip service?" How should I feel about that? "You're giving me whiplash, Drew."

He rubbed his hands along in my arms, leaving goose flesh behind. "I know. I'm a hypocrite. But I can't help it. You know I've had a thing for you since the day we met. I can't just turn off those feelings, Zel, even though I know that's unfair to you." He kissed my forehead and hugged me. "It's my problem, not yours. You keep doing what you're doing, even if it makes me crazy and horny as hell."

I nodded and went back to vacuuming because I didn't really know what to do about his confession. I enjoyed Drew, probably way too much considering he had a longtime girlfriend at home in New York. I didn't want to give him up, and I didn't want to take advantage of the confusion he'd confessed to and push him into a corner about us. Especially when there wasn't really an *us* yet.

"Well, I asked Aithan over for dinner tomorrow night. And you didn't exactly come up in the conversation, so what do you want me to do?"

"Me? It's not up to me what you do. Yeah, I'm cuckoo for Cocoa Puffs about you, but that doesn't mean I'm going to get between you and another guy. And, no, I definitely don't expect to be asked to eat with the two of you. That would be really fucking awkward for him."

I laughed. "Yeah, I can't imagine explaining that." I gestured to him. "Aithan, this is Drew. He's my author and my fuck buddy. You don't mind if he eats with us, right? Later we can all screw like rabbits in the guest room."

Drew's shit-eating grin returned. "Actually, that sounds like fun."

I shook my head. "For you, maybe, but I'd like to see where this thing with Aithan is going. Throwing him into a ménage à trois on the second date is probably asking a bit much."

"True. It's not like he's me, after all." He tapped his chest.

"Nobody is like you, Drew Katterman." I kissed him.

He went downstairs. When I was finished vacuuming I found him on the balcony, working on a manuscript. Not wanting to disturb his flow, I sat on the couch and researched recipes online. Aithan hadn't said if he had any allergies or dislikes, so I pulled out my phone to text him, and discovered that Greer had sent her itinerary.

> My flight lands at SeaTac @ 4:35pm Friday (10/25). I'm expected at the convention Sat & Sun. I'm flying home Mon @ 11:05am. So we have Fri eve to sort out this whole Tristan mess.

"Christ on a crutch," I muttered and typed:

> I hope u don't think I'm picking u up from the airport. I told u, I have a guest. Stay at a hotel. AND I don't want Tristan back.

A few seconds later she replied.

> Zel, don't be an idiot. He's hot & employed & you're not ready to be alone.

> Do u srsly think I'm better off with an abusive a-hole?!

> Abusive how? Did he hit u?

> No.

> Then suck it up, Buttercup. Take what u can get, little sis. They're not exactly lining up at your front door & u need someone to take care of u. You're incapable on your own.

"Fucking bitch!"

"Me?" Drew stood in the doorway, laptop in hand.

"No, my goddamned sister. Greer thinks I'm better off

with a guy who treats me like dirt than alone. Apparently, I can't take care of myself."

"Well, that's bullshit. Is she for real?" He took the phone and his eyes widened as he scanned the message. "What. A. Bitch." He glanced at me as if to judge how I took that criticism of a family member. "Sorry, to be harsh, but …."

"Oh, no. You're one hundred percent on target. Greer's a bitch."

He dropped beside me on the couch, snuggled up, and raised the phone to take our picture. "Bitch can get a clue from this." He licked my cheek and I squealed as the camera clicked. The pic was hilarious. He sent it and typed:

> Dunno, this one can't keep his hands off me, so I'm not worried about becoming a lonely old spinster. Don't come to my place. The guest bed is wrecked from all the fcking.

I laughed. "Oh, shit. She'll forward that to our parents, for sure."

He shrugged. "I'm guessing Mom and Dad know you're not an innocent flower."

"Hmm. Truth."

10

A GENTLEMAN AND A VERY SEXY ROGUE

I PUT the last knife on the table as Drew wandered into the kitchen, sniffing the air like a famished mutt. "Whatcha making? It smells damn good."

"Pot roast with parsnips and sweet potatoes." The oven timer buzzed. I put on oven mitts and opened the door. "And pumpkin drop biscuits," I added as I pulled a cookie sheet from the oven.

"Mmm, Daddy likes." He stole one from the sheet, juggling it between his hands before dropping it on a napkin. "What do you use instead of butter?"

"Honey." I handed him my glass honeypot.

"Oh, fuck yeah." He sat at the table and drizzled honey on the biscuit then hummed as he motored through it, remarking between bites, "This is some real gourmet shit, Brick."

"I'm glad you approve. Leftovers are for tomorrow. I made plenty."

He tilted his head back, a silent plea for a kiss, and I obliged. "You're bad for my girlish figure," he said.

"No, I'm not. AIP is excellent for your ass and your gut."

"And my brain. My word count has almost doubled since I started eating your home cooking."

I grinned. "You sure it's not the sex?"

Drew eyed me, or to be precise, he eyed my ass. "That's definitely inspiring." He popped the last bite into his mouth and glanced at the clock. "Damn. I'd fuck you before he arrives, but there's not enough time, and I will not be rushed."

"So considerate." I put the last biscuit in the bread basket and covered them with a towel. Casually, I remarked, "There's time for a blowjob." I put the basket on the table and laughed at the feral look on his face.

He squeezed his eyes shut and shook his head. "No, no. I won't break my rule." He sounded like he was convincing himself.

I wiped the counter. "Where will you be while Aithan is here?"

"Gonna take my laptop to Liquid Mud." He had his computer bag by his feet. "Text me when the coast is clear?"

"I thought you wanted to watch."

Drew's gaze sharpened and his grin turned predatory. He stood and caught my waist, pulling me against him. "If sexy times start, text *SOS*, and I'll come running. I do not want to miss seeing you get fucked by Mr. Fitness."

The way he purred that made me horny. He was so unabashed about his desires. It was a turn on. "Okay," I said and couldn't stop a little moan from escaping me as he captured my lips. He grabbed my ass and ground his hips against mine, his erection obvious.

"Christ." He forced himself away. "I'm leaving before I bend you over the table and fuck the shit out of you."

I nodded, breathing a little too hard. The man was magnetic and sexy as hell. "Go. I'll text you."

"One way or another, Zel, you're getting fucked hard tonight. That is a promise."

I nodded stupidly. It was my turn to wear a shit-eating grin as he retreated down the stairs.

Not ten minutes later, the doorbell rang.

I turned off the crockpot, took off my apron, and hurried to the front door, checking my hair in the mirror beside it before looking through the peephole.

Aithan. And he had flowers.

I opened the door. "Hey." I suddenly felt shy.

He offered the flowers — gerberas — pink, yellow, orange, and white. "I know it's a bit old-fashioned, but you know I'm wholesome like that."

"I do." I took them and felt the return of the shit-eating grin. "They're beautiful and you're thoughtful. Thank you."

"And they're non-toxic, so the kitties won't get sick if they sample them."

He kicked off his shoes and left them beside mine — more thoughtfulness — and hung his coat on one of the wall pegs. "Whatever you're cooking smells amazing."

"Pot roast. I stuck with something simple, since I wasn't sure what you like or dislike."

"I'm a polar bear. I'll eat anything."

I glanced over my shoulder at him as we went upstairs. "Good, 'cause I make a helluva good pot roast."

"My nose already agrees."

I put the flowers in a vase and set them on the table. "These are so lovely, Aithan."

"Almost as lovely as you." He grimaced and shook his head. "Can't believe I said that." He squinted at me. "Too cheesy?"

"No. Wholesome, which I like, remember? Can I get you something to drink?"

"Water is fine."

"Sparkling or flat?"

"Flat. I'm not a fan of the bubbly stuff."

"Really? Why not?"

He shrugged. "Dunno. Probably because we never had

carbonated drinks when I was a kid. My mom believes it weakens bones."

"It does?"

"No, but there are healthier drinks to choose from, so I humor her."

"Fair enough. Water it is." I poured glasses for both of us then checked the roast. "Hungry?"

"Starving, actually. Wednesdays are heavy for me. I start with back-to-back private sessions at six in the morning and the day doesn't let up."

"Well, then let's eat."

I plated the roast and the veggies, told him what was in the biscuits, and we sat. The food was terrific, maybe my best roast yet. Aithan had only praise and second helpings to show his pleasure. He even liked the carob brownies I offered for dessert.

"It's not chocolate," he remarked, "but it's a helluva a lot better than the weird hippie carob my sister tries to give me."

"It takes some getting used to, especially if you go into it thinking it'll taste like chocolate. But I buy the best quality organic carob available and add a little cinnamon to the recipe. It makes a big difference."

He nodded. "Definitely."

After dinner, we sat on the sofa, drinking tea and talking.

My phone buzzed on the side table. Aithan picked it up and passed it to me. "SOS? Is that an escape code in case this date goes south?"

Doh! I hadn't expected him to see a note from Drew. "No, far from it. That's just my friend Drew asking if it's safe for him to return to the townhouse. He's visiting from New York."

"Ah." He paused. "Friend?"

I chewed my lip. I didn't want to fuck this up and wasn't sure which was better, lying or the truth. I decided neither. "He's an author I've done some recording for. He's in town for a book signing. We've known each other for a few years."

Aithan nodded, but I couldn't tell if he was satisfied with that answer. He yawned. "Sorry. I probably should get going. I've got a seven-thirty class."

I stood and he did, too. "Okay." *Crap*. Had I just scared him off? I cleared our cups to the kitchen. He followed. When I turned around, he was right behind me.

"Hey." He cupped my chin and tilted my face. "This was a great meal and I had a really nice time just chilling with you, Zel."

"I had a great time, too. I'm glad you came over."

His eyes were so blue and so intense. He shifted closer, leaned in and kissed me. It was light and sweet, gentlemanly, but his lips lingered on mine and curved into a smile as the front door creaked. He pulled back just a little. "Your author friend?"

A muttered, "Whoops," drifted up the stairs, then the sound of the front door closing. I wasn't sure if Drew had stayed or left.

I giggled. "Yep, that's him."

Aithan stepped back. "I'll text you tomorrow."

"Okay."

He brushed his thumb over my lower lip and my breath caught. "Can I see you again, Zelda?"

I nodded. "I'd like that."

"Good."

I walked him downstairs. There was no sign of Drew. Either he was hiding in a closet or he'd gone back out. After another lingering kiss from Aithan — the man stole my breath — I closed the door and he started his SUV.

My office door opened. Drew poked his head out. "Did I chase him off?"

"Maybe." I sighed, feeling mostly content.

"Aw, crap. I'm sorry, Brick."

"Not your fault."

"Kinda is."

"Yeah." I gave him a fake sour look then headed up to the second floor. "Kinda is."

He followed. "Do you like him?"

"Huh?"

"Do you like him?"

"Yes." I watched his expression, afraid he'd be mad.

"Then ask him out again. Push the relationship."

I flopped onto the couch and yanked off my socks. "What about us?"

"What about us?" He sat beside me, pulled my legs across his lap, and started massaging my feet.

At least he didn't think there wasn't an *us*, but still …. "I'm confused, Drew. What are we doing?"

"We are having a very enjoyable relationship, Brick."

His thumb slid along the ball of my foot and a delicious sensation crawled up my leg. "Don't you mind if I'm seeing another man?"

He laughed. "I write reverse harem romance with sexy space bitches. If you want to screw another person's brains out, I'll be the last guy to stop you."

"You don't care?"

He looked at me from beneath his brows. "Oh no, that's not what I said. I care that you're happy and feel good. I like fucking you, and I like you. That doesn't mean I want to control you. It's not my place to decide who you screw, Zel. Just warn me if you're bringing him home, so I don't mess up your mojo again."

But everything I'd experienced with other men made me doubt him. "You *really* don't mind?"

"Nope. Strong chicks. Hot sex. Those are my jam." He grinned. "I do like to watch, though, so let me enjoy the show when you let him fuck you." He chuckled at the wide-eyed expression I wore. "I get off when someone I care about gets off, babe. I feel your pleasure."

"Okay, that's ... kinky."

"Is kinky bad?"

"No. Especially the way you explain it. It's sweet really. Thoughtful. But you're even dirtier than I thought."

"And you're sexier than you realize." He got to his knees and pulled me down flat on the couch.

"But I don't know how Aithan will feel about being watched. He seems way too gentlemanly to be into kink."

Drew busied himself with removing my jeans. "You'd be surprised who's kinky, but we can ease him into the idea. I don't wanna get my ass beaten and he looks like he'd do a thorough job of it. Could probably snap me in half. Which is another reason I want to watch you getting rammed by him. I mean, damn, I'm hot just thinking about it." He started on my shirt's buttons.

I squirmed beneath his touch. "Why do you write reverse harem? I don't know very many men who write romance, let alone romance where the woman has most of the power and lots of partners."

"There was no love between my parents. My dad beat the crap outta my mom, my sister, and me every day. I still don't know why she stayed with him; it wasn't for my sake, that's for damn sure." With my shirt open, he hummed as his lips trailed from my bra down toward my belly button. "But I grew up and figured out that I *love* love, that I fucking love women, and I love fucking women." He hooked his thumbs into my panties and pulled them down.

I stiffened under his inspection, but he ran his hands gently along my inner thighs. "Relax. I've seen lots of pussies. Yours looks just as good as the rest." He met my gaze. "You know it's okay to feel good, right?" He lifted my right leg over the back of the couch and hooked the left over his shoulder. "I've gone way too long wondering what you taste like, Brick." He slid his tongue down my thigh and into my folds.

Jeebus, I almost climbed off the couch. I grabbed his hair and held on, gasping as his tongue flicked over my clit and he slid his fingers into me. Still humming, he started a rhythm that had me mewling. I wanted to lock my legs around his head and hold him there forever. He licked and stroked. I moaned and rocked. The pressure of release built in me fast and the only thing I knew was his amazing tongue and the rhythm of his fingers pumping me. Finally, I couldn't take any more. My hips jerked, my body arched, and I shook as a cry escaped me.

I collapsed on the couch, trembling and panting as waves of orgasm shivered through me. "God*damn*. How'd you do that so fast?"

Grinning like a madman, Drew produced another condom, stripped off his shirt and pants, and crawled up my body. "Oh, that was just the warmup." He kissed me and for once I wasn't grossed out by the taste of me on a man's tongue. He slid his cock into me, taking his time, letting me feel the stretch as he buried every inch of himself inside my body.

"Oh, fuuuck." I groaned as he rocked his hips in the same rhythm his fingers and tongue had used to send me screaming over the edge only minutes ago. My already excited flesh sent bolts to my brain. Bolts that exploded when his teeth grazed the thin skin of my neck and he bit down. Pleasure flooded me, so intense it was almost painful. I gasped and pushed against his mouth and his cock.

I'd never felt so free to enjoy a man's attention. With every other lover, I'd worried about my tits jiggling or my stomach looking flabby. I'd tried to suck in my gut while sucking cock — not an easy feat — and cringed at every slap of flesh, every drop of sweat.

But Drew licked the sweat from between my breasts. He

thrust even harder when our skin slapped together. He worshiped my tits, kneaded my thighs, and grabbed my ample ass every chance he got. Drew made me feel desirable, not disgusting, as he touched me almost reverently.

He captured my wrists and pinned them above my head. "What are you thinking, Brick?" I blushed and he smiled. "Tell me," he coaxed and moved his body with mine.

"That you make me feel sexy."

"Because you are." I started to deny it, but he pulled out and sat up. "Come here." He guided me onto his lap facing him. "Ride me, Zel, so I can watch you fuck me. I want to see the pleasure on your beautiful face." He pulled me down and his dick slid into me, putting pressure in places I hadn't felt it before.

"Goddamn, you feel good," I murmured.

"Close your eyes. Focus on our bodies. Feel everything."

Straddling his lap, I did as he asked and let my head fall back. I rode that thick cock while he held my waist and sucked my nipples. Writhing atop Drew Katterman, I wasn't fat or ugly. I wasn't the greasy-haired teen who hid beneath baggy sweaters and slouchy sweatpants. I was naked and sensual, I was making him moan, making him thrust and sweat and pant.

His fingers slipped between our bodies and found my clit. He stroked me as I stroked him and, with a strangled cry, I arched. His teeth found my throat again, they nipped my skin, his cock thrust into me, and his fingers kept circling until my orgasm finally broke. With a long moan, my body stiffened as pleasure rolled through me, then my muscles let go and I collapsed against him.

Without pulling out of me, Drew grabbed my ass, stood, and laid me back on the couch. He thrust into me, hard, fast, and deep until I thought I'd crawl off the sofa as a laser light show fired off in my brain. And, finally, when I couldn't take anymore, when pleasure was threatening to drown me, he pushed into my body one last time and came with a growl and an unintelligible curse, eyes closed, agony and ecstasy chasing each other across his face.

Drew slowly raised his head and smiled, his light-green eyes bright and his skin flushed. "Damn, I love fucking you."

I traced his lips with my fingers. "I love getting fucked by you."

He kissed me tenderly and I sought out more, hungry for the feel of his lips. He smiled and complied, sliding his mouth over mine, kissing to the corner of my lips then across my jaw to my ear. "You're perfect, Zelda Gordon," he whispered, then sat up and pulled me atop him. He wrapped the soft orange couch blanket around us. "And that was some exceptional sex. I'm gonna miss you when I leave, Brick."

It was funny how accustomed to him I'd become. "Me too. I like having you around. You're ... easy."

"You slut shaming me?"

"No, I'm saying you're like one of my cats. There when I want attention, happy to do your own thing when I'm busy."

He laughed. "That's a first. Never been compared to a house pet before."

"It's a compliment. I adore my cats."

He kissed my temple. "I know. You dote on them. Means I'm held in high standing and you'll always feed me well."

"Very high standing." I lowered my voice. "Don't tell Lulu, but I think you may have replaced her as the alpha in this household."

"Beta," Drew said. "You're the alpha pussy, for sure."

I swatted him with a pillow, but he just laughed and pulled me close again.

I snuggled against him. "You make me feel amazing, Drew Katterman."

"Good." He folded his hands behind his head and looked smug. "Then my mission here is done."

"Does that mean you're leaving soon?" We hadn't

discussed his travel plans. Obviously, I knew he'd have to return to New York sooner rather than later, but I'd hoped to have at least another week with him. I hated the idea of Drew returning to his girlfriend, Livi, and forgetting about me. Call me selfish and insecure, but I couldn't help it.

"Friday afternoon."

I sat up. "That soon?" I fetched my shirt from the floor and pulled it on so I wouldn't have to meet his eyes.

He ran his hand down my back and over my hip. "Unfortunately. I have a signing in Boston on Saturday, then I go to Detroit, D.C., and Philly, before returning home to New York on Tuesday." He caught my hand and pressed it to his lips. "Plus, you have to work. I'm not the only author you do."

I knew he meant narration, but I still said, "Yes, you are."

He chuckled. "Cheeky."

I found my undies and slipped them on. "You're right, but I'm still sad to see you leave." I had no right to feel possessive, but I couldn't help it. I liked Drew more than any man I'd ever known. But it was way too soon to expect a commitment.

He sat up and cupped the nape of my neck, forcing me to meet his gaze. "Brick, I'll be back."

I studied him for a long moment. "I'd like that, but I'm not going to pine away by myself while you're globetrotting with other lovers."

"Good. You're better than that. Stronger. And you have Aithan to capture."

I laughed. "You say that like he's a conquest."

"Isn't he?"

I pulled on my jeans and stood. "Aithan Mazur is a gentleman." Leaning over him, I murmured, "Unlike you, sir."

He slid his hands into my hair and brought our faces close. "Oh? What am I, Zelda Gordon?"

"A scoundrel. A cad. A very sexy rogue, Mr. Katterman."

"I like that," he said, and pulled my mouth to his.

11

KINKY LIKE THAT

AITHAN TEXTED me Friday morning as I was heading downstairs and out for my run.

> Lunch today? Tobias wants to meet & feed u. He says his chef can accommodate your AIP needs.

I had to think of who Tobias was, then remembered he was Aithan's best friend.

> He owns a restaurant?

> Scumwater in Ballard. It's a gastropub & microbrewery. His chef offers a paleo menu.

> Really? That sounds wonderful. What time?

> Is 1:00 too late?

> Not at all. I'll meet u there.

> Excellent! Did u ever find your author friend Wed. night?

> Yeah. LOL! He was hiding in my office, watching us smooch at the front door.

He's into watching?

I snickered.

> He's kinky like that.

Reeeally.

...

Are u?

I shifted as excitement made my unmentionables twitch.

> Depends.

On what?

Sitting on my office couch, I chewed my lip and debated about being blunt. Old Zel wouldn't. She'd never have the guts to have this conversation. Of course, Old Zel wouldn't get fucked on her sofa by Drew Katterman, either.

> On who I'm getting kinky with.

My phone marked the message as read, but Aithan didn't respond for a looong minute. My excitement turned to nerves. Had I just screwed everything up?

> U still there?

Yeah. But my pants are suddenly tight.

I burst out laughing and sent him a laugh-cry emoji.

> Should I apologize?

> Definitely not. Unless you're a habitual blue-baller.

> No. I'm not that heartless.

> So, your author friend likes to watch u in bed. (Taking a deep breath here & hoping u don't delete my number.) Would u let him watch us?

I licked my lower lip.

> Before I answer that, tell me if you're truly OK with me seeing other men.

> I am, if that's the kind of relationship u want. Some things are worth sharing.

"Aww."

> That might be the sweetest thing anyone's ever texted to me.

Smiley emoji.

> So? U gonna answer my question?

I pressed my lips and my thighs together. The thought of Aithan fucking me while Drew watched made me wet.

> Yes, I'd let him watch that.

> Damn, girl, lunch cannot come too soon.

> LOL! I'll see u at 1pm. Time for me to go running.

> Okay, bye, beautiful.

> Bye.

I lowered the phone. Had I really just agreed to have sex with one man while another watched? I pressed my fingers to my lips and realized I was trembling. Was it from fear or excitement? "Both," I whispered. I sucked a deep breath and let it out slowly. "You can always change your mind, Zelda. Drew would understand. I think Aithan would, too."

I slowly stood and slipped my phone into the pocket of my running pants. Looking at nothing but my own feelings, I had to acknowledge the surprising truth. "I want to do this." The thought of being with both men turned me on more than anything I'd ever considered doing before.

It was scary, but in an exciting I've-got-butterflies-the-size-of-turkeys-in-my-belly way. Not an oh-god-I'm-gonna-barf-in-the-corner-and-cry way.

I shook my hands, trying to settle the trembling, as I headed for the door. I definitely needed that run to calm my nerves.

When I returned home, I found Drew sitting on my living room floor in his boxers and my blue terrycloth bathrobe, typing away, headphones on, head nodding, lips moving. Lost in his own world, he chuckled at something he wrote.

I plopped down opposite him and opened my mail, sorting junk from bills and trying to act casual.

Finally, he saved his file and looked up. "You look shiny and sweaty."

"Running does that to me."

"So does fucking."

I bit my lower lip. "When is your flight?"

"Eight-fifteen tonight. I've got a car picking me up here at three forty-five. Gotta go back to the hotel for my shit."

I nodded. "I have a lunch date with Aithan."

"Nice!" He high-fived me.

"He asked about you."

His brows arched. "Jealously?"

"No, more curious. I let slip that you like to watch."

"Oh?"

"He's okay with it. In fact, it turned him on."

"Ooh." He grabbed my ankle and his pupils were like saucers. "That is one hundred percent hot. You bringing him home after lunch?"

I swallowed and nodded. "Yeah." My voice sounded breathy.

Drew put his computer aside and crawled over to kiss me, tongue sweeping my lips before plunging hungrily into my mouth. "That will be the best damn going-away present ever, Brick," he said against my lips.

I smiled and stroked his jaw. "Gotta keep you coming back for more."

He laid me back. "Oh, I want more, alright. A whole lot more."

Lunch consisted of chicken taquitos with guacamole, jicama-avocado salad, carrot-bacon fritters, and berry crisp topped with vanilla coconut milk ice cream. All AIP compliant and all delicious. Aithan had even finagled the recipes from Tobias's chef, and I sent profuse praise and thanks back to the kitchen.

When I was getting ready for my date, Drew had discovered a dark-blue trench coat dress at the back of my closet. I'd paired it with my leopard print wedges and pulled my hair up into a sloppy chignon.

"You need more sexy shoes," he'd remarked while sorting most of the ones I owned into a pile beside the door for the Goodwill. "You've got legs going on forever, Zel, but no one knows it 'cause you don't flaunt what nature and your momma gave you."

I'd laughed. "My momma's itty-bitty. I got my height and curves from my Dad. All the women on that side of the family are Amazons."

"Remind me to thank that man," Drew had said.

Now, Aithan leaned across the table. "You're killing me with that dress," he said, proving Drew's fashion sense was far better than mine.

"Because you like it or because I look like Columbo?"

"You look nothing like Columbo." He laughed. "Oh, man, I love that show. Peter Falk was an amazing actor."

I grinned. "I know, right? It's one of my favorites. My dad and I binge watch reruns when I visit my parents."

"Are they nearby?"

"Bellingham. That's where I grew up."

"Oh, nice. I grew up in Los Angeles."

"Really? Do you miss it?"

"No way. Too crowded, too hot, too much traffic."

"More traffic than Seattle?"

"Definitely. I laugh when people complain about Seattle commuting. This place has nothing on L.A. Rush hour there is twenty-four/seven."

"Ugh. I don't think I'd like to live there."

"It's nice to have sunshine in the winter, but I prefer the changing seasons. You don't get fall color in SoCal. Autumn is hot and windy and everything's on fire."

"Yikes."

A good-looking Black guy crossed the restaurant and approached our table. Aithan stood and exchanged hugs with him. "Hey, man, thanks for accommodating Zelda's diet." He turned to me. "Zel, this is Tobias Peters. Tobias, meet Zelda Gordon."

I offered my hand and he shook it. "The food was fantastic. Thank you."

His smile revealed dimples. "I'm glad you liked it. Sam, our head chef, was excited to try some new recipes."

Holy shit, the man's voice was as smooth as silk.

Aithan pulled out a chair and Tobias joined us. He was a bit taller than Drew but not as tall as Aithan. His eyes were so dark they were almost jet and his skin was dark brown. His hair was close-cropped, and he sported a neatly trimmed black beard. He was fit like Drew, but not as ripped as Aithan.

"I wish I could enjoy one of your brews," I remarked. Tobias's brews were award-winners, especially his Foggy Autumn IPA.

"It's all good. Aithan drinks more than his fair share of Dark Brew Juju. I'm just glad to meet you, Zel. He's been talking my ear off about you." He leaned in and lowered his voice. "Sorry you had to go through some shit with Tristan."

I shrugged. "It's in the past." I glanced at Aithan. "I'm moving on." He took my hand and kissed it.

Tobias said, "Tristan's loss—"

"Is my gain," Aithan finished.

"And it's one helluva gain." Tobias winked at me. He started to add something, when a child's voice carried across the restaurant.

"Daddy!"

Tobias turned and his face lit up as a little girl raced across the room. He scooped her into his arms and planted a kiss on her cheek. "Little Bit, I've asked you not to run in the pub."

An elegant, older White woman followed. "Child, you know better than that," she said as she reached the table.

"Hi, Dianne." Tobias squeezed her hand. "Are you staying?"

"No, I left John in the car. We've got shopping to do and he has a meeting at four." She smiled. "Hello, Aithan. How've you been?"

"Good. Thanks." He introduced us and I learned she was Tobias's mother-in-law.

The little girl pouted. "Gammie, don't be mad at me. I

wanted to see Daddy." She must have been four or five years old. She had her father's brown skin, but stunning hazel eyes and insanely long eyelashes. Her black hair was pulled into two puffs atop her head.

Tobias nodded solemnly. "And you can see me while you *walk* across the restaurant. You don't want to trip a waiter and get hurt, right?"

"Right." She caught his face, turned it just so, and planted a big kiss on his cheek. "I'm sorry."

"Don't be sorry, be smart," Dianne said.

"Okay, Gammie."

The woman excused herself, and the child turned on Tobias's lap. "I wanna hug, Uncle Aithan."

Aithan grinned and reached for her as the girl squirmed out of her father's arms. "Hey, little Amara, I wanna give you a hug, too."

She wrapped her arms around his neck and squeezed as hard as she could, then gave him a kiss on the cheek. Turning, she considered me. "You're so pretty. Are you Uncle Aithan's new girlfriend?"

Aithan rolled with it. "Zelda and I just started dating."

She held out her hand and I shook it, charmed by the adult mannerism. "Nice to meet you," she said.

"The pleasure is all mine, Amara. You have lovely manners."

"Thank you." She turned to Tobias. "Daddy, I'm hungry."

"Well, let's get you a snack." Tobias stood and she hopped off Aithan's lap. He took her hand, then excused himself to take her to the kitchen.

"She's so stinkin' cute," I said when they were gone.

Aithan smiled wistfully. "Yeah, Amara's a hoot. She's so much like her mom. I wish Juliette was still alive."

"Oh, wow. Tobias is a widower? That's rough."

He nodded. "Juju was amazing and she would've been a

phenomenal mother. She's the reason Tobias has Scumwater. She pushed him to take a chance on marketing his beer. Brewing was just a hobby he started in his parents' kitchen. Juliette helped him grow it to national distribution while we were all still in college."

"That's amazing. Has it been long since she passed?"

"Five years. She died three days after Amara's birth."

"Shit. I don't even know how I'd go on after that."

Aithan shrugged. "No choice. He was suddenly a single dad. Amara needed him. Family and friends stepped up, too. Those first three years were hard, but he was managing just fine." His scowl and his bitter tone surprised me.

"Until?" I prompted.

Aithan shook his head. "Tobias decided Amara needed a mom when an old girlfriend returned to Seattle. He thought he was making a good choice, but Maeve turned out to be a real …. Mmm." He cleared his throat rather than cuss. The man never uttered a curse word. "She didn't like being second to Amara. Tobias got sick of her selfishness pretty quickly. Now she's fighting for partial custody."

"What? Why?"

"Alimony and child support."

"Cripes. Poor Tobias."

He sighed. "It sucks that Maeve won't take a settlement and just disappear. She contributed nothing to Scumwater but wants a share in the profits. They were married for a year and she bitched non-stop about the things moms do, like driving to and from school, making Amara's lunch, and taking care of her when she was sick. But when he filed for divorce? Oh, suddenly Mari was *precious* to her." His expression darkened. "The court granted her partial custody because she argued that Amara needed a mother's presence."

"How did she win that?"

He swigged his beer. "She has the money for a better attorney."

"That's awful."

He nodded. "Maeve was so unreliable about bringing Amara over for his weeks that he petitioned the courts to step in. That's why Dianne had her. She and John agreed to do drop-offs, so Tobias wouldn't have to see Maeve. She just loves to trigger him."

"They're her parents?"

"No. Juliette's. They try to shelter Amara from the worst of it, but Maeve likes to make scenes, if you know what I mean."

I did. "She sounds like a more manipulative version of my sister Greer."

"Every family has one, eh?" Aithan shrugged. He finished the last sip of his beer, then caught my hand. "Hey, let's not end our lunch on a downer."

I nodded and squeezed his fingers. "You wanna come back to my place?"

His lips curled into a slow, sexy smile. "Definitely. Lemme get the check."

I pushed back my chair and stood. "Okay. I'll run to the ladies room." I glanced back before entering the washroom. Aithan was watching me and he looked hungry. His expression freed the butterflies in my stomach again.

As I checked my hair and makeup in the mirror, and tried to calm my nerves, my phone buzzed. I pulled it from my purse and the fluttering excitement of the moment died. It was a text from Tristan.

> So how long have u been fcking my boss?

"Shit." I wanted to tell him I hadn't yet but would be in about thirty minutes. Instead I responded:

> Since never. I only met him the other day when he picked up your shit. And that's all I'll say about my private life. You're no longer a part of it. Who I date isn't your concern.

I turned off the phone and headed back to the table and the man I *wanted* to be with.

12

MOMENTS OF TRUTH

AITHAN'S SUV was right behind my car as I pulled into the townhouse garage. He parked in the carport and reached my door just in time to open it for me. His gaze traveled from my legs to my breasts to my eyes as I got out. He closed the car door then caught my waist with one hand, the nape of my neck with the other and kissed me.

I wrapped my arms around his neck and pressed against him, wanting to feel his whole body. I couldn't miss his erection. He was as excited as I was and his kisses were more demanding this time as his tongue caressed mine and promised more.

His hands went to my hips and he put a little space between us. "You drive me crazy."

I grinned, feeling more than a little naughty. "In the best or worst way?"

"Both." He took my hand. "Let's go inside."

I stopped him. "Wait. You should see this." I turned on my phone. Tristan had sent four more texts, each more vicious than the last.

"Not good." Aithan ran his hand through his hair as he

scanned them. "I'll have a long talk with him." He handed the phone back. "Why'd you show me that now?"

"I thought you should know this could get ugly if we keep going. It wouldn't be fair to keep you in the dark."

He nodded. "Thanks. But I'm not scared away that easily."

"Why do you want me?" The question slipped out before I had time to decide if I really wanted to hear the answer.

"What do you mean?"

"I mean, look at you. And look at me." My gesture went from his rock-hard physique to my pillowy one.

His gaze roamed my body. "I'm looking, Zel. And I love what I see."

"Don't you want some hardbodied woman?"

He shook his head. "We've discussed this already. I'm surrounded by women all day. All shapes and sizes. I know the difference between healthy and unhealthy and it's not about washboard abs. You're fit and gorgeously curvy and have this sultry voice that makes me want to close my eyes and soak it in for hours. You're smart and funny, Zel. You're successful and a helluva good cook, and you don't spend every minute counting macros, tracking your steps, and refusing to enjoy life because it might be a little unhealthy. I've had more than enough of *that*." He caught my waist again and pulled our hips together. "What I want is more of *this*."

I stared at him.

"You look surprised."

"Shocked, I think."

"Because I know sexiness and beauty come from what's inside a woman?"

I pressed my lips together and nodded. "I owe you an apology."

Now he looked surprised. "Why?"

"Because a part of me assumed you were shallow. I've had

too many shitty experiences with other men who were. I was wrong and I'm sorry."

He smiled. "Apology accepted. I honestly don't know why you'd bother with a relationship, especially after Tristan dumped all over your confidence. You don't *need* a man. That's obvious."

"Need and want are different things."

"True." He cupped my jaw. "So what do you want, Zel?"

"Not to screw this up."

"Me, too." He kissed me again then murmured, "And to go inside."

"Fair enough." I led him into the hallway and hung my purse on one of the coat hooks above the padded bench beside the door. When I turned, Aithan captured my face. He backed me into the wall, his mouth and hands firm but not cruel. Trapped between the wall and his hard body, I gasped as he kissed his way along my jaw, down my throat, to my chest. His fingers played across my nipples, teasing them hard.

"You're so beautiful, and this dress is sexy as hell, but it has got to go." He caught my hands and placed them on the tie at my waist. "Pull." I did and the bow unraveled. "Now the buttons," he said against my throat and moved my hands to the top one.

Trembling, I started moving down the buttons, slipping each wide, silver disc through its hole. I'd never had a man tell me to undress like this. He wasn't demanding, just certain. He knew what he wanted and giving it to him excited me.

When I was finished, Aithan eased the dress open and caressed me with his gaze. I'd chosen a matching bra and panties, blue-and-cream striped silk with tiny decorative bows. "Goddamn, that is the sexiest thing I've ever seen." His mouth crushed mine and his jacket hit the floor followed by his shirt.

Aithan sought the pins holding up my hair, and he made quick work of removing them. He tossed each aside then took down the chignon and ran his fingers through my curls. Pressing his lips to my ear, he murmured, "You don't know how beautiful you are."

He held my gaze for a long moment, then he growled and pinned me against the wall again, lifting my left leg over his hip and grinding his erection against me through his jeans. His fingers found the catch at the front of my bra. With a deft twist, the cups separated and he slipped my breasts free. He palmed them, humming happily as his fingers teased my sensitive nipples and my hips jerked against him.

I started to step out of my shoes, but a voice from the office doorway said, "No. Those stay on."

My eyes flew open, and I met Drew's gaze. He stood in the office doorway wearing my bathrobe, an impressive erection tenting his pajama pants.

"Drew." The reality of my situation crashed over me like a wave.

He saluted me with a steaming coffee cup. "Don't mind me, Brick, I'm here for the show."

"Isn't she amazing?" Aithan purred.

"Oh, you have no idea." Drew's voice was husky. He took a sip of coffee, his gaze never leaving mine, and slid his free hand into his pants.

I couldn't believe how casual they were while my brain pinged between turned on and freaked out.

"Hey." Aithan gently touched my cheek, recapturing my attention. "Are you okay with this, Zel? If you're not, just say so. It's alright to change your mind."

He wanted me, that was obvious. But if I said, "No," he would step back, cool off, and respect my choice. I glanced at Drew. He nodded. I could count on him. Always.

These two men put me first, even now, as I stood naked and vulnerable before them. And that gave me courage. This was another thing Old Zel never would've done. But New Zel? She was a bit more like Juno Galore than I'd realized. Bolder, braver, willing to take this risk.

I exhaled. "I'm more than okay," I said and captured his lips with mine.

Aithan groaned and returned my kiss. He hooked his fingers into my panties and shimmied them down my legs, helping me step out of them. He kissed his way up my thighs and belly, then straightened, captured my mouth with his, and slipped his fingers between my legs and into my folds, growling appreciatively to find me so slick and ready. He worked my clit in gentle circles, making me writhe. His mouth moved to my left breast and he licked and suckled as I moaned and pushed against his hand.

My voice pitched up as tension mounted inside me, and Aithan's fingers stopped circling. He kicked off his shoes and released his own pants. His erection stood free as he shed his underwear. His thighs and ass were smooth and muscular, his cock was thinner than Drew's but longer.

Drew offered a condom. "Need a sheath for that sword?"

"That's very gentlemanly of you." Aithan took it, tore open the little packet, and handed the condom to me. "Do me the honor, Zel, since you're already there?"

He meant since my hand was already wrapped around his cock. I wanted to suck him off, but I remembered Drew's rule. Instead, I placed the rubber against the tip of his dick, then rolled it down the length, taking a moment to caress his balls and watch his eyes roll up with ecstasy.

Aithan murmured something in a foreign language, then slipped my dress and bra off. He surprised me by sitting on the bench and pulling me onto his lap, facing Drew. Draping my calves outside his, he spread his legs, opening me for my other lover to see.

"Lean back, beautiful. Put your arms around my neck. You can trust me. I'm here to make you feel good."

I shivered. Those were the same words Drew had said. How were these men on the same wavelength? I exhaled and reached back, shoving my fingers into Aithan's thick, dark hair. My head fell back against his shoulder. The position arched my back and lifted my breasts. He moved his hips and his shaft slid across my folds, not entering my body, but teasing a sigh from my lips. His fingers danced across my ribs and stroked the fullness of my breasts. They flicked over the hard peaks of my nipples, eliciting another sigh. His lips moved along my neck, nipping and sucking as his fingers and his cock stroked me, pushing me closer and closer to release, but not giving me what I really wanted.

Still leaning in the doorway, Drew stroked his cock, his gaze sharp and hungry, his hand slow and sure. His movements matched the languid glide of Aithan's dick across my flesh.

His excitement made my heart pound harder. I wanted to wrap my lips around his cock while Aithan fucked me, but I couldn't. Drew had a rule and I wouldn't make him break it. He would watch while we fucked. This time.

Aithan's fingers found my clit again and I moaned his name. "Aithan. Please."

"What, beautiful? What do you want?" His tongue flicked over my ear. "Tell me. I won't do it unless you tell me."

God, he was relentless and it was making me so fucking horny. "I want you inside me."

"Thought you'd never ask." He shifted my body just enough to slide his cock inside me, slowly easing me down, and letting the entire length push deeper and deeper, all the way to the base.

I groaned with the exquisite pressure of his flesh filling me.

"Fuck." Drew fondled himself and drank me in with his gaze. "You're absolutely perfect, Brick."

Pinned by Drew's hungry gaze and drunk on the feel of

Aithan's skin, I bit my lip and drove down onto him, feeling every inch of my newest lover. He met each thrust with his own, holding my hips and keeping me steady, bouncing me onto his rock-hard cock.

"You like watching him, too," Aithan said, panting with each thrust. "Don't close your eyes, Zel. Watch him cum."

I moaned and thrust. Drew stroked his thick cock faster. Aithan rammed into me so hard his ass left the bench with each stroke. It was so fucking erotic. I mewled and gasped. A tremor took hold of me. Pressure built inside me then broke free. I arched and screamed with overwhelming pleasure. Aithan kept thrusting inside me, riding the waves as my muscles clamped onto his dick.

I opened my eyes to see Drew cum over the head of his cock and down his hand, pure bliss on his face. Aithan pressed his mouth against my back, grasped my hips, and pushed into me one last time. His low groan rumbled through me as he came, buried deep inside my body.

"Whoopsies," Drew said and disappeared into the downstairs bathroom. "Did I interrupt something between you two?" he called from the small room.

I laughed, but my voice sounded weird. Who was I? Zaftig Zel, the fat girl who was mocked by her classmates and dismissed by men? Or Zaftig Zel, the sexy woman who watched one man pleasure himself while watching her being pleasured by another man, which gave that man pleasure? Good lord, I was the center of a Gordian knot. No wonder I felt off-kilter. I needed time to unravel what I'd just done with Drew and Aithan and figure out where I – *we* – went from here.

Aithan hugged me close for a long moment, as if knowing I was freaking out a little. "Thank you," he murmured.

"For what?"

"Trusting me."

I turned my head and kissed him.

Drew emerged from the bathroom sans robe. Aithan lifted me to my feet, steadying me as I staggered a bit. "Your author wears your robe?" He pulled on his underwear and picked up his jeans.

"My author is eccentric and horny."

Drew held the terrycloth garment open and I stepped into it. He tied the sash then cradled my face between his palms. "You okay, Brick?"

I nodded. "Yeah, just … overwhelmed." I introduced them. "Aithan Mazur, this is Drew Katterman. Drew, this is Aithan."

Aithan gaped at him, his pants halfway up his thighs. "Wait. *The* Drew Katterman? You write the *Starship Steam* series. And the *Dragon Domination* books, right?"

Drew grinned suddenly bashful and it was a freaking adorable look on him. "Yeah, those are my books." He picked up my dress and lingerie.

"Dude, I love your battle babes. They're *amazing*."

Drew eyed me. "You ever listen to the audiobooks?"

"Only. Best thing to do while stuck in traffic." Aithan pulled his pants all the way up. They looked nice riding low on his hips. The man's physique was a God-given gift. He smiled like an angel and fucked like a demon, and I felt mighty blessed.

"Well, you just pleasured the narrator." Drew jerked his thumb toward me.

Aithan turned, his expression as bright as a kid's on Christmas morning. "No. Way."

It was my turn to blush. "Way."

"Now I know why I love your voice so much. I can't believe I didn't put two and two together." He grinned at Drew and confessed, "I've jerked off to all your books."

"Nice!" Drew high-fived him. "You know, in here is where the voiceover magic happens." He flicked on the office lights.

Aithan followed him into the room. "So you record everything here, Zel?" He peered through the window of the recording booth.

"Yep. Record, edit, and mix all my files. Everything's done here." I was still reeling a little, still off-kilter.

He moved to the shelf where I kept soft cover copies of all the novels I'd recorded, as well as the awards I'd won. "Damn, beautiful, I didn't realize how successful you are."

Before I could downplay my accomplishments, Drew said, "Brick's one of the top five fiction narrators in the industry. She records for the big publishers, too."

"Whoa. That's cool." Aithan grinned at me.

"I've been fortunate. Recording for Drew put me at the top of a lotta lists." I changed the subject. "So you like romance novels?"

"Sure." Aithan looked at all the award plaques on my office wall. "My sister, Paulina, got me hooked on reverse harem. I like strong women who know what they want and ask for it. Our mom's that way, so it's what I look for in a woman."

Drew flopped onto the loveseat. "That's why you were good with me watching you bang her."

Aithan shrugged. "I work hard to be fit, man. Why would it bother me to show off my skills?"

Drew folded his arms behind his head. The tattoos on his chest flexed with his movements. "In my experience, having another man in the room freaks out a lot of guys."

Aithan shrugged. "If Zel gets off being watched and sharing her body with more than one guy, I'm totally okay with that. I get off when she gets off."

Drew's head tilted. "So you're okay with ménage." His gaze drifted to me and Aithan's eyes followed. "Zel?"

I chewed my lip. *Here we go.* "Moment of truth."

Drew leaned forward and caught my hand. "You're safe with us, babe. You're still in charge. I promised you that, and I don't break promises. You know that."

I nodded. I trusted him.

Aithan stroked my jaw then tipped my head up to look at him. "You're in control. I'll never forget that."

Drew got up and moved behind me. "Turn off your brain, Zelda Claudette Gordon," he whispered in my ear.

How had I gone from barely attractive to Tristan, to pursued by two incredible men? I shivered and decided not to question my amazing fucking luck. They wanted me, even after seeing me naked. Even after my earlier hesitation. I swallowed and wished away the butterflies in my belly. "The more the merrier, boys."

Drew hugged me and kissed the back of my neck. "Tease. You know I have a car coming in twenty minutes."

Aithan laughed. "You blue-balled yourself, man."

I escaped them and dropped onto the loveseat. "You planning to get dressed before leaving, or are you gonna wear your PJs all the way to Boston?"

"Tempting," Drew replied, "but no. I was heading upstairs to get dressed when I heard the garage door open. Glad I waited."

I tucked my hair behind my ears, trying not to blush. "Me, too."

Aithan changed the subject. "Does he know about Tristan?"

Crapola. "Yeah, but not about the newest messages." I fetched my phone from my purse and showed the latest nastiness to Drew.

He scanned the texts, his expression darkening. "Fucking hell, Brick. Send these to your dad."

"I don't want to drag him into this mess."

Drew shook his head. "Maybe not, but that's not normal behavior."

"He's right," Aithan agreed.

I chewed my lip. "I'll text him after you leave."

Arms folded across his impressive chest, Aithan arched a

brow at Drew. "You're leaving just when things are heating up?"

Drew groaned. "Afraid so. I have book signings on the East Coast this weekend." He pulled me into his arms. "Rerecord those chapters when you're ready to get your head into them, okay?"

"I will. Don't worry. It won't take long."

"I know. I've got a few weeks of wiggle room before I have to pub that file, so you have time."

"Thanks."

He kissed me, then glanced at the clock. "Shit. Gotta put clothes on."

"Not the words usually coming out of your mouth," I remarked.

He gave me a threatening look. "Don't make me bend you over your desk."

"You and your idle threats," I said, then squealed and ran up the stairs, laughing as he lunged after me.

13

NO SECOND GUESSING

AFTER A QUICK SHOWER and clean clothes, I headed downstairs but stopped on the second floor landing as the guys' voices drifted up.

"I've got other commitments on the East Coast," Drew said. "You're here, man. You have the luxury of seeing her every day. That makes it easy to know the next steps. But my home is on the other side of the country. I don't know if a commitment is what Zel wants right now, and I can't drop everything and move to Seattle after one amazing week of fucking. That wouldn't be fair to either of us."

Aithan's voice rumbled in response. "You can't just leave her hanging. *That's* not fair. You're not responsible for her decisions, but you *are* responsible for bringing her into this relationship."

"Yes, but she needs to tell me what she wants. I won't second guess her and I promised her long ago that I wouldn't push."

"Come on, you know she wants you to stay."

"No, I don't. She hasn't said that. And I can't anyway. Not now. Zel isn't the only person I'm with."

"Does she know that?"

"Of course."

I did, and I'd deliberately shoved aside that fact. I knew his girlfriend lived with him in New York City, but it was more fun to pretend I was special rather than just another notch in his belt, albeit one he'd spent years trying to drill.

"What if, ultimately, you are just a fling, Zel?" I whispered. "That doesn't make all the things he said lies." That was true, but my confidence was still too shaky, my willingness to let him in still too new.

Drew added, "We have a professional relationship, too. I don't want to screw that up. We've been very good for each other's careers."

I sucked in a deep breath and squared my shoulders, then trotted down the stairs to the landing. "Hey, you ready to go?"

"Yes, but actually, no." Drew pulled me against him and pressed his lips to my ear. "I like him, Zel. Hold onto this one. He's good for you because he's all about you."

I leaned back and looked between my two lovers. "You know what? I don't want it to be just about me. If there's going to be an *us*, it needs to be equally about all of us. I've already had the relationships that had a *me* and a *him*. They don't work. I'm not making that mistake again."

Drew beamed at me, like a proud papa. "See, Aithan? She's amazing."

"Definitely."

I shook my head. "Why? I'm just being logical. Are relationships so fucked up these days that trying to find balance between everyone is exceptional?"

"Yeah," they said in unison.

"Shit," I muttered.

Drew kissed me again. "Promise you'll keep Aithan?"

"Absolutely, if he wants to stay."

Aithan caught my hand and gently tugged me away. "I want to stay."

Drew's phone chimed. "That's my ride." He opened the door and nodded to the driver waiting in the driveway, then stole me back from Aithan and kissed me hard, his tongue caressing mine, his hands on my back and my ass.

I pressed against him, wanting to remember the feel of his body molding to mine, the woodsy-citrus smell of his skin, and the tickle of his beard. "I'm going to miss you so fucking much."

"I'll text you once I'm home. We'll figure out the next time we can hook up."

"Tell me this is more than just a hook up, Drew." I pulled back and searched his eyes. "After all our history, say it's something more."

His gaze sharpened and his expression grew intense. "Do you want it to be more, Brick?"

"I … want both of us to be sure." I pressed my hand over his mouth. "Think about it. Take your time. Let me know." I stepped back and caught Aithan's hand. "I'll do the same, Playboy."

The car honked. Drew gave the driver the middle finger, even as his gaze searched mine. "I hear what you're saying, babe, and I won't rush in. I promise."

"And you don't break promises."

"Exactly." He offered his hand to Aithan who gripped it. "Take care of her."

"You know I will, man."

Drew grabbed his computer bag, kissed me quickly, and went out to the car.

I watched it pull out of the driveway, feeling melancholy. "I miss him already."

"I see that." Aithan's arms went around me from behind. "He'll be back."

"You think so?"

"I think he's crazy about you and trying to figure out how to make this work with his East Coast life."

I started to close the door but glanced down and saw a package tucked behind the planter on the stoop. I picked it up. "Well, crap. It's for Tristan."

"Why'd he have it shipped here?"

"Because the mail keeps getting stolen from his place. He had all his valuable items shipped here."

"I'll take it to work."

I arched my brows at him. "And he'll lose his shit. You don't want that kind of scene at the gym."

He grunted. "True."

I closed the door and pulled my keys from my purse. "I'll drive it over to his place."

"I'll go with you."

"You will?" I stared at him. "Is that a good idea?"

"We'll have to talk it out eventually and you're right, it's better if that conversation happens privately."

"May as well rip off the bandage. Unless ...." I studied his expression, looking for any hint of hesitation.

Aithan cocked his head. "Unless?"

"Are you sure you want to do this? I mean, it's messy, what with Tristan freaking out and me having another lover ...." I trailed off, afraid he'd take the out now that he had a chance and wasn't under Drew's scrutiny.

He cradled my face with his hands. "Unless nothing, Zel. I'm in this for as long as you'll have me. And you're right. Better I talk with Tristan privately—"

"Than in front of the entire gym," I finished for him. I turned my face and kissed his palm.

Aithan pulled me against him and kissed me, running his tongue across my lower lip.

"Stop that unless you want me to need another shower."

He chuckled. "Tempting, but let's get this delivery over with." He handed me my purse. "I promise to make you sweat later."

"Mmm, you better keep that promise."

He flashed that amazing smile of his. "I'll drive, you text your dad."

As we headed toward the Central District, I reread Tristan's texts. Some were just general bitching, but several were meant to embarrass me and threaten my publishing contracts.

> Do your mom and dad know what a slut you are, Deep Throat?
>
> I've got video I bet they'd love to see.
>
> Maybe I'll sell it to PornViews.
>
> Your agent would love to know about your new career, Skull Fucker. And those NY publishers you're so proud of. Do you think they'll like employing a porn star?

"Goddamn him." I let the phone fall into my lap. "Why's he being such a dick? He obviously never gave a crap about me, so why's he being a jerk about me seeing other men?"

"Because *you* dumped *him*." Aithan drove over Portage Bay and exited the freeway. Traffic wasn't too bad; we were just ahead of rush hour. "You took control from him, and if there's one thing I know from working with Tristan it's that he does not like to be out of control."

I tapped my phone screen. "These messages tell me that's exactly what's happening. He's losing control."

Traffic stopped for a red light and Aithan looked at me. "Do you think he's a threat?"

"Honestly, I'm not sure. He's really good at hiding his emotions."

"Not lately."

I nodded. "And that's probably good. Better he vent than let his anger build up. I just don't know how much anger he has toward me, or us. If this is just venting and bluffing, then it's nothing to worry about."

"But he's been verbally abusive in the past?"

Aithan turned right on Montlake and accelerated.

I sighed. "Yeah, I guess he was. I mean, you get accustomed to being belittled. It's not something that starts on Day One of a relationship. It just kinda creeps in. It doesn't mean he's suddenly turning into a monster though." I watched Seattle flash past the window, Craftsman and modern homes worth millions of dollars blurred by the rain that had started falling as we drove toward Stevens. "He was never physically abusive. I can't imagine him *hurting* me."

Aithan said nothing for a long moment. The SUV's tires splashed through puddles and its windshield wipers kept up a steady, squeaking rhythm. "Threatening to humiliate you and jeopardizing your work contracts isn't hurtful?"

I glanced at him. He was right, and I hated it. I shook my head. "I don't even know if this video really exists."

"You're making excuses for him."

Fuck. "Yeah. I am." I looked down at the black screen of the phone in my lap. "It's just that I hate to think I've been so completely wrong about him. You know?"

"I know. And I understand. I'm not sure what to do about his employment, either. I sent an email to my attorney yesterday."

I looked back at him. "Oh, crap. Really? I'm sorry you've been dragged into this. I don't want Tristan fucking up your business."

He shook his head. "Us dating isn't why I contacted him. I told you his behavior is contrary to Blue Water's policies. I need to understand my rights as his employer, regardless of my relationship with you."

That made sense. Employment law was tricky. We rode in silence, each consumed by different sides of the same problem.

Aithan circled Tristan's neighborhood until he finally found parking a block from the house. He shut off the engine and turned to me. "So you don't know if he really has a video of you?"

"No, not that I know of. Definitely not that I gave him permission to film. Honestly, I think he's just trying to embarrass me. He knows my dad's a lawyer and will demand to see these messages."

He leaned closer, his gaze holding me in place. "And if you're wrong?"

I swallowed. "I could lose my contracts with four major publishers. He could cost me a hundred thousand dollars."

Aithan's eyes widened. "Seriously?"

"Yeah."

"That's not a minor threat, Zel." He shook his head. "That's a huge financial blow. You need to bite the bullet and send those messages to your father if you think he can help you shut down Tristan."

I blew out a slow breath. "I'm sure it's the smart thing to do, but would you want your dad to read messages about you giving head?"

"If it meant protecting my career? I wouldn't hesitate. It's not like your dad doesn't know you've had sex, right?"

I laughed humorlessly. "Right. He knows I'm not an innocent flower. But, still." I held up my phone. "Deep Throat? Skull Fucker? It's humiliating."

"Exactly. And it'll enrage your dad. Hell, if it was my dad, he'd break Tristan's kneecaps and knock his teeth down his throat."

I gaped at him. "Your dad sounds charming."

"My dad's a retired Army master sergeant."

"I guess that explains his charm."

He laughed. "Yeah, Mama and Babcia didn't let him discipline us the way he really wanted to."

"Babcia?"

"Grandma. It's Polish."

"Ah." I took his hand. "Why haven't you walked away

from this? You can. I will totally understand. I won't be mad at you. I couldn't."

He raised my hand to his lips and kissed my fingers. "No, Zel. I don't run from problems, and I'm not leaving you."

"That's chivalrous, but not necessary. I don't need a man to take care of this bullshit."

"I know. And that's why I'm staying. Because you *are* capable of handling this. You're tough, and I find that incredibly sexy. I'm staying because I want to be with you, Zelda Gordon, not because I have some misguided idea that you need my protection."

I shook my head. "I'm not *that* capable. I'm still going to my dad for help."

"Because he has the resources you need to put Tristan in his place and end this mess before it gets out of control."

"True." I glanced at the Craftsman houses lining the block. Several were under reconstruction — more of Seattle's endless remodeling. "Okay, let's get this over with. If we're lucky, he won't be home."

Aithan nodded toward my phone. "Text your dad first."

"Right." With a sigh, I started typing.

> Hi Dad, I'm about to forward you a set of text messages I got from Tristan today. They're awful & embarrassing & I really hate sharing them, but I need advice on how to deal with him. I'm with a friend right now & not home, so it might be a while before we can talk. I'll call you later. Sorry. Thx.

With that I forwarded the texts and stuck my phone in my pocket. "He's gonna hit the roof." I grabbed the package and got out of the SUV. The rain was coming down hard and I raised my jacket's hood.

Aithan exited, too, and zipped his jacket. "Yeah, but not

because you did anything wrong." He caught my arm and we started walking. "You know that, right?"

I nodded. "Yep, that much I do know. I couldn't ignore Tristan's insults and disinterest any longer. The relationship was broken, but he wasn't going to end it, so I did. It's his fucking problem if he can't handle the way I cut him off."

"Except he's making it your problem too."

I covered his hand with mine. "And yours." We'd reached Tristan's rental.

Aithan grunted at that and we climbed the stairs to the old, tan house's front door.

With every step, I prayed my ex-boyfriend wasn't home.

14

THIS MESS WITH TRISTAN

A PETITE BLACK woman with a glorious halo of black curly hair answered the door. "Hey, Aithan, what's up?"

"Hey, Candy. Is Tristan here?"

Her gaze jumped past his shoulder to land on me. "Oh, man, are you Zelda?"

I nodded and proffered my hand. "Zelda Gordon."

She shook it, then stepped back to admit us into the small foyer. "Come in from the rain, but you shouldn't stay. He's down in the basement and *pissed* off."

Aithan introduced her. Turned out Candy was Candace Peters, Tobias's sister. She was pretty and had a definite don't-fuck-with-me air about her, and I liked her immediately. It made no sense that Tristan hadn't introduced us before, but he'd never even taken me to his place and barely mentioned her. I cringed realizing how far I'd shoved my head up my own ass to avoid the blindingly obvious signs of his contempt.

"I'm just dropping off a package that belongs to him," I said.

The stairs creaked, and I looked toward them.

"What the fuck are you doing here?" Tristan snarled as he came up them like a mad dog.

I scowled. "Regretting doing you a favor." I dropped the wet package on the table beside the door. "That came for you today. I thought it would be rude to return it to its sender."

"Rude?" He laughed cruelly. "What's rude is you showing up at my house with my boss who you're fucking."

Aithan raised his hands like he was trying to calm an enraged bull. "She thought it was better than sending it to the gym with me."

"Did she really?" Tristan sneered. "Because you didn't want a scene?"

"Looks like we're getting one anyway," I muttered.

"Thought I'd be grateful? Maybe even happy to see you? Are you fucking crazy, Deep Throat?"

Fuck you. He'd never called me that when we were together; maybe he'd said it behind my back. Maybe he'd joked about it with his loser Bellingham friends. He obviously meant to piss me off with it now, and it was working. "Yeah, I must be nuts. It's the only explanation for putting up with a dick like you for so long."

"Well, I can't believe I wasted so much time with a fat slut."

"Fuck you. I just had the best fuck of my life, so I know what a limp-dicked asshole you are. The comparison isn't flattering." From the corner of my eye, I saw Candace wince; this was not heading down a good path.

I grabbed Aithan's arm. "We should go. This was a mistake."

"No shit," Tristan said.

Aithan turned to open the door.

I shook my head. It was hard to look at my ex. Anger distorted his face and knowing I caused it made my stomach churn. "I didn't come here to piss you off, Tristan. And, for what it's worth, I'm sorry I didn't see sooner what a train wreck our relationship was."

"Fuck off, cunt." He stepped forward and spat in my face.

I gasped and jerked back.

Aithan moved fast. He pinned Tristan against the wall, forearm across his collar bones, hand locking Tristan's fist to his side. "Calm down, man," he said, his own voice remarkably controlled. He was the taller and broader man and used that to his advantage, leveraging his weight against Tristan.

"Get the fuck off me!"

"Not until you chill out. I'm not gonna let you hurt Zelda. You know that."

"Fuck you, man."

"That's not helpful." Aithan leaned into the hold and Tristan gasped. "Does Candy need to call the cops?"

"What?" Tristan's eyes widened, fear replacing anger. "Fuck no. I'm no threat."

"You spat in Zel's face, and you threatened to wreck her career. What part of that makes you not a threat?"

Breathing slowly to control my nerves, I wiped his saliva off my cheek with my sleeve. "You're not thinking straight, Tristan." My voice was even, thank God. "This is assault and the text messages are cyberstalking. I'll let them go uncharged, but I'm seeking a protection order against you."

"Are you fucking kidding me?" Tristan's gaze fell on me and he looked trapped, wide-eyed and at the end of his rope. I knew involving the police could mean unsealing his juvenile record.

Candace rolled her eyes. "Her dad's a lawyer, dip-shit. Of course she's not kidding."

"Let's leave, Aithan," I repeated.

His gaze pinned to Tristan, he spoke to Candace. "You gonna be alright with him here?"

"Yeah. I'm not worried."

"I'm not a fucking threat to anyone, man!"

Aithan obviously didn't believe that. "Are you sure, Candace?"

She nodded. "Yep. Tristan and I are cool. You guys go. I'll work this out with our boy."

Aithan didn't look happy, but he released Tristan and took a large step back. "Okay. Call me if you need anything."

"I will."

Tristan said nothing. He just glared at us and massaged his chest.

When we were seated in Aithan's SUV, he fished a packet of facial wipes from his glove box. "You okay?"

"Thanks." I took it, pulled one out, and scrubbed my cheek. My hands shook a little but it felt more like adrenaline than fear. "Yeah, I'm good."

"Freaking out?"

"Not as much as you'd expect. I don't know why. Maybe it's coming. Maybe I'll flip out in the middle of the grocery store or something. But I'm mostly sad that he's fallen apart like this. Tristan just seems lost."

"He's always been that way. Like a lot of what he says and does is an act to fool everyone into thinking he's got his life together."

I looked around for someplace to throw away the used wipe.

Aithan started the engine and pointed out a little paper bag on the floorboard. "Trash goes there." He was so fucking put together.

I stashed the wipe. "The only person Tristan is fooling is himself. And not very well." I didn't say anything about the trouble he'd gotten into during high school. It wasn't my place to tell his boss about that. As big a dick as my ex was being, he'd worked hard to put his messed up childhood behind him. "He needs to get back into therapy."

My phone rang as Aithan pulled away from the curb.

I answered, "Hi, Dad."

"Get a protection order, Zelda. Today. And stay away from him. Don't return his texts or his phone calls. Don't have any communication with him. Period. Get your goddamned locks changed — I'm sure you haven't yet — and save all his messages. I've got a call in to Ross Henderson. He's an excellent defamation attorney. I'll give him your number. You need to retain his services about this video threat."

"Yeah, my next stop is the courthouse."

"Good." He hesitated. "*Is* there a video?"

"Not that I know of. If he has that, he never got my permission to film it and he sure as hell doesn't have my permission to show it to anyone or sell it. I'll sue his ass off."

"That's right. That young man has shit for brains."

"Yeah, he does." I didn't mention the spitting. My dad would lash me for going over to Tristan's place.

"Talk to Ross. He can advise you on informing the publishers and your authors about this situation. I'm not sure what the best approach is and I don't want to steer you wrong."

"Okay. Thanks, Dad. I appreciate the help. And ... I'm sorry you had to read that."

"I'm glad you trust me to help, Punky. It's not like I think you're *inexperienced* or anything."

I laughed. "No, I guess not. Does Mom know what's going on?"

"Some. I didn't share the messages. She'd drive down there and cut off Tristan's balls."

"Yeah, she would."

Then he zigged on me. "Zel, who's the tattooed fellow you're hanging out with?"

"Huh?"

"Your sister forwarded a picture of you with some tatted up loser. Is that circus sideshow what this mess with Tristan is all about?"

We'd stopped at a light and Aithan must've heard,

because I could see him pressing his lips together, trying not to laugh.

I rolled my eyes. "That tattooed loser makes more money in a month than you earn in a year, Dad. He's not a freak or a deadbeat. And he's not the reason I kicked Tristan to the curb."

Aithan shook his head and stepped on the gas.

"Oh. Is he that author you do a lot of racy work for?"

I laughed again. "Yeah, Dad, Drew Katterman. He's a really good friend and not nearly as freaky as you think."

Aithan side-eyed me and I sucked a deep breath, struggling not to crack up.

My dad grunted. "He need any IP advice?"

IP was Dad speak for intellectual property. "Probably."

"Good. Give him my office number."

"I will."

"And get that protection order."

"I will, Dad."

"And be careful."

"I definitely will, Dad."

"Very good. Okay, I'll call you later, Punky."'

"Thanks, Dad. Bye."

He ended the call, and Aithan cracked up. I started laughing, too. It felt damn good.

When he finally stopped snickering, he said, "To the courthouse downtown?"

I sobered. "You don't have to do this, you know."

"I want to, Zel. I'm part of the reason Tristan's so bent right now."

I rested my hand on his thigh. "Thanks. It helps having backup."

"I definitely have your back." He turned right on Madison. "And your front."

A slow smile lifted my lips. "If you promise to repeat today's performance, you're welcome to both."

Traffic slowed and he risked a glance at me. "You like it from behind, beautiful?"

My cheeks heated as I remembered my first experience with Drew. "Yeah, actually. That's one of my favorites."

"Ever done anal?"

"No." Now I was seriously blushing. "That's kinda, I dunno, scary?"

He looked back at traffic and accelerated. "Not if it's done with the right guy."

I bit my lip. "You asking to be that right guy?"

I didn't know how he stayed so focused on his driving.

"When you're ready, yeah."

"That one of your favorites?"

"Oh, yeah. But I won't rush you. I know it's pretty intense for some people."

"Thanks."

We fell silent again. The rain eased as we passed Seattle University and Swedish Hospital. He and Drew were so different and yet the same. Aithan was quiet and cool but not cold. Drew was touchy-feely and gave no shits what others thought of him. But both men deferred to my wants and needs. They were free with their affection and their compliments, supportive and giving.

Aithan slowed and turned right. "What else do you like?"

I looked back at him. "Are we really having this conversation?"

"Yes." His voice and expression were matter-of-fact. "I want to know how to make you happy."

"Oh. Okay." I watched his face and said, "I really like sucking cock." His cool broke. His eyes widened and he licked his lips.

God have mercy, those lips were made for sin.

"I'll gladly help you out with that." He turned the SUV into a parking garage.

"You'll have to wait. I have an agreement with Drew, but I promise you won't regret it."

"I'm sure I won't." Aithan parked, turned off the engine, then caught the back of my head and pulled my lips to his, kissing me fiercely, his tongue in my mouth. He eased back and tucked my hair behind my ears. "Now, what's that agreement you have with your author?"

His intensity made my head spin, and I cleared my throat, buying my brain a second to realign after that toe-curling kiss. "No BJs and cocks stay wrapped until STD testing has cleared our jibblies."

He laughed. "Okay, off to the doc to get my jibblies examined ASAP, because you can't tell me you love oral, then think I can wait to see what you do with that talented mouth."

I leaned close and dragged my gaze from his lip to his eyes. "There's truth behind that fucked up nickname Tristan gave me."

"Damn." He exhaled and his expression turned hungry. "Let's get this court thing done, 'cause now all I can think about is getting you home and naked."

15

MORE THAN HE COULD SWALLOW

DREW DROPPED his travel bag in the foyer and stared around his trashed apartment. "Nine grand a month and it looks like a homeless psychopath lives here." His nose wrinkled. It stank of stale cigarettes and rancid meat. He'd been gone less than two weeks. How the hell had it turned into a cesspool in such a short time span?

He pulled his phone from his jacket pocket and texted Livi.

> WTF happened to the apt?

> Huh?

He scowled. "Fuck her and her 'huh'."

> The cleaning crew is supposed to be here every Mon. That was yesterday. It's a fucking pig sty & smells like a chain-smoking cow died in here.

> Oh. That. I told them not to bother me.

He gaped at his phone.

> Because???

> They woke me. It's annoying.

> You know what's annoying? Coming home to find my apt looks like addicts have been partying in it. Where the fuck are u?

> London. Don't get snippy w/me. You're the one who told them to come at 10.

> U can't haul your lazy ass outta bed by 10am one day a week?

> OMG. Obvsly u didn't get fcked in Seattle. Did the fat Amazon reject ur dick?

God, could she be any more of a bitch? Drew leaned back against the front door and scrubbed his palm over his face.

> When are u coming home?

> Dunno. Noos & I are in Oslo til nxt mo. Maybe I'll b back @ Xmas. I'll text u a list of gifts I want. & pics so u don't fuck up.

He stared at Livi's crap strewn across their living room.

"*My* living room. I pay for everything and she treats this place like a fuckin' flophouse."

He texted her a pic of the room:

> WTF?! Do you srsly not see all this shit?

The message was delivered but remained unread.

Cussing under his breath, Drew went to take a piss, but the bathroom was in even worse shape.

A brownish-orange ring encircled the toilet bowl and streaked its sides. Piss yellow stains marred the white marble floor. And there were shit stains on the seat.

He stared into the toilet. How the hell had a spoon gotten in there? And who the fuck had just *left* it? His gaze traveled the room and stopped on the walk-in shower.

"Oh, for fuck's sake!"

Dirty dishes sat in crusty piles, mold creeping over their surfaces and across the shower floor.

"This is beyond the pale," he said. "Beyond. The. Fucking. Pale."

He took more pictures, then shaking his head, Drew shoved up his sleeve and reached into the toilet for the spoon. As if in slow motion, his phone slipped from his coat's breast pocket and plunged into the water. He watched it sink and settle, clinking against the spoon and giving rise to a little stream of bubbles.

"Well, fuck me," he muttered, fishing out the phone and the spoon.

He washed his hands and the phone and headed for the kitchen. It, too, was a mass of unwashed dishes, unwashed counters, unwashed everything. Filthy pots sat on the stove, cooked pasta glued to their surfaces. A pizza box with four slices of moldy pizza occupied the oven. The microwave stank of burned plastic and was coated with something brown — peanut butter he hoped. He scrounged uncooked rice from the pantry, opened its plastic bag, and shoved his phone into it. Clipping the bag shut, he left it on the counter then returned to the bedroom. He changed into old sweats and a ratty tee shirt, then started cleaning.

Six hours later, the apartment was scrubbed enough to invite the cleaning crew in. Drew showered, changed back into clean clothes, and headed for the concierge office.

"Welcome home, Mr. Katterman." David Browning greeted him as he entered the small, neat room. "How can I help you?"

"Afternoon, David. Three things. Can the cleaning crew come in tomorrow morning? Can you recommend a good iPhone repair shop? And Olivia Isaak is no longer welcome in the building as my guest."

The man nodded, his expression utterly neutral. He considered his computer, clicking through several screens before replying. "The crew's calendar is full in the morning, but there's a two o'clock opening tomorrow. Will that do?"

"Yes. Book it, please. And tell them it'll be a deep cleaning. Extra charges are expected."

"Very good, sir. As for the phone, Cellular Stop is affordable and does a quick job." He wrote the address on a slip of paper. "And Ms. Isaak's status is noted. I'll inform management, security, and the doormen. May I suggest rekeying your apartment's front door? I can have someone from Maintenance there by four-thirty this afternoon."

"Do it. I'll drop my phone off for repairs and be back to let them in. Thanks, David. You're always saving my ass."

"That's my job, Mr. Katterman." He looked over the rims of his reading glasses. "Would you like to leave a message for Mrs. Ashton regarding the complaints?"

Drew frowned. Mrs. Ashton was the building's senior manager. "Complaints?"

"Oh. I see. Perhaps those weren't shared with you by Ms. Isaak. There were six complaints while you were away. I'm afraid the matter has been referred to the management team for violating your tenancy agreement."

Drew squeezed his eyes shut and sighed. "No, they were not brought to my attention."

"I'll print copies for you."

"Thanks. I should meet with Mrs. Ashton about this."

"That would be wise." He generated the notices and pulled them off the printer.

Scowling, Drew scanned them. Four noise complaints, one for rude behavior, and one for smoking in the halls. Livi had invited *friends* over to party while Drew was on the West Coast. "Does Mrs. Ashton have time this week?"

David considered her schedule. "Thursday at eight forty-five in the morning?"

"I'll take it. And apologize for me when you see her next."

"Of course, sir. She is aware that you were away on business." He gave Drew another slip — the meeting date and time — as well as a knowing look.

"Thanks."

After seeing the repair guys about his phone, Drew returned home and set it atop the living room radiator cover to dry. They alleged it was waterproof and should be fine once it dried completely. But they advised him to keep it powered off for three to four days.

As he wandered around the apartment, his mind compared Livi to Zel, and the former came up short each time.

His gaze hopped from item to item. Her things occupied every surface: clothes, fashion magazines, jewelry, purses, shoes, makeup. All crap Livi had purchased with his money but not his permission. "Zel wouldn't tolerate this shit."

Why did he put up with his girlfriend's excesses?

"Fuck this." He poured scotch over ice. Scotch he hadn't bought. "Fuck her."

He downed the drink, then gathered everything Livi had brought into his apartment. He piled it in the office. Dresses. Pants. Boots. Bags. Cosmetics, overpriced lingerie, art, and magazines. Bedding. Chairs. Electronics. Video games, hair products, nail polish, and all her motherfucking cigarettes. So much crap crammed into his three-bedroom apartment that he didn't buy or want.

A few of the items he'd gifted to her, but the majority she'd purchased. Livi was so addicted to spending his money that he'd placed a limit on her credit card the previous year. That had caused the first seismic fracture in their relationship. Six years together and she'd gotten increasingly greedy, lazy, and insensitive. The fracture spread as she complained about the constraints and ignored his attempts at reason.

And now this filth? The noise and rudeness? They were more than he could swallow. Livi had other lovers; Magnus was her favorite. That was fine with Drew. They'd always had an open relationship. But there were rules. Primary among them was not bringing people back to his apartment without his consent, and *never* when he was traveling.

That rule was unbreakable.

The maintenance man arrived to rekey the apartment while Drew finished searching out all of Livi's belongings. He'd have David send up a team to pack all her crap into boxes, then ship them to her parents' home in Connecticut. Her mom and dad could deal with her and her shit.

He. Was. Done.

With new keys in hand and Chinese takeout spread across the small kitchen table, Drew gazed around the apartment. It was sparse without Livi's clutter, but he felt like he could breathe again.

"This must be how Brick felt after she dumped Tristan. Feels good, Zel. Real good." He opened the white boxes of Chinese food and dug into sticky rice and General Tso's chicken. It was fucking delicious.

The next day, Drew emailed *Meteors and Mistresses* to his editorial staff and touched base with his marketing team while the cleaning crew scrubbed the last traces of Livi's mess off his floors and counters.

He checked his social media accounts and remembered his soon-to-be-ex had access to all of them. He changed the permissions and sent her a message telling her she was off them. They needed to talk, but breaking up with her through social media would be shitty. He'd call her once the phone was working.

Drew wasn't a dick.

Or an idiot.

He called his credit card company and cut her spending limit by two-thirds. She'd be pissed. He wasn't leaving her penniless while overseas, but she might have to cut her trip short.

"Too fucking bad." He opened the file of his latest book, *Rocket Rendezvous*.

Even with the cleaning crew running the vacuum and working around him, Drew finally felt focused in his own home. He got in ten thousand new words before the sun set. His rumbling stomach pulled him from his deep focus. The cleaning crew had left. The apartment smelled clean and looked shiny.

He showered, sans fucking moldy dishes, and crawled into bed. The crew had even put fresh sheets on the bed and laundered the dirty bedding and towels. Man, he loved those guys. He opened the building's payment portal on his laptop and left the cleaners a hefty tip.

Drew skimmed his news feeds. He responded to messages on social media, replied to emails from his teams, and started to send a quick note to Zel. But his inbox refreshed and a new one popped up.

It was from Livi.

*You fucker! Answer my texts! I need **more** money, not less. How the fuck am I supposed to survive in Paris on this pissy little amount?! What the fuck is wrong with you?!!!*

He replied.

My phone got wet. No texting for a few days while it dries. And I don't want to do this over email.

She emailed back immediately.

Do what? Be a little bitch?!

Drew scowled.

Have this conversation, but here we are, so fine. Learn to stretch your money, Livi. This is the last month I'll underwrite your lavish lifestyle. When you get back to the States, go to your parents' house, that's where all your shit will be. Our relationship is over.

What?!!! Fuck you!!! You fucking fucker!!!

Drew bared his teeth at the computer.

Use fuck or exclamation points one more time and I'll close that card and cut you off completely. I'm trying to be civil about this, Liv. You knew the rules. You ignored them. Again. I'm the one handling the fallout with my building's management team. If I lose this apartment, it'll be because you screwed me over. I'm sick of your greed and laziness.

Asshole. I'm done with you. You suck in bed and you're boring. Magnus said he'll pay for my trip.

Good. And good luck to him. I'll ship out all your crap tomorrow. You might want to warn your parents that a shitload of boxes are coming their way. Goodbye, Livi.

Fuck you!!!

Drew laughed. He signed out of his email and went onto his credit card's website. He found Livi's information and cancelled her card. He knew her dad had an emergency account for her, so she wasn't truly stranded, but it felt good to shut her out.

"Yup, Brick. I see why you cleaned house so thoroughly. There's nothing better than throwing out the trash."

He plugged in his computer to charge, turned off the bedside light, and settled into clean sheets and blankets.

Tomorrow he'd go for a run, then finish drafting *Rocket*.

"And email Zel," he said around a yawn.

16

THE FATKINI

AITHAN and I didn't have anal or oral, but we did have sex on every level of my house, every night for the rest of the week.

"Why does Drew call you Brick?" he asked Friday morning after we'd returned from a run and eaten breakfast. We sat at the kitchen table. He sipped coffee and I snuggled Lulu while Frank snoozed on the sunny windowsill.

I said, "Computer, play 'Brick House' by the Commodores."

The AI responded and the song filled the kitchen with funk.

Aithan laughed. "Seriously? He nicknamed you after this song?"

"Yup. We met at a conference. Before he even introduced himself, he said, 'You have the sexiest voice I've ever heard. You're hired.'" I laughed. "I was so confused by him."

"Had you done romance before that?"

"Oh, yeah. I was there to speak on several panels about voiceover, including one about narrating explicit sex scenes, so Drew's work wasn't shocking or anything. But he was even more brash back then, flush with success and partying with fans. He's learned to tone it down, believe it or not. A certain amount of jealousy dogs him, though he's the nicest, most generous guy."

"I guess that's par for the course when you're at the top of the sales charts."

"Yeah, and Drew's prolific. He churns out one or two books a month, and they're good. His fans are rabid and insanely loyal. There's a certain amount of fan-girling and more than a few women who think they just need to get his attention, suck his cock, and that'll be the ticket to being Mrs. Katterman and having a huge fortune to spend lavishly."

"How much success are we talking about? He's pretty rock-n-roll, but he doesn't come across as super-rich or anything like that."

"He'll probably top eight figures this year alone."

Aithan paused with the mug halfway to his mouth. "Seriously?"

"Seriously. He gives a lot to children's charities and funds a writing project for rural kids. That program pays college tuition for a dozen students each year."

"Damn. And I thought I was doing well by holding a yearly fundraiser for Seattle's children's hospital and doing monthly blood drives."

I squeezed his arm. "You're doing great. Don't compare your success to Drew's. He'd be the first person to tell you that. Not even he can fully comprehend his fortune, but he does understand it comes from hard work, persistence, and a whole helluva lotta good luck."

He studied me. "You really like him."

"I do. He's done a lot for my career. But I also value his friendship. He's been kind to me, and it doesn't hurt that he's an amazing lover."

"Don't make me jealous."

I giggled. "If you wanna fuck him, I won't get in the way."

He shook his head but chuckled. "He's not really my type. No breasts and too much tackle."

"You have nothing to worry about in the banging department, Aithan Mazur. I'm blessed with two extraordinary lovers." I finished a glass of water and listened to Lulu purr. "I'm just afraid I'll screw up everything. And there's a lot on the line with Drew and me. I don't want to lose him as a friend or an employer. I worry about crossing a line and not being able to go back to just professionals, ya know?"

He nodded. "If it makes you feel any better, before he left, he mentioned the same fear about losing you."

Being reminded that Drew shared my concerns should've eased my worries, but I hadn't heard from him since he landed in Boston. "I guess seeing how quickly things turned ugly with Tristan makes me anxious."

"Would Drew get mean like that? He doesn't strike me as that kinda guy."

"No, I can't imagine that. He's much more kind-hearted than Tristan ever was. He cares about me, that's a certainty. But he has a long-term girlfriend in New York. I'd like to pretend I'm the only woman in his life, but I'd be lying to myself."

He nodded. "So what do you want to do about it?"

I focused on the silkiness of Lulu's fur under my fingers before answering. "Ask him to commit to me. But I won't pressure him anymore than he'd pressure me. We've been down that road before."

"You two have history."

I nodded. "We do. He tried to make more of our friendship once before, but I wasn't in the right place at the time." I looked up. "I didn't respond well."

"Yet, he's still here."

Lu stretched and rolled off my lap. She hopped onto the sill and started bathing Frank.

"Yeah." I got up, lifted the kettle off the stove and made

tea. Then I sliced a Honeycrisp apple to share. "The same 'no pressure clause' applies to you, you know," I said around a bite as I sat back down. "I'd love for us to be exclusive, but I won't demand a commitment. You decide. I'm not going anywhere."

He swallowed the last of his coffee. "Neither am I, Zel." He reached across the table and twined his fingers with mine. "I like sharing your life and your bed. I like being with you. I like us as a couple. And I don't mind you being with another man, as long as he's good to you."

His phone chimed on the table by his elbow. He glanced at it. "Mm. I forgot about that."

"What?"

"Tobias and I are supposed to grab lunch. It's his day off from the brewery and his parents have Amara this weekend. We usually get lunch the second and fourth Fridays of the month when his folks or his in-laws have her."

"Invite him here. I'll make something for all of us."

"You sure? You don't always have to feed me, you know."

I laughed. "I'm used to cooking everything from scratch. Feeding one or two more people is easy. And you guys are better company than the last jerk I regularly cooked for."

He leaned across the table and kissed me. "You know how to make me happy."

"Don't you know that saying about a man's heart and his stomach?"

He grinned. "Yeah. It's a lie. Everyone knows the way to a man's heart is through his pants."

I pushed him back into his chair. "Degenerate."

He took his coffee cup to the sink and rinsed it. "No, no. That's Drew. I'm the gentleman, remember?"

"I do. And I'm happy to have such a wholesome man in my life."

Grinning, he returned to the table, leaned down, and kissed me, letting his lips drift along my jaw to my neck.

I squirmed. "Tobias? Lunch? Remember?"

"Screw that guy."

I laughed. "I don't think he's the type to jump into bed with his best friend's girl."

"You'd be surprised."

I leaned back and considered him. "What're you saying?"

"You're a very attractive woman, Zel. Tobias isn't blind and you're very much his type."

I shook my head and started to question that, but his phone rang.

"Yeah, man," he answered then mouthed, "Tobias," to me. "I'm at Zel's. She invited you over here for lunch." He listened. "I'll ask, but I don't think that's a problem." He looked at me. "Okay if Candace comes, too?"

"Sure. I like her."

"She's one hundred percent welcome." He listened more, then asked me, "Can they bring anything?"

"Hamburger buns and cheese. Drinks, if they want alcohol or soda. I have ground beef and the rest of the fixings. I'll make a salad, and brownies for dessert."

He relayed that and hung up after giving them my address. "They'll be here in an hour. Put me to work, beautiful."

I sent him downstairs to the back patio to fire up the barbecue.

After lunch, Candace and I loaded the dishwasher while Aithan cleaned the grill and chatted with Tobias.

She handed me a rinsed plate. "Just so you know, there's never been anything between Tris and me." I glanced up and she added, "I'm in a committed relationship."

"Yeah, I know. He told me you have a girlfriend."

"Oh. Okay. Cool." She laughed a little nervously. "I was worried you'd think I was behind his pissy behavior."

"Ha! No, no. I've known Tristan too long to blame anyone else for his bullshit."

"It's like that with some people." She passed over a glass. "You just know how they're wired, right?"

"Definitely. My friend Drew's that way with me. I swear he sees right into my soul."

She leaned against the counter and twisted the damp towel around her hands. "I'm disappointed with Tristan. I thought he was better than all this shit."

"Yeah, I did too."

"Are you pressing charges?"

I sighed. "No. He needs help. He needs to learn how to treat other people better. But will ruining his life accomplish that?"

She shrugged. "I think he's depressed."

"He has been for a long time. He's on medication, or supposed to be, but I'm pretty sure he stopped taking it."

"I think you're right." She frowned. "I don't remember seeing him take anything, though he could hide that from me. It's not like I pry into his business or snoop in his medicine cabinet. I wouldn't want to embarrass him or make him think I'm kicking him out."

I added soap to the dispenser. "Will you now?"

"Nah. We're on good terms. As long as he pays his rent and keeps the house clean, I have no reason to make him leave. He's actually the best roommate I've ever had."

"Huh." I closed the dishwasher and set its cycles. "He never picked up around here. Rarely helped with dishes or cooking, and definitely never offered up a dime toward expenses."

"Ugh. It's like there's two sides of him. You must hate him."

"No. I probably should, but I just feel sorry for him." I

started the dishwasher. "I know what a fucked up childhood he had."

Tobias and Aithan came into the kitchen.

"Tristan?" Tobias asked, picking up on the last of our conversation. I nodded, and he added, "You're a better person than I am. I'd bust his chops for the shit he's pulling."

"You've been burned by Maeve," Candace pointed out. "You're still licking your wounds."

"Exactly. Don't put up with it, Zel. He'll just push harder if you cut him any slack."

Candace cocked her head at me. "What was the last straw?"

"Before what?"

"Before you kicked him out."

"He didn't tell you?" When she shook her head, I told them about the fatkini insult and how it made me realize what a turd Tristan was.

"What a shithead," Tobias muttered.

"Yeah," Candace said.

"Absolutely." Aithan grinned at me. "But I wanna see this bikini." Candace snapped the wet towel at him.

I bit my lip and looked down, suddenly feeling insecure. "I'm not comfortable wearing it in front of anyone."

Aithan's expression fell, but he came and leaned against the counter beside me. "Remember when you were a kid and you fell off your bike or busted your butt roller skating?"

"Yeah?" Where was he going with this?

"That bikini is just like that. Tristan knocked you down, Zel. He kicked the confidence out of you."

Candace nodded. "You gotta put that thing back on and flaunt what you've got in a great big fuck you to him."

Tobias nodded. "They're right."

I shook my head. "He's never going to see me in it."

"Of course not," Candace said, "but that's not the point.

You bought it because you knew it would make you feel sexy, right?"

I pressed my lips together.

Aithan asked gently, "Are you're gonna let Tristan steal that feeling from you forever?"

I stared at my striped socks and considered their words.

"Think about it, Zelda," Candace continued. "He insulted you to assert power over you. And you're still letting him."

That felt like a kick in the tits because it was true. I looked at her. "I thought you were his friend."

"Nah. I'm his roommate. That's not the same thing. We get along, but it's not like we hang out or anything. He does his thing. I do mine. Tristan isn't the type of person I'm friends with. He's too insecure and selfish."

She was right — they all were — about Tristan, about the bikini, and about me giving up power to him. I tucked my hair behind my ears. "Okay. I'll put it on."

Aithan brushed a kiss against my temple. "Good. Get back on that bike. I think you'll be glad you did."

I went up to my bedroom and pulled the bikini from the back of my lingerie drawer then sucked in a deep breath before changing. I didn't look at myself in the mirror, afraid I wouldn't like what I saw. Facing the bedroom door, I closed my eyes and gave myself a mini pep talk. "You can do this, Zel. You'd planned to wear this in front of a beach full of strangers. You can wear it in front of friends." I blew out another slow breath but sat on the bed instead of heading downstairs. "Fuck." I was shaking. Maybe this was that delayed post-Tristan freak out.

I jumped to my feet at a tap on the closed bedroom door.

"You okay?" Aithan was in the hall.

Was I gone that long? "Maybe?"

"Can I come in?"

I swallowed. "Yeah. Okay."

The door swung open, but Aithan just gawked. "Holy

moly, woman." His face lit up with the dopiest grin. "You're stunning."

I shrugged and looked away, feeling profoundly insecure. I sank back onto the bed.

He closed the door and came to sit beside me, all delight smothered. "Not feeling it, huh?"

"No. Feeling more like the girl who hid in her bedroom eating cookies after another really shitty day at school."

He put his arm around my shoulders, and it felt so good to be sheltered like that. "I wish you could see yourself through my eyes, Zel. Then you'd know there's no reason to feel self-conscious."

"It's weird. I'm totally secure in my work. But in my appearance?" I raised my hand and rocked it back and forth. "I guess I just heard too many lumbering elephant jokes when I was growing up."

"From?"

"The kids at school. They called me Zaftig Zel. I was tall and fat, had zits and braces and long greasy hair. I wore the baggiest clothes I could find. And it got worse when my thyroid went wonky. I had anxiety attacks and gained eighty pounds in six months. My high school boyfriend dropped me 'cause I was embarrassing. I ended up hospitalized and stopped going to school." I shrugged. "After that, I just didn't want to be *seen*."

"That's rough, especially since I want everyone to see me with you, beautiful."

I rested my head on his shoulder. "I really need to get over this."

"How can I help?"

I tilted my head to consider him. Aithan was so good to me; I hoped I deserved him. "Hold my hand? Maybe my hair, too, if I throw up?"

He chuckled. "Wouldn't be the first time I've done that. At least you won't be drunk and obnoxious." He stood and offered his hand. "Coming down?" I took it and let him pull me to my feet. He grabbed my robe from the back of the bathroom door, "so you don't get cold," then led me downstairs. I shouldn't have been anxious, but I couldn't shake the shame Tristan had attached to the bikini and my body.

Candace and Tobias were still in the kitchen. We entered the room and he stared. "Damn, Zel, you're a knockout times ten."

His sister's eyes widened. "I wish *I* could fill that out the way you do. Belinda Emory has nothing on you, girl."

I fought the urge to snatch the robe. "Who?"

She arched a brow at me. "Belinda Emory? She's a plus-size cover model."

Tobias nodded. "She's built like sex on two very long legs."

"Just like you," Aithan added.

I stared at them. "I am?"

Candace and Tobias stared back at me, and she said, "Seriously? You really don't know how hot you are?"

"Um, no?" I replied, wondering deep down if they were just being nice.

As if reading my thoughts, she said, "We're being one hundred percent honest, Zel, not blowing smoke up your ass."

Tobias nodded. "You could be a super model."

"You're tall and curvy and gorgeous," Candace added. "And if you don't put on that robe, I'll be forced to leave because Aithan and Tobias will jump you like horny dogs smelling a bitch in heat."

"Candy!" Tobias looked mortified and shoved her as she laughed.

Aithan just nodded, his expression thoughtful. "She's not wrong."

I chewed my lip, still trying to decide if all of them were complimenting me to spare my feelings.

Candace pulled out her phone. "Here. I'll show you Belinda Emory." She did a quick search and held it out to show me a stunning, curvaceous brunette in a string bikini.

"Oh, I've seen her." I scrolled through a few more pics of her in other swimwear. She was sexy and confident, obviously comfortable in her skin in a way that I so was not.

"Now, look at her then look at yourself." Candace indicated the mirror in the powder room opposite the kitchen.

I stared at the model then slowly took a step to the side to see myself in the distant mirror. Same high cheekbones and long, wavy hair. Same small waist, curvy hips, and ample boobs. Same long legs.

"How tall are you?" she asked.

"Five-eleven."

Tobias said, "Goddamn, woman, I can't believe modeling agents aren't chasing you down the street."

I crossed my arms over my chest. "I was approached a few times when I was in New York on business. I just — I don't know — didn't take them seriously. I thought they were creepers."

Aithan shook his head. "The only reason you're not walking runways is your lack of confidence."

He was spot-on about my total lack of self-assurance. I shook my head. "That's not a lifestyle I'd want. I like narrating books. I like living in other peoples' worlds, and I'm paid well to do it. I'd never return those calls. I don't want to be noticed like that."

Candace leaned against the kitchen counter. "That's fair, but can you understand now what those scouts saw in you? Can you see what makes Aithan and Tobias, and your friend Drew, pant when you're around?"

Tobias palmed his face. "Can you stop?"

She answered him with a wicked grin.

I shrugged. "Maybe?" I turned away from my reflection. "I don't know, Candace. I'm not confident like you or like my half-sister." I laughed humorlessly. "She's petite, blonde, and *oozes* self-assurance. Men fall at her feet, and she walks all over them."

"You hate her?" Aithan asked.

I tilted my head and gave a little shrug. "Sometimes. Definitely did when we were teens, though I adored her when I was little. But she thinks I can't do anything for myself."

He scowled. "That's absurd."

"I know."

And like the devil herself had heard me, my phone buzzed with a message from Greer.

17

THE DEVIL HERSELF

> I'm boarding the plane now. Pick me up in front of the Alaska terminal at 4:45.

> No. I told u to stay downtown. I have company & I don't want your help.

I GROWLED and turned off my phone, leaving it on the kitchen counter. "God, she can't take no for an answer."

"Wait," Candace said, "was that from your sister?"

"Yes. She has the most annoying timing."

"Wow." Tobias peered at my phone. "That's kinda freaky."

"Believe me, I know. She always shows up when I don't want her in my business."

"Family can be like that," he said drily, and Aithan and Candace laughed.

She rested her cheek on her brother's biceps. "Tobias is the youngest of five kids and the only boy. Just ask him about nosy sisters and no privacy."

I shook my head sympathetically. "Oh, man, that musta been miserable when you were a teen."

"Understatement." He side-eyed his sister.

Her smile was evil. "We were cruel, it's true." Then she sighed and wrapped her arms around his waist. "I'm just glad he listened when we told him Juju was the right woman for him."

Tobias pulled a face and waggled his head. "You have your moments." Then he returned her hug.

Aithan picked up my phone. "But that's not why Zel's wearing a bikini in her kitchen. Has Drew seen it on you?" I shook my head and tucked my hair behind my ears. He murmured, "You know he'd want to."

I laughed, a little embarrassed. "No doubt."

He held out the phone. "Why don't you send him a pic?"

"I don't know, Aithan."

He caught my hand and placed the phone in it. "He's nuts for you, beautiful, and this'll get him on the next flight to Seattle."

I laughed again. "Probably true."

Candace said, "Zel, if this is the infamous fatkini, you need to buy more of them. I mean it, girl. You are killing it … and Aithan. And you'll kill Drew if you send him a selfie."

Aithan jerked his chin at Tobias. "You're also slaying him."

"Annnd that's our cue to leave," Tobias said as Candace and Aithan cracked up again.

"What?" I asked. "Why?" I really enjoyed talking with him and his sister.

Candace caught her brother's arm. "I'm managing Scumwater tonight. I cover when Tobias is off. He promised to drive me over." She nodded at the phone again. "You really should send a selfie to your other guy."

"I'll take it." Aithan tilted his head, a soft, encouraging smile on his lips. "Whaddya say, Zel? Pic for Drew?"

I sucked in a slow breath. He was right. Drew would love the photo, and I needed to see myself in a new light. I had to find my spine if I wanted to hold on to these two amazing guys. I held out the phone to him. "Okay."

"Yeah?" There was no denying the delight in his voice and on his face. The guy genuinely loved the way I looked in the fatkini.

"Yeah." Maybe sounding confident would make me feel confident.

He held up the phone. "Little sexy smile, beautiful?"

Candace added, "Better hurry before he and Tobias melt from the heat."

I felt awkward, but her comment and the dopey grin plastered across Aithan's face made me giggle.

He snapped a pic and his grin widened. "This is perfect." He held up the phone for me to see.

I had to admit the photo looked pretty fucking sexy. "That's *me*?"

They all laughed, but not in a mean way.

"Yeah, Zel." Aithan wrapped his arms around me. "Now do you see what Drew and I see?"

"Maybe?" I stared at the photo, trying to justify my mental self-image with the real deal.

He turned the phone to show Tobias. "She's hot, right?"

"Oh, hell yes." He shoved his hands into his pockets and peered at me from beneath his brows.

"Why's it so hard for you to see how beautiful you are?" Candace asked.

"I guess because I heard how ugly and weird I was from all the kids around me growing up. Like I told Aithan upstairs, I was the tall, fat girl with braces and zits. I grew up in a wealthy neighborhood. A lot of the girls were beautiful, like you and my sister. I was a bull in a china shop and a lot of kids reminded me daily that I wasn't petite or pretty."

"Forget that," Aithan said. "You can't let your childhood bullies mess up your whole life."

I shrugged. "They generally don't. Hell, I'm more

successful than any of them. I guess I just can't get past this whole fucked up body image thing. Having a thyroid disorder doesn't help."

"Why?" Tobias asked.

"It messes with my head." I tapped my temple. "Graves' disease and mood disorders go hand-in-hand."

Aithan fetched my robe from the back of a dining chair. "What do you see when you look in the mirror?" He held it open for me.

I slipped into it. "Seventeen-year-old obese Zel, the girl whose thyroid was a disaster, whose boyfriend dumped her for getting too fat, the girl on the verge of being a shut-in."

"That's not what any of us see." He hugged me from behind. "You have body dysmorphia, Zel."

"Ever thought about counseling?" Tobias added.

I shook my head. "It's not stopping me from living my life and running my business, so no. I used all those negative comments to drive me. Maybe that's not emotionally healthy, but success does taste pretty fucking sweet."

Aithan nodded. "We all have history that's made us miserable, but it also made us who we are." He tied my robe's belt. "The thing is some people want to be unhappy and drag you into the gutter with them. It's the only way they can feel good about themselves."

"When they're pulling other people down?" Candace asked.

"Yeah." Tobias nodded. "That's Maeve."

"And Tristan," I added.

Candace glanced at her watch then grabbed Tobias's arm. "Come on, little brother. I gotta get to Scumwater."

"True dat." There was hunger in his dark eyes when he met my gaze. "Thanks for the awesome lunch, Zel."

"My pleasure. You're welcome back anytime. Both of you."

Candace elbowed her brother. "She means you."

"And you," I protested. "I really enjoyed chatting with you. I don't have many female friends."

Aithan and I walked them out then returned to the kitchen to unload the dishwasher.

A cellphone sat on the counter beside the fridge. I picked it up. "Whose is this?"

"Uh-oh." Aithan took it. "That's Candy's." He pulled his own phone from his pocket. "I'll text Tobias."

I kept unloading the dishwasher, wiping moisture off the glasses as he texted.

I looked up when he muttered, "*Kurde*." His brows were furrowed.

"What's wrong?"

"Something at the gym. I gotta deal with this." He went out to the balcony and made a call. I kept busy and tried not to eavesdrop.

"It's Aithan. Is Juan free?" He paused, waiting. "Hey, man, what happened?"

Finished with the unloading, I changed into yoga pants and a loose sweater then fetched my laundry and sorted it across the kitchen floor. The laundry room was adjacent to the kitchen. After putting up the first load I took a few minutes to clean the litter box in the first-floor bathroom.

I was coming out of the garage after dumping the stinky stuff in the trash, when the doorbell rang.

It was Tobias.

"I came for Candy's phone."

"Sure, come on in."

He followed me upstairs where we found Aithan sitting on the couch, wearing a scowl.

"Everything okay?" I asked.

He rubbed the back of his neck. "Tristan got written up."

"Oh no." I washed my hands at the kitchen sink and poured a glass of water. "What'd he do?"

"He was talking about me and my personal life in front of

clients." He shook his head. "First time Juan's had to warn a trainer."

I sat beside him. "Think he's trying to get fired?"

He shrugged. "I have no idea what he's thinking."

"He's not," Tobias replied. "He's just pissed off and doesn't know how to handle being mad."

"He spat in Zelda's face Wednesday afternoon."

"What?" Tobias looked from him to me, his eyes wide. "You fucking serious?"

"Yeah," Aithan replied. "I drove her downtown to file for a protection order."

"Holy shit," he muttered. "The guy's losing it."

"I don't understand why," I said. "He really didn't give a shit about me when we were together, he made that abundantly clear. And, yeah, I took the initiative and dumped his ass, but not getting his way or not getting to make that move doesn't really explain why he's so hellbent on fucking up his life and mine." I snuggled against Aithan and he wrapped his arm around my shoulders.

"You know what, Zel? This part of this mess is my problem, not yours." He turned my face toward him and kissed me, his lips caressing mine, his tongue sweeping my lower lip and eliciting a little moan from me.

"Ahem, still here, lovebirds," Tobias said.

I giggled and sat back. "He came for the phone."

Aithan fished it from his pocket and held it out. "I told you I'd bring it to the gym tomorrow."

Tobias took it but his gaze remained on me. "Yeah, I know."

"But you couldn't stay away," Aithan murmured.

I patted the couch. "There's room."

Tobias slowly shook his head though his desire was obvious in his intense gaze and the way he adjusted his jeans before pocketing the phone. He shrugged and looked down. "As tempting as that is, and you are tempting me,

Zel," he met my gaze, "my daughter comes before my dick."

I stood and grabbed his hands. "I totally respect that."

A slow smile spread across his face. His eyes were bright, but he looked down again, bashful in a way that made me melt. "Thanks, lady, you've got a good heart to go along with that rockin' body." He drew me into a hug. Glancing over my shoulder, he said, "Come on, man, get some sugar." Then Aithan's arms were around me from behind.

"Awww. Friendwich." I sighed. "This is nice." The guys laughed.

From the landing of the stairs, a voice said, "What the hell, Zelda. You couldn't bother to pick me up because you're screwing a bunch of guys?"

Tobias jerked away. Aithan's arms tightened around me.

Greer stood at the top of the stairs wearing a dark-green jumpsuit, her makeup and hair perfect.

Goddamn her timing. I sneered at her. "Did you consider knocking first?"

"Why should I? I have a key." She shook her keyring at me.

"Remind me to kill Mom for giving you that. And we were hugging, not screwing. That comes after you leave." I gestured to the guys. "Aithan Mazur and Tobias Peters, this is my half-sister Greer Gordon-Rosinski. She's a pain in the ass and not staying."

"Yes, I am," she retorted.

"No. I told you no, Greer. You don't get to make decisions for me. I'm not five anymore, and I'm sick of you not listening. I told you I had company. I told you I don't want or need Tristan in my life. I told you to stay downtown."

She glared at me, a host of emotions rolling across her beautiful face like Midwestern weather. Shock. Confusion. Annoyance. And, finally, defensiveness. She crossed her arms.

Tobias said, "And that's my cue to leave."

I touched his arm. "See you soon?"

He smiled softly and kissed my cheek. "Definitely." He and Aithan bumped fists. "See you tomorrow morning, man."

"Yep. Be ready to work hard. Burpees are on the plan."

Tobias groaned. He pocketed his sister's phone, nodded to Greer as he went around her, and disappeared down the stairs.

"Are you leaving or staying?" I asked Aithan as I went to the kitchen and put my glass on the counter.

"Whatever you want, beautiful."

"Stay. Greer's leaving."

She gaped at me. "I am?"

"Yes. You have a room booked."

Greer scowled. "How do you know that?"

"The fucking cab idling below my kitchen window is how I know that. I'm not an idiot, despite what you think. And I don't need you here to handle my life."

Her head cocked and she smiled smugly. "That's not what Mom said."

"I don't care what Mom did or didn't say. I'm managing fine without you."

"Yeah, I see that. Throwing yourself at every dick you meet?"

My jaw dropped. "That was rude, even by your weak standards. Show a little respect? Aithan is my guest."

He finally spoke up. "I asked Zel out, not the other way around."

Greer snapped, "Stay out of this, pretty boy."

I slammed my hand on the dining table. It made a satisfying thwack and she jumped. "Leave the key and leave my house. Now, Greer. This conversation is over."

"What? You can't throw me out."

"Bitch, I just did." I held out my palm. "Key."

She rolled her eyes. "You're such a child, Zel."

"I'm not the one insulting a man I don't know."

"I insulted you, not him."

"Get. Out."

With another dramatic eye-roll, she dropped the key into my hand and turned for the stairs. "Don't come crying to me or Mom when these guys use you and throw you aside like the trash you've become. I came here to help. But if you don't want the truth and my guidance, I can't be held responsible for your misery, Zelda."

"Don't let the door hit you on the way out," I replied.

She tossed her blonde hair over her shoulder and huffed down the stairs. I followed and locked the door behind her. The cab door shut and the car pulled out of the driveway.

I turned off the porch light and rested my head against the door.

"You okay?" Aithan had followed me. He rested his hands on my shoulders.

I started laughing. What a fucking rollercoaster ride the last few days had been. "Yeah, though I'm wondering what the hell I did to deserve an overbearing bitch of a sister." I turned. "I'm sorry you had to see that. Seems like you're bearing the brunt of the crazy in my life. I swear it's not always like this."

He dropped his arm around my shoulders and steered me toward the stairs. "Everyone has crazy. Most just hide it a bit better. At least I know when and where it's coming from with you."

"Thanks, I think."

18

SPINNING OUT OF CONTROL

I SAT in bed with Lulu and Frank. Aithan had gone home. He had an early start in the morning and we both knew it was better if he didn't spend the night boinking me. Besides, I had my own work to do over the weekend. I still needed to rerecord the two chapters for Drew and there was an erotic short story due Wednesday that I hadn't even read yet.

Thinking of Drew reminded me of the bikini picture. I pulled it up and forwarded it to him, hesitating for only a moment before typing, "The fatkini says hurry back," then hitting the blue SEND button.

Before snuggling down into bed with the short story, I checked my email. Mostly ads. An automatic payment reminder from Seattle's electric company and one from my business credit card. My agent had sent me four scripts to audition. Checking their deadlines, I winced. All were due Monday. "I know what I'm doing on Sunday." It served me right for ignoring work for a few days. That wasn't like me. But Tristan's crap and the unexpected relationships with Drew and Aithan had thrown me completely off schedule. "Get your shit together, Zel," I lectured myself.

Frank looked up with sleepy eyes. He yawned, showing a

killer's teeth, then stretched and slunk across the bed to settle beside my hip. I obliged him with chin scratches and continued browsing my email.

I also had an introductory email from Roush, Guthrie, & Henderson LLP. Ross Henderson wanted to meet to discuss my problems with Tristan. I chewed my cheek, debating about my next steps. Deciding talking to a lawyer wasn't a bad idea, I responded with my availability and my contact information.

I found a brief email from Drew. He was back in New York and things were messy. I worried about what that meant. Was it his girlfriend? His manuscript? His marketing? I wrote back:

That sucks. I'm sure it'll work out. Check your phone for a message. I think it'll make you feel better.

Closing my computer, I settled in to read a bit of paranormal hanky-panky.

The next morning, after my usual routine, I stepped into the recording booth and knocked out the short story. It was pretty steamy and had me wishing Drew or Aithan was around. I sent the first ten minutes of "Haunted Cravings" to the author for approval, then opened Drew's manuscript and reread the final chapters.

But instead of focusing on the story, my mind kept wandering to the man. I checked my email, but he hadn't responded. Nor had he seen the message with the fatkini pic yet.

I chewed my cheek and poked at my worries.

"Fuck, Zel, this isn't helpful. Watched pot and all that bullshit. He's probably buried in his manuscript." Or in his NYC girlfriend. Livi couldn't be ignored, no matter how much I wished it.

My email updated with a message from the short story author:

Great work, Fannie! I love it. You're approved to finish the file. Thanks!

I replied:

Sounds good. I'll edit the rest of the story and have the files to you this afternoon.

I put the story through editing software then addressed each of the edits the proofing program flagged. I checked my levels and listened to the final file, then saved it to the cloud and an external drive, and sent a download link to the author. Finally, I generated an invoice for her and closed the files and apps.

Sitting back on the office loveseat, I sighed and stretched. It felt good to have a finished project. Drew's incomplete novel nagged me. I didn't like having projects hanging over me like that, but I also knew forcing the performance wouldn't make me, or him, any happier. I still had a few days to deliver the finished book.

I skimmed Fannie Gordon's social media accounts, posting a note about life's craziness and how happy she was to have another finished project releasing soon. Between my pseudonym and me, I had a ton of regular listeners; enough to guarantee most of my audiobooks became bestsellers. That was another reason I had contracts with the big publishers.

I browsed the accounts of some of my friends and groups then, out of habit, opened one of Drew's profiles. I was greeted with a picture of him and a gorgeous platinum-blonde woman dressed for an evening event.

Olivia Isaak, his East Coast girlfriend.

Great night at the Girls with Toys *launch party. Thanks for the invite, Toni and BGG. Livi and I had a blast!*

The post was three weeks old.

I considered the petite woman hanging on Drew's arm. I'd seen her in person only once, but we'd never really met. Livi wasn't someone I ever wanted to know. A short silver dress hugged her body, reminding me exactly how slim she was. The woman didn't have an extra ounce of fat on her.

"She's about as opposite from me as he can get."

I logged off. Closing my computer, I stared at the bookshelf, chewing my bottom lip. No wonder he hadn't bothered looking at my picture. His sexy little NYC girl was keeping him plenty happy.

I groaned. "Stop it, Zelda." My mind was running down the drain, but I couldn't help it. I wanted to be more than just a fling for Drew. He'd said there was more between us. I saw proof of that in the years he'd pursued me. So why couldn't I believe it?

Because old thought patterns were hard to break. I considered texting Aithan, but that was stupid. He had clients to help and a gym to run. "God, you're being such a baby."

Deciding busy was better than idle, I returned to the booth and knocked out the raw recordings of the four auditions my agent wanted. When I was finished, I put them aside to edit Sunday. By that time it was five o'clock and my stomach was rumbling.

Upstairs, I fed the cats and warmed up empanadas I'd made and frozen the previous weekend. I batch cooked every other weekend, so I had plenty of food in my freezer. The scents of garlic and onions and fried dough filled the kitchen.

While I ate, I contemplated my reaction to seeing Drew with Livi. Maybe I was infatuated with him, but did I *love* him? That seemed impossible. Sure, we'd known each other for a few years, but our interactions had been for business.

In reality, the last two weeks were the most time we'd spent together. Was that enough time to fall in love with someone? I'd never been in love, I knew that now. I wasn't sure I'd even *liked* Tristan; he'd just been available. I scowled at that ugly truth. I hadn't loved him. He hadn't loved me. He'd been someone to fuck, and even that hadn't been satisfying.

I definitely felt differently about Drew and Aithan. I wanted to be with them, and when we were together, I felt good about myself. They encouraged me to feel that way. Both were generous, in bed and out. Both treated me like I was special. I'd certainly never gotten *that* from Tristan. He was too damned selfish to give me that kind of attention.

"Ha! And now that I have his attention, I don't want it."

My phone rang, interrupting my spiraling thoughts.

"Hi, Mom. What's up?" I knew the answer before she said anything.

Greer.

"What did you say to your sister?"

"I threw her out of my house. She insulted me and my friend, Aithan. She refused to listen when I told her I had a guest and she wasn't welcome here."

"But why not?"

"Because she's a bitch, Mom!"

"Honey, she's your sister."

"So? How does that make her behavior more acceptable?"

"Greer just wants to help you, Zelda."

"No, Mom. Greer just wants to be right. She doesn't listen to anything I say. She jumps to conclusions always predicated on me being an idiot who can't take care of myself."

"She's worried about you."

"Oh, bullshit."

"Zelda."

"It's true, Mom. If she was worried and really cared, she'd hear the words coming out of my mouth. Instead she dismisses everything I say as stupidity and tells me I'm a slut."

"She didn't."

"Yeah, she basically did."

My mom was silent for a moment. "So you *are* seeing a few guys?"

"Yes, I'm dating two men. Drew and Aithan. They're good to me in ways Tristan never was. Greer should be happy that I'm happy. She should trust my judgment when I say I don't want Tristan back. That he was a crap boyfriend. Instead, she told me to take what I can get 'cause men aren't lining up outside my door, like I'm some hideous, pathetic monster who's destined to become a crazy cat lady."

"Oh, dear. I didn't know she was so harsh to you."

"Oh, Mother. You just don't want to know that your eldest daughter treats your youngest daughter like shit."

"Well, I still think her heart is in the right place."

"I still don't think she has one."

"Zelda Claudette Gordon, don't be mean. Greer has always tried to take care of you."

"Greer has always tried to micromanage my life. Have you forgotten that I'm the one who went to speech therapy because she talked for me? Or that I'm the one who wasn't allowed to dress herself until I was ten because she decided I was color blind. I'm the one who almost repeated sixth grade because Greer did all my homework because I was 'too slow to understand the problems.' I'm the one who didn't get her driver's license until I was eighteen because Greer decided I wasn't capable of passing the driving test."

"She thought she was doing what was best for you."

"Mom, do you know why Greer getting married and moving to San Francisco thrilled me so much? It wasn't because I was happy for her. I was happy for me. I finally got her out of my hair."

Mom sighed. "Will you ever forgive your sister for trying to take care of you?"

"Not until she stops trying!"

The doorbell rang. "Hold on. Someone's at my door." I went down the hall and saw Aithan through the peephole. "I gotta go, Mom. Aithan is here."

"Oh. Well, call me later, honey. I think we need to talk about this more."

I opened the door. "Hi, I'm on the phone with my mom."

"Okay," he mouthed and stepped into the foyer. He'd brought me roses. Red. Fucking. Roses.

"Oh my God. Aithan brought me flowers, Mom. Tristan never did that in the two years we were together. You know what he brought me? His dirty laundry."

"Zelda, call me later?"

"Okay. Tomorrow. Bye, Mom. I love you."

"I love you, too, honey. Bye."

I hung up and took the flowers, burying my face in them and breathing deeply. "Are you for real?" I kissed him hard.

He slid his hands around my waist and returned the favor, nipping my lower lip and grabbing my ass. "I think so." He followed me upstairs. "I take it Mom's worried?"

"Greer called her. My mom wants my sister and me to be friends and has a thousand excuses for her bitchiness." I searched the cupboards and finally found a vase from flowers my Dad had sent me when I signed with my agent. The roses went into the vase with water and the little packet of weird crystals florists insist keep them alive longer. I put them in the middle of the dining table next to the gerberas. Lulu and Frank immediately jumped up to inspect them. They sampled the leaves then decided they weren't tasty enough to bother with and head-butted Aithan for love instead.

He happily obliged, rubbing ears and chins, and eliciting purrs of delight.

"I thought you'd be at the gym all day," I said.

"I was. It's seven. Did you lose track of time?"

I glanced at the clock. "Shit. I totally did." I fed the cats while he inspected the contents of the refrigerator. "Empanadas?"

"Yeah, beef. You want to try one? They're made with cassava flour and lots of garlic."

"Mmm, sounds awesome." He pulled the container from the fridge. "What kept you so busy?"

"Recording and editing. My brain spinning out of control. My mom pissing me off." I waggled my head. "You know, the usual."

He laughed. "Your brain's always running rampant?"

"My brain is unreasonably overactive."

He brushed my hair back and kissed my forehead. "Stovetop, oven, or microwave?"

"Microwave works great." I wrapped four in paper towels and plated them. He put them in and started heating them while I pulled out leftover salad from our lunch with Tobias and Candace, and sliced an avocado.

"How's everything at Blue Water?"

"Quiet. Which is good. No one seems bothered by Tristan's tantrum."

"What will you do about him?"

"Juan gave him the rest of the week off." He set out plates. "It means I have to cover his classes, but I'm hoping he'll screw his head on straight with the paid break."

I sniffed. "I hope so too."

"Any word from that lawyer?"

"Yeah. I'm waiting for him to confirm an appointment time next week."

"Good."

The microwave beeped and we sat down and ate. Aithan loved the empanadas. "They're different from the ones I've had, but I like them just as much. The filling is delicious."

"These are one of my favorite AIP foods. Easy to make, they last a long time, and everyone likes them."

"Did you finish Drew's novel?"

"No, not yet. But I finished and sent off an erotic short story."

He paused in clearing the table. "Erotic?"

"Yeah." I grinned, liking the spark in his eyes. "You wanna hear it?"

"Yes, please."

"You know how this will end, right?"

"Oh, I sincerely hope so."

19

MOJO FOUND

I AWOKE to the most delicious feeling, fingers gently stroking my left breast. I sighed and stretched. Lips and tongue replaced the fingers and I arched my back, pressing against Aithan.

He chuckled and surged up to capture my lips with his. "Good morning, beautiful," he murmured before giving my right breast its due ministrations.

Every flick of his tongue zinged straight to my crotch and made me squirm. His fingers slipped between my legs and he murmured approvingly at the dampness he found. "Someone's awake and," he flicked his tongue over my right nipple, "perky."

Deciding to return the favor, I reached beneath the sheets and found his cock, hard and throbbing, a little slickness of its own proving he was just as awake. "I'm not the only one, Mr. Fitness." I stroked him, squeezing and releasing. He pulsed beneath my fingers.

He groaned. "Damn, woman, you know what you're doing. No doubt about that."

My other hand grabbed his jaw and pulled his face up. I wanted those lips, wanted to bite and suck them, run my tongue over them then capture his mouth. I wasn't gentle, but Aithan met my ferocity with his own, biting and sucking, thrusting into my hand and sliding his fingers through my folds and into my body.

I groaned and arched. He ran his lips over my throat and down my chest.

"Get a fucking condom."

"Yes, ma'am." The bedside drawer scraped open. A package crinkled. Then Aithan settled between my legs. I wrapped them around him, hooking his thighs with my calves, and moaned as he slid into me. Every goddamn inch of that impressive cock slowly pushed deeper until he filled me all the way to his base. He pinned me that way, holding his body over mine and gazing into my eyes.

"You're so beautiful, Zelda." He rocked his hips back and thrust them forward, a slow, steady rhythm that made me pant. My hips met his thrusts. My legs tightened and pulled, encouraging him to move faster, delve deeper. But Aithan would not be rushed. He pulled out to the very opening of my body, thrust his cock in fast, shallow movements that made my nerves sing, then plunged hard, 'til he was balls deep.

"Oh, God." I moaned and pushed against him, reveling in the feeling of fullness. I squealed as his mouth found my nipples and his fingers found my clit. The world fell away. I knew only the pleasure filling my body, the pressure for release building with each thrust.

I started pushing back harder, faster, and Aithan matched me, his focus on my clit and my core as he pumped into me. His breathing sped, his muscles trembled. I knew he was working my body to climax first, but he wasn't far from his own release.

His lips found my neck and sensation overwhelmed me. The tremors broke free and ripped a cry from my throat as they took over. Pleasure surged through me. Aithan couldn't ride it out the way he had with Drew watching. Two more deep thrusts and he settled into me, groaning low and pressing his face to my chest as he came hard.

Even after coming, my muscles continued to spasm. Aithan pulled the yellow comforter up and wrapped it around both of us as he spooned me and kissed my shoulder.

The tremors finally subsided and I made a little squeak as he kissed my neck again.

"You okay?" he whispered.

I nodded. "Very. Just overwhelmed." I rolled over and looked into his blue eyes. "That was a big orgasm."

He smiled like the fucking Cheshire Cat. "I aim to please, Ms. Gordon."

"Mmm. You definitely did that, Mr. Mazur. I'm well pleased." I stretched, reaching over my head and pointing my toes toward the bed, arching off the mattress, and sighing as I let the stretch go.

"Goddamn, that's sexy." He ran his hand over my belly. "You do that again, and I'll roll you over."

I laughed and sat up just as Frank appeared in the doorway. He zoomed across the room and leaped onto the bed, landing in my lap.

"Oof!"

Aithan laughed.

Frank head-butted my face and purred loud enough to be heard downstairs.

"I know, I know. It's breakfast time." I dumped the cat at the foot of the bed and fetched my robe from the floor. I shrugged it on and followed Frank to the kitchen as Aithan headed for the shower.

"Helluva way to start the day," I said to the cats as Lulu trotted into the kitchen, tail high and crooked. They meowed and circled as I opened a can of lamb pâté and divided it between their bowls. I rinsed and refilled their water bowl then put the kettle on to boil.

Leftover bacon went into the microwave, followed by grain-free apple-plantain fritters. Aithan wandered into the kitchen, barefoot but dressed for the gym as I was microwaving a cassava flour English muffin. His hair was wet and he ran a hand through it, slicking it back.

I stared. Fuck me, he was so damned sexy.

He caught me looking. "Whaaat?"

I smiled. "I like having you around in the morning."

He returned my grin. "I like being here. It's a helluva nice way to start the day."

"My sentiments exactly." I poured cold brew into a cup and topped it off with hot water. "For you, sir." I passed him the mug. He took a sip then set out plates and silverware at the breakfast bar.

The bacon and fritters were plated, along with fresh blueberries and the first muffin while a second cooked.

"Honey, ghee, or jam?" I asked.

"All?"

I nodded. "Good choice."

The microwave beeped and I plated the second English muffin then sat beside Aithan. We ate in companionable silence while the cats bathed.

"I'll be at the gym all day." He indicated his empty plate. "And this was amazing. Best homemade breakfast I've had in a long time."

I smiled. "I'm glad you enjoyed it. Come back any time. I'm batch cooking and baking all day, so there'll be lots of delicious food in the freezer."

"You do that every weekend?"

"Every other. But I'll make more this time, since I expect to have a regular visitor."

He sipped his coffee and nodded. "Yep, you'll have company. More than you can stand. Kick me out when you get sick of my face."

I kissed his cheek. "Never. I can't imagine tiring of this

amazing man."

After Aithan left for Blue Water, I went grocery shopping. I didn't need staple items, but I was low on meat, vegetables, fruit, and avocado oil. Back at home, I gathered all the ingredients I needed to cook four breakfast dishes to spread throughout two weeks. I had a large freezer in the garage. It held ingredients for my meals then held the pre-made meals once they were cooked.

After making all my breakfasts, I'd go on to make lunches and dinners, plus snack foods and desserts. I had this down to a science with specific meals I enjoyed enough to eat over and over without losing my mind, and snacks and desserts to help me through the rough days, like when I had PMS so bad I could kill and stuff the body in the freezer to be eaten later.

Once I got the bacon and a dozen sweet potatoes into the oven, I mixed up a huge batch of pork sausage patties — I made the best, hands down — and got that frying in leftover bacon grease. Between the bacon and the smoked salt I used in the sausage patties, the house smelled delicious.

It felt good to be busy. It stopped me from scratching the scab that Tristan had gouged into my psyche and kept me from chewing on my own insecurity over Drew's continued silence.

I plugged in my phone and started an audiobook — a romantic fantasy narrated by my friend Amanda Bright. She'd asked me to give it a listen and provide feedback. She was in her second year of pro work and I was her unofficial mentor.

Amanda's husky British accent filled the kitchen:

"It was the kind of night when thieves and lovers slipped through open windows, taking what wasn't theirs. The kind of night when kings felt their mortality while plotting assassinations and sorcerers brewed potions and raised the dead. The kind of night when Halina jerked awake, unsure if she'd called out in her sleep,

struggling to escape the nightmare that had wrapped her in her worst fears."

I cooked, baked, and listened, making notes of what worked and what she needed to focus on improving for the next title. Overall, the narration was excellent and I was absorbed in the story while making sweet potato brownies. So when my phone rang, I jumped a little and stared at it in confusion.

Then I saw the caller ID. I paused the book and answered on the third ring.

"Drew! Where've you been? I was starting to worry."

"Ah, hell, Brick. I'm sorry. I dropped my phone in the toilet and had to wait four days to be sure it was totally dry before using it. Plus, Livi made a fucking mess of my apartment. I had to meet with building management and grovel so I didn't get booted outta my digs."

"Oh, man, that sounds awful."

He laughed. "Understatement. I cut off Livi's credit and ended our relationship over email. Which is really shitty, but, goddamn, she left dirty dishes in the shower, Zel. The *shower*, for fuck's sake!"

"Eww. That's so gross."

"Right?"

He'd left his girlfriend? My stomach fluttered. "I'm sorry you had to split up with her."

"Nah, don't be. It was time to move on. You know she was a head case and jealous as fuck. Wanted to control who I saw and when but didn't give me the same say in her relationships. The only thing she liked about me was my bank account and the cushy lifestyle it afforded her. No ambition, that one. I didn't realize how much it was pissing me off until spending time with you. You've got your shit together, babe. That makes you so fucking sexy. You have no idea."

"Well, I'm still sorry you had to go through all that. I just want you to be happy, Playboy."

"I know. That's what's so amazing about you. You've got such a generous heart. And, fuuuck, that bikini pic! I almost dropped the phone in the shitter again when I saw it. Had to jerk off in a coffeehouse bathroom while looking at you."

I couldn't help but laugh and blush. "You didn't."

"Hell, yes, I did. I'm coming back to Seattle next month. You better be wearing that when I ring your doorbell."

My heart jumped. He was coming back. "Really? I get to see you that soon?"

"Only if you promise to wear the fatkini and fuck the living daylights out of me."

"I'll fuck you raw."

"I love it when you talk dirty. You're the best girlfriend I've ever had."

I bit my lip. "I'm your girlfriend?"

"Hell yes, you are." He paused. "Aren't you? Say, yes, Zel."

"Definitely yes. I've been going nuts without you here."

"What? You've got Aithan."

"Yeah. And I want you, too. I'm a greedy girlfriend, Drew. Get used to it. Greedy and demanding."

"Yes, ma'am. You know I like women who know what they want—"

"And aren't afraid to demand it?"

"Bingo."

We chatted until the oven timer went off.

"You're cooking?"

"Baking. Carob chip tiger nut cookies are coming out. Brownies go in next. Donuts and apple bars are on the docket, too. Then I have dinners to make."

"Oh, right. I forgot you batch cook. And now I'm fucking hungry."

I laughed. "Go. It's past dinner time there."

"Yeah, I've got leftover pizza."

"Mmm, I do miss pepperoni pizza."

"Sorry, babe."

"That's okay. I can splurge when you're in town."

"But you'll get sick, right?"

"Maybe. A bit. But some things are worth the antacids."

"Well, you know you best. I'll call you tomorrow night, babe. And dream about you tonight."

"Don't wear out your hand."

He laughed hard at that. "As if."

I baked and cooked for three more hours, stopping when I'd made everything and my back was too sore to keep going. I groaned and stretched. It was sore across the middle at my bra line. That was another drawback to having big boobs that no one ever mentioned. The weight of my tits pulled on my back muscles. Day to day, it wasn't a problem, but on batch days, it got to me.

Finally sitting down to eat my own dinner, I mused, "He left Livi and I'm his girlfriend." I could not stop a shit-eating grin from taking over my face.

Amanda's book ended and I sent a quick feedback email to her, then I put my dishes in the sink. Feeling sassy, I ran upstairs and put on the fatkini and my robe. I took the last of the batched food out to the garage freezer and went to my office.

Sitting down in the booth, I opened *Stars and Strippers*. I put on my headphones, set up a new file, and recorded those last two chapters.

And I fucking *nailed* them.

I finally remembered what it felt like to be sexy and strong. I finally reconnected with Juno Galore in all her blaster-toting, alien-screwing, badass glory. And I did it wearing a sexy-as-fuck fatkini.

Screw Tristan. Obviously, he didn't know good thing when it was right in his lap.

I took a selfie — headphones and cleavage — and sent it with the chapters to Drew. I followed up with a text message.

> Check your inbox. Upload links & a little surprise. Let me know what u think. Xoxoxo

He replied immediately.

> Oh? Hold please ... Ohhh! Nice & are u trying to make me drop my fking phone again?

I sent the laugh-cry emoji.

> I'll give these a listen & get back to u ASAP.

> OK. Thx!

I read my email and responded to my agent. She'd booked me to narrate two of the books I'd auditioned for. One of the producers wanted me to record in-studio in New York, but they had a production delay and were asking for a February date. The other book I could do from home. I confirmed both bookings and added them to my calendar. Maybe Aithan and I could hang out with Drew in NYC. "That could be fun," I said as Lulu wandered into the office. "Right, Lu?"

She looked up at me and got all crazy eyed. With a flick of her tail, she charged from the room and up the stairs. The sound of feet scurrying overhead and some hissing meant Frank had ambushed her. After a good tussle, they'd curl up on the wing chair beside the window and enjoy a lovefest and spa day.

"Weirdos."

My phone rang. It was Drew.

"Nice fucking job, Brick! You got your mojo back. That's some of your best work yet."

"Yeah? I think so, too. I don't want to brag, but you're lucky to have me."

"Oh, I know. And I plan to have you again and again. Got my hands down my pants just thinking about fucking you."

"You're unbelievably perverted."

"Just the way you like me. Aithan's the gentleman, remember?"

I laughed. "Yeah, he is, but he's not vanilla."

"Oh, definitely not. I could watch you getting banged by him for days. That's hot shit."

"Why do I think we'll end up in your next book?"

"Zelda, you've been in the last fourteen books. Every time Juno Galore gets some tail, I'm picturing you. Expect the sex to get steamier, babe, 'cause now I have the real deal for reference. It's so much better than my imagination."

"You keep going and this'll turn into erotica."

"Nah, too much plot. These chapters are approved and I'm signing off on the whole novel. Finish and send it over. My readers are gonna love this one."

Bouncing in my spot, I felt giddy. "Sweet! Okay, I'll finish up and have it to you tonight. Not much left to do. Thanks to you and Aithan, I'm feeling pretty effing good."

"You *do* feel good, especially when I'm effing you."

I got off the phone and happily edited the files. I uploaded the finished novel, sent Drew a link, and closed my computer. It felt amazing to finally have my groove back. I headed upstairs, took a quick shower, and debated between comfy and sexy pajamas.

Opting for comfy — they wouldn't be on for long once Aithan came home — I plugged in my phone to charge then returned to the kitchen to brew a cup of tea. It was just after eleven-thirty, but I was a little too amped up to crawl into bed.

"Home," I mused, realizing I'd thought of Aithan living here without hesitation. I let myself dream of Drew and

Aithan with me. "Would you like two new daddies?" I asked Frank as he hopped up on the counter and shoved his face into my hand. I scratched his chin, smiling as his throat vibrated and his eyes closed in contentment. "You're a sweet kitty, Frank, even if you do get a bit jealous."

He bathed my hand then jumped down and went for a late-night snack.

I returned to musing about Drew and Aithan and some very naughty group activities.

20

JUMP

AITHAN LOOKED up as Juan knocked on his office doorframe. "I'm heading out, boss. You leaving soon? It's eleven thirty-five."

Glancing at the time on his phone, Aithan nodded. "Right behind you. Thanks, again, for handling Tristan this week."

"Yeah, man, no problem. I hope the break does him some good."

"Me, too."

"You want me to wait for you?"

"Nah. Go ahead. You pulled a long day. Get some rest and come in late tomorrow. I'm gonna text Zelda, then head home."

"Okay. See you tomorrow."

"Yep. Goodnight." Aithan closed the gym's financial files and shut down his computer, then he texted Zel.

> Looong day, beautiful, & I gotta be in early tomorrow. I'll swing by your place tomorrow night, if that's cool with u. Let me know. Gnight.

He almost added, *I love you,* but paused and sent the

message as it was. He pocketed his phone, shut off the office light, and locked the door. Shouldering his duffel bag, he doubled-checked the front entrance lock then headed for the employee entrance and the back lot.

He liked Zelda more than any other woman he'd been with since college. She was so open and giving, and she made him want to open up and give back. She never seemed to be after anything from him, which was refreshing. The few women he'd dated over the last eight years had left him feeling like a hood ornament — a show of status. Or like a piece of man meat — brood stock to make and support their babies. None of them made him feel accepted or ... loved. Zelda did. She was strong but also vulnerable, smart, funny, and fun. And she was confident in her career. Her success made her sexy. Hell, so did her gorgeous body. The woman was a modern day Valkyrie.

Aithan smiled to himself. Maybe he really did love her. Maybe he needed to find the balls to admit that to himself and her.

And he was surprised that he didn't mind sharing her with Drew. He really didn't know the guy, but Zel obviously cared about him, and he seemed to be good for her. He definitely made Aithan step up his game when it came to sex.

"Nothing like a little healthy competition, I guess." He laughed. Plus, he actually liked the idea of another man being around to take care of Zel; not that she needed a man. But Drew seemed like the kind of guy who would pamper her. And Aithan was sure Zelda Gordon needed more pampering in her life.

He set the gym alarm, turned off the last hall light, and stepped into a quiet, moonless night. He closed and locked Blue Water's employee door, frowning up at the row of security lights. They weren't on, and the back lot was pitch black. The lights should've been glaring back at him, illuminating the entire lot.

"Damn things." He reached up to see if the bulb was loose on the main light above the door. If it burned out, the others didn't work. It was a flawed design he kept meaning to have rewired.

Something hard slammed into the back of his head. Pain flared through his skull and down his left shoulder. He hit the wall then the ground, his head bouncing off both. More pain ripped through his ribs as a foot met his chest, again and again.

The world faded while rough hands pulled at his pockets.

21

THE WRECKAGE

I WAS STEEPING a tea bag when the doorbell rang.

Smiling, I trotted downstairs, looking forward to a night with a hot personal trainer in my bed.

But when I glanced through the peephole, I froze. The wrong trainer stood on my doorstep with his bike over his shoulder.

Inhaling against the sudden lurch of my gut, I opened the door. "What are you doing here?"

Tristan wore a pained expression as he stared at his feet. "I came to apologize." He looked up. "Can I come in?" It was pouring, and he looked like a water-logged dog waiting to be kicked.

I bit my lip. "It's late." And I expected Aithan any minute.

He cleared his throat and fiddled with the gloves he wore when he biked, a birthday gift from me. "I know. But I really need to apologize, Zel. This is hanging over me. Please? Give me a chance to explain."

I sighed. Everything told me I should close that door and order him to stay away. Hell, the protection order said that. My father would scream it. Drew and Aithan would shake me for not listening to my own reasonable inner voice.

Instead, I stepped back and let him in.

Tristan was a dick. And he was rude. But he'd never been violent. I didn't truly believe he would've hit me the other day.

I crossed my arms and glared at him. "You spat in my face." I could acknowledge his regret but still nurse my own anger; the two were not mutually exclusive.

His expression fell and he squeezed his eyes shut. He shook his head and, somehow, looked even more hangdog when he met my gaze. "And I'm really, really sorry. That was such a complete dick thing to do. God, Zel, I've never acted like that before."

Still, I wasn't quite willing to let him slide into forgiveness so easily. "Is there a video?"

"A what?" He looked genuinely confused.

"Deep. Throat. A video."

Tristan's expression crumpled again. "Ugh, no. Hell no. I'd never do that. I'm not that big a douchebag. Besides, I was always too focused on you, uh, sucking my cock to think about filming it. And no way I want the whole world seeing my dick."

"Then why'd you say that?"

He leaned his bike against the wall and took off his cycling shoes and his jacket. He blew out a long, slow breath. "Because I'm an asshole." He shook his head and his eyes darted around, as if searching for answers. "Honestly, Zel, I've screwed up so much. I don't know what I was thinking."

"You weren't." I headed up the stairs without waiting for him. "I'm making tea and there's still cold brew."

He followed. "Thanks."

He pulled off his gloves as he sat at the kitchen counter. When I passed him a cup of coffee, I saw the knuckles on his right hand. They were bloody, swollen, and skinned. The entire back of his hand was black and blue.

"Tris, what did you do?" I grabbed his wrist and inspected the damage. "Road rash?"

"No." His shoulders slumped and he swallowed. "I punched a wall."

"Seriously? That was stupid."

"Yeah, I'm good at that lately."

I shook my head. "Go wash your hand. I'll get bandages and ointment."

He went to the kitchen sink while I got the first aid kit from the powder room. "You can't do this to yourself," I said as I put the kit on the kitchen counter. I blotted fresh blood from his hand. "Not again."

I didn't need to turn over his wrist to know about the scars. Tris was a cutter all through middle school and a delinquent through high school. He'd done a lot to inflict harm on himself, including running with a really rough crowd. He'd gotten into a lot of shit, even spending a few months in juvie for theft. But he'd moved down to Seattle to get away from those guys and escape a home filled with drugs, alcohol, and violence. He'd gotten into personal training and therapy to fix what he hated about himself, which was pretty much everything.

He sighed. "I don't know how *not* to wreck everything, Zel. You were good at that."

"At what?" I poured hydrogen peroxide over his split knuckles.

"Making me face my bullshit. You've been doing that since we were kids." He caught my gaze. "You know that's why I always admired you?"

"And you showed that admiration by giving me shit every day at school?"

"I never claimed to be the smart one." He cocked his head, his damp blond bangs falling to the side. "That's always been you."

I put down the bottle. "Stop. If you're trying to get back into my good graces, you have a long road ahead of you."

"I know, I-I just feel like I've screwed up the best friendship I've ever had." He was scrambling to explain. "And, I don't want you to hate me, Zel. I just," he grimaced again, "I just don't know how to be happy. It's like I can't have anything nice or good in my life. If it lasts too long, I kill it. Every. Fucking. Time."

I blotted his knuckles. "They might be broken. Have you considered getting an x-ray?"

"No, that never crossed my mind. 'Cause I'm an idiot." He sniffed. "I know that's what you're thinking."

"Being self-destructive *is* idiotic." I searched through the first aid kit for the bandages shaped for knuckles.

"You always call me on my bullshit. You've been doing that since first grade."

I found two of the bandages I wanted. "I can't fix your problems, Tristan." I met his gaze. "You know that, right?"

"Yeah. And you shouldn't have to. FYI, I'm not a complete moron, I called Dr. Stoneman."

"Really?" Stoneman was his therapist. "Good. Do you have an appointment?"

He nodded. "Tomorrow morning. He fit me in."

I tore open the paper around the first bandage. "I'm glad you're taking care of your mental shit again."

"I thought you'd be happy. You were always after me to take my meds and see Stoneman." He caught my hand. "I know I haven't shown it, but I've been thinking, and I'm actually glad you're with Aithan."

My eyes widened. "You are?"

"He's a good guy. He'll take care of you and treat you well." He took a bandage. "Fuck. I don't know why I'm such an asshole to you."

"Maybe because I fight back."

"Yeah, you're fiery." He smiled, though it was sad. "That's my favorite thing about you."

"Not my deep throat?"

He groaned, and not in a happy way. "God, I am such a douche canoe." He covered his face with his hands.

"I'm sorry." I pulled his hands down.

"What?" He stared at me. "Don't apologize, not to *me*. You have nothing to be sorry about." He pulled a face and applied the bandage to the back of his hand. "I was a shitty boyfriend for you, and I definitely deserve every smack you've got with my name on it."

I nodded and gave him the other bandage. "You really do."

Lulu wandered into the kitchen. She jumped onto the counter and head-butted him.

"Hey, little cat." Tristan scratched her ears while she buzzed contentedly. "I miss these guys."

I capped the peroxide and put the bandages back.

"Zel? Any chance we can be friends?"

I closed the first aid kit. "I don't want to have this conversation tonight, Tris. Right now, the answer is no."

He nodded, but a little spark of hope burned in his gaze. "Okay. Then let's have it again in a year. That'll give me time to change your mind."

I moved Lulu to the floor and washed my hands. "Okay, a year. But I make no promises." I pinned him with a steady gaze. "I'm serious. Don't assume anything about us because, for the first time in a long while, I'm really happy where I am and who I'm with."

He nodded again. "That's fair."

"More than fair."

He finally sipped his coffee while I put honey in my tea.

"Zel?"

"Hmm?"

"Do you really need the protection order?"

I stiffened and considered the slowly swirling tea in my cup even as I considered his question and my answer. I turned and I sounded pissed even to my own ears. "Is that why you came here? To convince me to drop it? To let you off the hook for the bullshit you've pulled over the last few weeks?"

He shook his head and raised his hands, as if fending off an attack. "No. That's not it. I really came here to apologize. I never meant to hurt you ... I mean ... I know I've been an ass, but I'd never *hit* you, Zel. I'm not my dad. I'm not like *that*. You know I'm not."

I nodded. "I know."

Tristan skipped school almost as often as he attended it because he was hiding bruises, afraid that a report to CPS would only worsen the abuse. He was the oldest child and he took the worst of the punishment, willingly. As much as he was a dick to me and everyone else at school, he'd taken all the hits at home to protect his younger brothers.

His mom finally divorced his dad after Tristan moved out of the house. He hated her for putting up with the man's violence for so long. His brothers hated him for leaving; it meant the abuse turned on them and then their family fractured.

I blew steam from my tea and took a careful sip. "Don't ask about the protection order. It's not something I'm going to discuss with you."

He nodded. "Okay. Sorry. That was selfish."

I put down my cup. "Listen, I know you're trying. I also know you suck at this because your family was a fucking disaster. But you had two years with me, Tris. And I tried to make it work. I tried so damn hard because I know you're not a monster. But I could not keep doing it alone." I leaned toward him. "You're not your father? Well, I'm not your mother. I won't put up with abuse, and constant insults *are* abuse."

He gulped more coffee. "You're right. You're one of the few people I know who always is. I have shit for brains, Zel." He didn't say it sarcastically. He sounded like he meant it.

"No. That's more self-pity. You need a lot of time with Stoneman. You were doing so much better when you were seeing him and taking your meds."

He grimaced and scratched his scalp. "I'll try to remember that."

"Please do. I tried, but you just tuned me out."

"You weren't the only one saying it." He shrugged. "But lifelong habits are hard to break."

"Tell me about it," I murmured, thinking of my body image issues.

"I'm sorry I lied to you so much."

"About what?"

"Lots of things," he muttered then clarified, "Your appearance. I've always thought you were beautiful, but I didn't have the balls to own it. I let the opinions of the fucks I called friends influence me more than my own feelings."

My mouth was hanging. I shut it with an audible snap. "No. You don't get to tell me that now. We dated for two years, Tristan. You had all those months to say it. I know you think this is confession time, but that's more than I can swallow."

He shrank in his seat. "I just needed you to know. Maybe someday you'll believe me."

"Maybe, but not tonight."

22

AFTERMATH

AITHAN'S SKULL THROBBED. His ribs screamed and every breath stabbed his chest and shot pain through his shoulders and back. The world vibrated and rocked. Disoriented, he opened his eyes, but the light glaring into his face hurt too much and he closed them again. The darkness was better.

"Mr. Mazur, my name is Jennifer. You're in an ambulance on the way to the hospital."

The woman's voice sounded distant. There was a wailing sound. A siren.

Ambulance?

He looked at her. "What happened?" The words came out garbled, weak, raspy.

"You were assaulted. You have head trauma and a punctured lung. Just remain calm. You're getting the help you need. We're pulling into the emergency entrance now."

The siren stopped wailing. The ambulance slowed and stopped.

Jennifer started shifting things around as another paramedic opened the doors.

Aithan closed his eyes again. Too much light and noise. Too much motion. Too much pain. It all made his head pound and his stomach churn. The hospital smells didn't help — antiseptics, rubber, and whatever strange soap all hospital sheets were washed in combined to nauseate him more.

The gurney rolled through hallways teeming with doctors and nurses. They asked questions.

"Do you know your name?"

"Can you tell me today's date?"

"Do you know what happened to you, Mr. Mazur?"

"Where do you hurt?"

"Mr. Mazur, do you use any recreational or prescription drugs?"

"Do you smoke?"

"Have you been drinking tonight, Mr. Mazur?"

"Do you have any health conditions the hospital staff needs to know about?"

They took x-rays, a CT scan, and an MRI. Having people poking and prodding him and shoving needles into his veins seemed bad until they pushed a tube between his ribs. That was worse than being cracked in the skull.

Finally, a doctor came to his bedside and sent the others away.

"I'm Dr. Emily Nathus. I'll be your attending physician for the rest of the day, Mr. Mazur."

"Aithan." He raised his hand. His voice sounded thick and slow, like his tongue didn't remember how to form words.

She shook his hand. "Nice to meet you. I wish it was under more pleasant circumstances."

"Me, too."

"I'm here to tell you about your injuries and discuss treatment. Think you can handle that?"

Breathing was tight and painful. He hated not being able to fill his lungs. "Sure. Not going ... anywhere."

She gave a small laugh. "No, not likely. You have a skull fracture and a concussion. Two broken ribs, three with hairline cracks, and a collapsed right lung. That's the bad news. The very good news is that you don't have intracranial bleeding or other internal injuries. I'm not gonna ask what happened. I have the general details and there's a detective waiting patiently to ask you questions."

Aithan grunted.

"You'll be with us until that lung and your skull are stabilized. That'll be five days at least."

He grunted again. This would cost a fortune he didn't have.

"Once you're breathing well, we'll remove that chest tube. And we want to monitor your brain for swelling. It took a good whack, but we're optimistic that you'll recover quickly and completely."

"Glad to hear that," he rasped, dragging in a shallow breath every few words.

"Me, too. Do you have any questions before I send the police in?"

"My family?"

"My understanding is someone from your company contacted your family, but the police officer can confirm that. If you need anything, summon the nurse." She showed him the call button, then let an officer into his room.

The man took the chair she'd abandoned and introduced himself as Detective Brian Kevlin.

"I'll tell you what I know and you fill in any gaps from your own memories. I know that'll be tough. From experience, I can tell you that details will emerge over the next days or even weeks as your brain heals. Nothing is insignificant. Okay?"

"Okay."

He set his phone between them, recorded the who, when, and where of the interview, and asked, "Do I have your permission to record this interview, Mr. Mazur?"

"Yes."

"Thank you. Alright. Angela and Jacob Guzman found you unconscious and bleeding behind Blue Water Fitness at one forty a.m. this morning."

Aithan recognized the names and knew he knew them, but his brain refused to give them context.

As if reading his mind, the detective said, "They're the gym's night cleaning crew. They recognized you, fortunately. Your wallet, phone, keys, and vehicle were missing. The good news is that your vehicle was recovered an hour ago, abandoned in Shoreline. The bad news is that the interior was set afire, the exterior was defaced, and the tires were slashed. A report with photographs will be sent to your insurance company."

"Bleeding?"

The officer blinked. "Uh, right. Yes. Whoever hit you used a blunt object that split your scalp."

Aithan slowly reached up to feel his head. Staples made an arc above and behind his left ear. He winced. Right. "Okay."

"We know your last employee," he glanced at his notes, "Juan San Miguel, left at eleven thirty-five p.m. He said he spoke with you just before leaving Blue Water Fitness and you indicated you'd be leaving within minutes. Do you know approximately what time you locked up the building?"

Aithan squeezed his eyes shut, trying to recall the previous night. "Everything's jumbled. I remember Juan leaving." He inhaled and coughed weakly, wincing at pain the meds couldn't quite mask. "Sorry."

"Take your time."

Finally, getting some breath, Aithan said, "Juan turned off the inside lights. And I sent a message to Zel."

"Zel?"

"Zelda Gordon. My girlfriend. I told her I was going home."

"And you sent that message after Mr. San Miguel left the gym?"

"I think so?" Something drifted through his mind, something about a light. It seemed important. "Wait." The officer nodded and remained silent, giving him time to think. "The lights weren't working."

"Which lights?"

"Outside. The security lights behind the building. When I left, they weren't working. They're motion activated, but didn't come on." Aithan winced, suddenly recalling the pain of being struck. "That's when I was hit. I reached up to see if the bulb in the master light had burned out."

"Did you see your assailant?"

He thought for a moment. "No. I didn't even hear him. I reached for the lightbulb, then I was in pain, then I was on the ground. I guess I blacked out."

The detective scanned his notes again. "You're sure about the lights not functioning?"

"Yes. Why?"

"There's no mention of it being dark in the back lot. In fact, Angela Guzman specifically noted that she saw you lying in front of the employee door as she and her husband got out of their car. She ran to help you. Could she have seen you if the lights were out? Is there other lighting in the lot?"

"No, it's all on the same circuit. A row of lights that are aimed down on that small lot. It's pitch black without them. There are only six parking spots back there for Blue Water's employees and a gated entrance. You can't drive in without knowing the code to open the gate."

Kevlin nodded and made notes. "I'll get over there to check the lighting. What you're describing implies your assailant climbed the fence or knew the code. Or he came through the gym, went out the back door, and waited for you." He nodded slowly. "Do you have any enemies, Mr. Mazur? Any disgruntled current or former employees?"

"Enemies?" Aithan drew a slow, labored breath. "Not that I know of." He stared at the IV line taped to the back of his hand. "I've never had to fire anyone, so I can't think of any pissed off employees."

"What about Tristan Blaylock?"

He looked up. "Tristan? What about him? He's a current employee. Good group trainer."

"Mr. San Miguel mentioned some interpersonal issues with him."

Aithan grunted again. It was less painful than nodding. "Tristan broke up with Zel."

"Zelda Gordon?" The detective's tone sharpened. "Your girlfriend?"

"Yeah."

"How long ago was their breakup?"

"Um, three weeks, I think?"

Kevlin blinked. "You're seeing the woman your employee broke up with less than a month ago? Had you both been dating her long?"

"No. I met her the week they split? I think it was that Saturday, but I'm a little hazy on days right now. It's in my phone. She was Tristan's girlfriend but broke up with him. She started seeing Drew and me around the same time."

"Who's Drew?"

"Her author." The detective gave him a blank look, so Aithan tried to explain. "Zel's a narrator. She records Drew's books for him. They started dating. Then I did too. Date her, I mean."

"And this was while she was dating Mr. Blaylock?"

"No, after they split up."

"Does this author know you're dating Ms. Gordon?"

"Yes."

"He doesn't take issue with her seeing you, too?"

"No."

"But Mr. Blaylock did?"

Aithan frowned. "He was upset about their split, but we haven't talked about it, I don't think."

Kevlin referred to his notes. "But he complained about your relationship with her in front of your gym patrons, correct? That's why Mr. San Miguel said you authorized him to send Mr. Blaylock home with a week of paid vacation. Is that right?"

"Did I?" Aithan muttered mostly to himself. "Yeah, I remember that." He met the detective's gaze. "I guess he does have a problem with me seeing Zel."

"I'd say so. And I'll be talking with him next."

23

A LIE AND AN ALIBI

> Looong day, beautiful, & I gotta be in early tomorrow. I'll swing by your place tomorrow night, if that's cool with u. Let me know. Gnight.

THAT MESSAGE WAS WAITING for me when I finally climbed into bed after two hours with Tristan. I snuggled under the covers then replied.

> Definitely a long day. I'll miss u tonight, but you're welcome here anytime. Xoxox

The next morning, I paid bills and caught up on social media, then called my mom. Our last talk hadn't been too happy, so I owed her an upbeat update on my life.

"Hi, Mom."

"Hi, honey, how're you?"

"Great, actually!"

"Ohh? What's happened to make you so chipper? The last time we talked you were raging about your sister, who's still very upset with you, by the way. You need to speak with Greer, honey."

"Yeah, yeah, Mom, eventually. Don't ruin my good mood."

"Right. Sorry. What's got you so happy?"

"Drew Katterman asked me to be his girlfriend last night." I rolled my eyes at myself; I sounded like a high school girl with a crush.

"Oh? Oh! Isn't he that rich author?"

"Mooom. There's more to Drew than his bank account."

"I'm sure there is, but his bank account certainly adds to his appeal, right?"

"No. I don't need Drew's money. Sheesh, when did you get so money hungry?"

She laughed. "Since I married your father. You know he's a tightwad."

That was true. "Whine, whine, whine. I don't think you're suffering much in your giant, ocean-view mansion."

She laughed again. "You got me there. So, you have a new fella. Was he one of the ones Greer caught you with?"

"Greer didn't *catch* me with anyone. I was hugging Aithan and Tobias. That's not hanky-panky."

"Wait, there are three men now? I'm confused."

"No, no, just Drew and Aithan. Only Drew is officially a boyfriend. Tobias is just a friend. Aithan is something in between, I guess?"

"I see. Does this mean Aithan is out?"

"No. Drew's totally open-minded about me seeing Aithan, too."

"Huh. So those fellas swing both ways? If you know what I mean."

"No, Mom, they're not bi. At least, I don't think so." I shrugged. "I'll ask."

"You can do that?"

"Uh, yeah. Why wouldn't you?"

"Well, I don't know. I'm not sure I'd have the courage to discuss that with my new boyfriends." She sighed. "Zel, this sounds very complicated. Are you sure this is wise?"

"A) What's wisdom got to do with sex and attraction? And B) I'm happier than I've ever been, Mom."

"Well, if you're that happy, I …." A muffled sound interrupted her. "Oh, hold on, your father wants to talk to you."

The phone rattled as she handed it off, then my dad came on.

"Did you get that protection order all set up?"

"It's in process. I have a court date next month."

"Good. What about your locks?"

Shit. That'd slipped my mind. "Calling the locksmith today." I bit my lip and rushed on to the next sentence before I lost my courage. "I had a long talk with Tristan."

"What? You shouldn't have any contact with him, Zelda."

I cringed at his disapproving tone, the one that made me feel like Eleven-year-old Zelda getting into trouble for sneaking liver to the dog under the table so I wouldn't have to eat it.

"I know, I know, Dad. He came over to apologize. And you know what a monster his father was and what he went through as a kid."

"Yes, I know all that. And I also know abusers are made, not born. I'm not saying Tristan is a bad person, Zel, but I am saying he's a bad person for you. He's never been your friend. Do you remember when he pushed you down at school and your tooth got chipped?"

"That was in third grade. And he apologized then, too. I can't believe you remember that." Memory like an elephant, that man, and as unforgiving as they get.

"So you're willing to set aside two years of verbal abuse because of one apologetic conversation?"

"I didn't say that. I just thought you should know that I'd

had a positive discussion with him. He has a therapist appointment today. So he's making an effort."

"Well, I hope so, for his sake. But I don't want you to cancel that protection order. He needs to know boundaries exist, Zelda. Don't assume he won't turn violent. That's all he learned growing up under Robert Blaylock's thumb."

"You mean his fist."

My dad grunted. "Yes, that's the sad truth. I just want you to be smart and safe, Punky."

"I know, Dad. I am."

"Good. So what's this I hear about you having a new rich boyfriend?"

I rolled my eyes. "Forget about the money, please? Drew asked me to be his girlfriend."

"But the other fella's still in the picture? The gym owner?"

"Aithan, yes. Drew's comfortable with me dating him, and I don't want to give up either of them."

"Well, eventually you'll have to choose." That was Mom. She'd gotten on one of the other house phones. "Men don't like to share for long, honey. Believe me."

"You know, I don't think that's the case here," I replied. "Drew's one hundred percent okay with an open relationship, and Aithan said he's fine with sharing."

Mom replied, "Yes, well, that's what they *say* …."

"I'm hanging up," my dad said and the phone clicked.

Mom giggled. "He's not comfortable talking about S-E-X."

I laughed. "Neither are you. You have to spell the word."

"Oh!" She giggled again. "I guess I'll have to get better if I'm going to meet your new boyfriends. Will you bring them here for Thanksgiving?"

"I dunno. I mean, I haven't even discussed boyfriend-girlfriend status with Aithan. It's still October, so we have time. And I don't know if they have plans with their own families. So I'll get back to you on that."

"Okay, well, your father's standing in the office doorway.

We're supposed to go grocery shopping. Please call your sister?"

"I will. Eventually."

She sighed. "I love you both equally, you know."

"Mom, this isn't about your love, okay? Greer needs to learn her place in my life."

She sighed again. "Call her, Zelda."

"I will! I will!"

"Good. Bye-bye, honey. I'm happy for you and your boyfriends."

"Thanks, Mom. Bye."

My phone buzzed a little while later as I was cleaning the kitchen counters.

> Hey, it's Tobias. Bad news. Aith is in the hsptl. Candy & I are heading there. U want to come w/ us?

"What the fuck?" I washed my hands and replied:

> OMG! Yes, I want to see him. Is he OK? What happened?

> Long story. I'm in your driveway.

> OK. I'll be right down.

I met them in the driveway and climbed into the back of Tobias's silver Outback. "What happened?"

Candace turned in her seat. "He got jumped leaving Blue Water last night. He's got a fractured skull, punctured lung, and a bunch of broken and cracked ribs."

"What the hell?" I couldn't believe what I was hearing.

Tobias accelerated. "The gym's cleaning crew found him out cold at the back of the building last night. The assholes who mugged him took his SUV, his keys, wallet, and phone."

My stomach felt hard, like I'd swallowed a boulder. "Holy shit. Is he really gonna be okay?"

Candace nodded. "That's what he said."

"I didn't actually talk to him." Tobias stopped at a red light, his turn signal clicking. "His sister Paulina called me. She's flying in from Dallas tonight but asked if I could get over to see him ASAP and send her an update that's not tainted by Aithan's optimism and painkillers."

I nodded. "Will the staff even let us visit him? We're not family."

"Paulina told them we were coming and that the family wants us to see him."

Part of me felt like an intruder. I'd only known Aithan a few weeks. Yeah, we'd fucked like rabbits during that time, but that didn't make me almost-family like Tobias and Candace were.

"There's something else, Zel," Candace said. "The police came to interview Tristan about the attack. They said it seemed premeditated. Like whoever did this was laying in wait for Aithan. Tristan is their primary suspect."

I went cold. "Oh, shit. Because of me."

"Because he mouthed off about the two of you at the gym and was given a week of mental health days to get his shit together," Tobias said. "They also know you requested a protection order."

"Fuuuck." I slowly shook my head. That belly boulder gained weight as I recalled Tristan's split knuckles. "What time did this happen last night?"

"Eleven thirty-ish." He pulled into the hospital's underground parking garage.

Relief washed through me. My ex wasn't a monster.

"Tristan says you can vouch for him." Candace shook her head in disbelief. "He says he was with you last night."

I bit my lip and nodded slowly. This was gonna get tricky. "He was."

She stared at me as Tobias said, "Huh?" and pulled into a parking spot.

"He came to my place to apologize for being a dick. He was there until one-thirty."

"You let him in even though you have a protection order out against him?" Tobias definitely sounded pissed.

"I applied for one. Still haven't had the court date for it. And he just needed to talk. He said he's seeing his therapist again."

Candace nodded. "He had a doctor appointment early this morning." She frowned. "But his knuckles were all busted up …."

"Because he punched a wall." Never would've thought saying that would be a relief.

Tobias's expression hardened. "So he says. How do you know he wasn't punching Aithan after cold-cocking him with a crowbar?"

I swallowed. "Well, he showed up at my house around the same time Aithan sent me a text. Tristan couldn't have been in two places at once." I held up my phone to show the time stamp of the last message I received from Aithan — eleven forty-two p.m.

Tobias didn't look convinced, but Candace nodded. "You need to take that to the police because, right now, Tristan is in deep shit."

"With good reason," Tobias snapped.

I touched his shoulder, hoping to calm him. "Aithan first, then the police. It won't hurt Tristan to be under the cops' thumbs for a little while longer." Maybe they could scare him straight the way they had back in tenth grade.

We got out of the car and rode the elevator to the lobby, then wended through a maze of white corridors to the Emergency Department.

"Why do hospitals always seem so huge and smell like you shouldn't touch anything?" Candace muttered.

"Sterile hell," Tobias agreed, scanning the crowded waiting area. People paced or talked in hushed tones. Others stared at their phones or at nothing. A few dozed in their seats, bodies hunched, faces lax.

After being directed to another floor on another wing of the sprawling building, and wandering through another maze of hallways, we finally found Aithan's room at the end of a quiet hall. The door was closed.

"Do we knock?" Candace asked. "What if he's sleeping?"

"Then we wake the fucker up." Tobias opened the door.

Aithan was alone and hooked up to machines. An oxygen tube rested beneath his nose, monitors were taped to his chest, and an IV was stuck into the back of his hand. He looked ashen, but he opened his eyes, spied me, and smiled.

"Hey, beautiful." He sounded raspy and weak. "Come give me some sugar." After every few words, he paused and drew in a labored breath.

I kissed him, trying not to dislodge any tubes or jostle him. "I'm afraid I'll hurt you," I said, wanting to hold him close but holding back instead.

"Nah, I'm on morphine, and you're the best medicine a man can get."

"Oh, boy." Candace laughed. "You're so loopy, Aithan."

"High as a kite, girl," he slurred and gave her a lopsided grin.

"Hey, brother from another mother." Tobias clasped Aithan's hand. "Glad to see your brain still works."

"Oh, yeah. No bleeding in my noggin, but I'm gonna have a gnarly scar." He turned his head and pointed to an area above his left ear where a long arc of staples closed a nasty wound.

"Fucking hell, Aithan." I dropped into the chair beside his bed. The left side of his face was black and blue from temple to jaw, and his left eye was swollen and black, the whites reddened by broken blood vessels. Someone had hastily wiped dried blood from his neck, but it still lingered in his scalp and around his ear. His chest was bruised where the hospital gown dipped low, as was his entire right arm and his jaw.

I pressed my lips together. Seeing him like this shook me. He was always so strong and solid. He seemed like the kind of guy you couldn't knock down, no matter how hard you tried. But someone had put him down hard and out cold.

He could've been killed.

His sleepy gaze drifted to me and turned concerned. "Hey, don't be upset, Zel. I'm still alive and s'posed to go home in a few days." He reached for my hand and I clasped his fingers. His grip wasn't as firm as usual, but it was still far from weak and that made me feel a little better.

I nodded. "You're right."

"And they found my ride."

"Where?" Candace pulled another chair close to the bed and sat. Tobias leaned on the back of it, his hand on his sister's shoulder.

"Umm, Shoreline, I think? I'm a little hazy on the whole thing." He looked back at me. "You'll hear from a police ocifer."

"You mean officer," Tobias said as we all chuckled.

"Right," Aithan said, "Ocifer Calvin or something like that. His card is here somewhere. Wants to ask you about Tristan."

"Yeah, I thought so," I said.

Aithan nodded, then looked confused. "You did?"

"They questioned him at my place this morning," Candace explained.

"Seriously?" He shook his head then winced. "Don't think he'd do this."

"He didn't," I assured him.

Tobias said, "You don't know that for sure, Zel."

"Yes, I do."

Aithan was watching us, confusion still on his face. "How?"

Fuck, I thought. He was not going to like my answer. *Rip the bandage off fast, Zel.* I sucked a deep breath.

"Zel?" Aithan tugged my hand.

"Tristan came to my place last night. To apologize. He stayed to talk for a few hours, then I sent him home."

"He went to see you?" His grip tightened.

"Yeah. He showed up around eleven-thirty."

He frowned. "You shouldn't've let him in."

I looked at our hands. "I know, but I did."

He nodded slowly. "It's good you did. Now you can vouch for him."

"Maybe that's exactly why he went to Zelda's house," Tobias said.

I looked up. "What?"

"You're an alibi." Candace slowly nodded. But the nod turned into a shake. "No, I agree with Zel. Tris is an idiot, but he's not a threat to anyone except himself."

"Absolutely," I agreed.

"How do you know?" Tobias argued.

"Because I've known him since I was six."

Aithan grunted. "Call the police, Zel. He's innocent."

I nodded and pulled my phone from my purse as Candace found the card the detective had left on Aithan's hospital table.

It was the right thing to do, even if Tobias's words had planted a seed of doubt in the back of my mind.

Is that what last night's apology was? A lie and an alibi?

24

DO YOU BELIEVE HIM?

I LEFT them talking about how trashed Aithan's SUV was while I went down the hall. A restroom seemed like the most private space available, so I locked the door and sat on the lowered toilet lid.

"This is Detective Kevlin." He sounded tired and a bit like my dad.

"Hi, my name is Zelda Gordon. I'm dating Aithan Mazur, and Tristan Blaylock is my ex-boyfriend."

"Yes. Thanks for calling me, Ms. Gordon. I'm guessing you spoke with Mr. Mazur? How's he doing?"

"Okay, I guess? He's talkative and high as a kite on morphine, so there's that. The doctors expect him to be discharged in a few days."

"Good, good. Glad to hear that. So, I have some questions about your relationship with both men, as well as clarification on Mr. Blaylock's alibi."

"Yes, I can vouch for him. Tristan was at my house last night until one-thirty in the morning."

"He was?"

"You sound surprised."

"Well, considering that you have a protection order in process against him, I am."

"He came over to apologize for being a complete dick, to ask for my forgiveness, and to say he was happy Aithan and I are together."

"Hmm. Do you believe him?"

His question caught me off guard. Did I? Was Tristan's change of heart genuine or convenient? Was his late night apology honest or manipulative? I chewed my lower lip, unsure how to answer.

"Ms. Gordon?" the detective prompted.

"I think I believe him? I mean, I've known Tristan since we were kids. He can be an absolute turd and he's done some really stupid things, but he's never been violent."

I could hear the keys of his keyboard clacking as he took notes. "What time did he arrive?"

"Eleven-thirty-ish."

"Can you be more precise?"

"Well, I plugged in my phone at eleven thirty-one then went downstairs to heat water for tea. It was still boiling when the doorbell rang, so I'd say eleven thirty-three is about right. And Aithan sent me a text message at …. Hold on," I put the phone on speaker and scrolled through apps to get to my messages, "eleven forty-two. I don't know who jumped Aithan, but it wasn't Tristan, Detective. He was sitting in my kitchen at the time."

"That's how it appears. Okay. Thank you for providing that information. We'll keep working the case, and I'll contact you if I have any further questions."

"Thanks for handling this. Aithan is the nicest guy. He really didn't deserve this."

"That's what I've heard from many people, including Mr. Blaylock."

We said our goodbyes and I hung up, but I didn't immediately return to Aithan's room. Instead, I swallowed and blinked back tears. It hadn't occurred to me until I said it aloud, that while Aithan lay bleeding and beaten in a dark parking lot, I was sitting in my warm kitchen, wearing comfy pajamas, and talking to my ex-boyfriend. "Fuck," I whispered. "That's so messed up."

Had it really been a random attack? The detective — and Tobias — didn't seem to think so. But Tristan had been with me. That was undeniable. He hadn't taken out his anger on Aithan.

"So who did?" I asked my reflection in the mirror as I washed my hands and blotted my reddened eyes. I drew a deep breath and let it go slowly, releasing irrational guilt. It was awful that Aithan had been beaten, but I didn't need to feel ashamed for not being there to stop it. That was ridiculous.

But a large part of me was afraid he'd cut me out of his life because I'd let Tristan back into it — albeit briefly — last night while *he* was being beaten unconscious. I shook my head. "Stop being a paranoid idiot, Zelda. Aithan isn't that knee-jerk." I met my reflection's gaze again. "Focus on getting him home and healed. Let the cops worry about catching the bastard who did this."

I stepped back and squared my shoulders. The pep talk helped.

When I got back to the room, the door was closed and Tobias and Candace were arguing in the hallway.

"No. I'm not going to kick him out just because you think he's guilty. Zelda proved he had nothing to do with it. You don't condemn a man without evidence."

"There's shit-tons of evidence. Just because he wasn't present during the attack, doesn't mean he wasn't involved."

"What are you saying?" I asked.

Candace turned to me. "What did the detective say?"

"That Aithan has no enemies and he was surprised that I could confirm Tristan's alibi."

Tobias said, "But he didn't say that cleared him of guilt, right?"

"We didn't discuss that. He's still working the case."

He nodded. "Because Tristan's still a suspect."

"Suspected of what?" Candace asked, hands on hips and chin jutting.

"Being an accessory to the crime," her brother replied.

She blinked and stepped back. Obviously, she hadn't really considered that. "You think he put someone up to this?" Tobias nodded, his jaw set in a firm line. She looked at me. "Zel? Does Tristan know people who would do something like that?"

I bit my lip as I met her gaze. "Yeah. He does."

"Fuck." She grabbed her head with both hands, like that knowledge physically hurt. "But would he do that?"

Both of them watched me while I thought hard about it. When we were kids he might have. He was hot-headed, and his friends weren't above beating the snot out of someone just for shits and giggles. But Tristan had never joined the brawls. He knew all too well what a beating felt like.

I shook my head this time. "No. He left home to escape violence and put distance between those people and himself. I really don't believe he'd put anyone up to beating Aithan, let alone almost killing him."

"You sure you know him that well?" Tobias asked.

"I've known him my whole life. Since first grade. He didn't ask anyone to attack Aithan. I'm sure."

Candace nodded, but Tobias still scowled, his doubt sticking like glue.

I jerked my chin at the door. "Is he asleep?"

"No," Candace said. "The nurse wanted to do some stuff and asked us to step out for privacy."

"Probably getting his ass wiped," Tobias said.

She elbowed him. "Don't be a dick."

"Should we wait?" I asked.

"You should, for sure," she replied. "He asked if you were coming back. I think he wants to grope you some more."

I gave her my fiercest Disapproving Mother look, the one I learned from my own mom, but she just grinned back at me, mischievous as shit and pleased with herself.

"Mother*fucker*," Tobias muttered, looking at his phone.

"Maeve?" Candace guessed.

"Of course. She told Amara about Aithan. Now Little Bit wants to see her uncle."

"Well, fuck. That bitch has less sense than God gave a goose." Candace shook her head. "What're you gonna do?"

"Call my girl and explain that she can't see her uncle today, but that he's gonna be okay." He looked around. "Where'd you make your call, Zel?"

I pointed down the hall. "The bathroom."

He nodded and raised the phone to his ear as he walked. "Hi, Dianne, can I talk to Little Bit?" He disappeared into the bathroom.

"Why does Tobias insist Tristan was involved?" I asked Candace. "Do they have history I don't know about?"

She looked surprised by the question. "No, he's just über protective of friends and family. He's always been the guy who put himself out there for other people. He'll fight tooth-and-nail for what's right."

"But he really seems to have it out for Tris."

She shrugged. "They've never been friends, ya know? They tolerate each other, but that's all. I mean, I doubt they've spoken more than a dozen words since Tristan moved into my place. I don't know what it is about him that rubs Tobias the wrong way, but treating you like shit definitely didn't help."

"Huh. I guess that makes sense."

"It does in my brother's mind. He's slow to trust and even slower to forgive. And some people will never earn his trust again. I think Tristan may be among them."

"It just seems a bit extreme without a more direct cause. I mean, you both hardly know me."

"True, but Aithan is stupid about you, and Tobias will do anything for him." She side-eyed me. "Plus, my little brother totally digs you, Zelda."

I was flattered but didn't really understand why Tobias felt that way. We'd spent maybe eight hours together, tops. And it still didn't explain why he disliked and distrusted Tristan.

The door to Aithan's room opened and the nurse came out. "You can go in now."

Aithan's eyes slowly opened. He looked ready to sleep for a week. But he lifted his hand and I took it. "Wish you could climb up here and stay with me," he murmured.

Candace grinned. "You are so stinkin' cute when you're wasted and in love, Aithan Mazur."

He slowly raised his other hand and gave her the middle finger. "Where's Tobias?"

"Talking to Amara," I replied.

"Ah. Tell him not to bring her here. She doesn't need to see me dopey and all busted up. Might scare her."

Candace rubbed his knee. "Don't worry. He's telling Mari her uncle will be fine and she can visit him when he's home and feeling better."

He nodded but his eyes drifted closed. I leaned over him. He shook his head. "Want you to stay, but too sleepy. Sorry."

"Don't be." I kissed him. "Sleep and heal. I'll come back tomorrow."

"You can meet Paulina." He tugged my hand to his face and kissed my fingers. "Want you to meet my family."

"Okay. I can do that." I kissed him again and Candace kissed his forehead then we left, closing the door quietly behind us just as Tobias emerged from the restroom looking thunderous.

"Uh-oh," she muttered.

"That goddamn twat told Mari what happened to Aithan. Little Bit was in tears thinking he was going to die."

"Cripes," I said. "Your daughter didn't need to know that. How could Maeve be so callous?"

"Oh, she's a motherfucking doozie," Candace snarled. "How'd she find out he was jumped?"

He shook his head. "Dunno. Guess Dianne said something."

"Ugh." Candace led the way to the elevators. "You'd think your mother-in-law would've learned not to share *anything* with that woman."

Tobias brooded as we made our way back to the parking garage. When we reached his car, he said, "I'll drop you at home, Zel, then we gotta pick up Amara, Candy."

"Yeah, totally. I'm all for hanging with Little Bit."

"Thanks." I squeezed his shoulder. "I appreciate the ride to and from the hospital."

"Of course." He glanced in the rearview mirror, then reached up and squeezed my fingers back. "Glad to have you around, Zel. You're good for Aithan."

25

HOME IS WHEREVER YOU ARE

THE SUN WAS GOING down when they dropped me off. I went through my mail and fed the cats, then decided to finish cleaning the kitchen. I was distracting my brain. Not that scrubbing counters and the stove was much of a mental stretch, but I could pretend it was a challenge. Keeping my hands busy always engaged my noggin.

My phone rang and my spirits lifted when I saw the caller ID.

"Hey, boyfriend."

"Hi, babe, how's your day going? I've been thinking about you non-stop. Got a lot of really good writing in, including two fucking amaze-balls sex scenes. I'm telling you, you are good for my word count."

I laughed. "And you always make me smile, which I needed. Today was awful."

"What? Why?"

"Aithan's in the hospital. Someone jumped him when he was locking up the gym last night."

"Holy fuck! Is he okay?"

"He will be. He's got a fractured skull, collapsed lung, and broken ribs. They tap danced all over his chest."

"Brick, honey, that's fucking horrible. What hospital is he in? I'll send him a stripper-gram."

That really made me laugh. "You would do that, wouldn't you."

"Yeah. I'm looow class like that." He paused. "But, seriously, he's really going to be okay?"

"Yeah. They expect him to go home in a few days. He's completely wasted on morphine right now."

"Ooh, nice. Maybe I'll fly home and climb into bed with him. Get him to share some of that good stuff."

"Bitch, please, you don't do drugs."

"No, I don't. But I've had morphine post-surgery. That's some good shit. When you're in major pain, the morphine fairy is your best fucking friend."

I sobered. "You said home, like Seattle is your home."

"Home is wherever you are, Brick."

"Aww. I think I just melted a little inside."

"I'm ready to return to the Pacific Northwest. It's been a long time since I lived west of the Rockies. I miss it. And I miss you."

"You do?"

"Hell yes."

He was melting me big time. "I didn't know you ever lived on the West Coast. I thought you were from New York."

"Nah. Born in Idaho. Raised in a shithole in the middle of nowhere."

"Huh. I did not know that. I mean, I knew your childhood was rough, but I didn't know about Idaho."

"Yeah. I don't miss it or anyone I knew from there, but I do miss the Pacific Northwest. I'm ready to leave New York. I used to think this was the place to be because I'm a writer and hipster authors are supposed to live in the Big Apple, or some bullshit like that. But, I dunno, maybe I'm mellowing in my old age. That dream doesn't seem so dreamy anymore."

I laughed. "Yep, you're *ancient*."

"I'm thirty-seven, babe. That's ancient compared to you. I'm fucking robbing the cradle with you. I mean, what are you, like, eighteen?"

"Twenty-four, fuck you very much. I'm much more mature than Eighteen-year-old Zel ever dreamed of being."

"Probably a lot sexier too. I like being your sugar daddy."

"Hmph. I can buy my own sugar."

"I know that. And I love it. Anyway, I'm coming out this week. You shouldn't be dealing with Aithan's situation alone."

"I'm not alone. His friends Tobias and Candace are one hundred percent in. And his sister Paulina flew in today."

"Well, it's an excuse to turn around and come back to Seattle. I miss your ass and your bed. Seriously, Zel, if I move there and buy a house, will you come live with me until I'm old and shriveled?"

I was stunned. He moved fucking faster than greased lightning. "Whoa. That's …. Really? Are you sure you want to jump into the deep end already?"

"Yes. I don't screw around. When I see something I want, Zelda Gordon, I make it mine. A relationship with you is something I've wanted since the day we met. You know that."

"I do. It's just that I'm not accustomed to men being so forward with me. They usually hem and haw, then disappear after one night of bad sex."

"Yeah, well, I'm not one of those assholes. I'd marry you, but you shouldn't have to choose between me and Aithan."

I laughed. "Wait, wait, wait. Are you serious? You're already talking about marriage?"

"Oh, hell yeah. There's something about you that makes me want to get married, adopt pets, can fruit, and make babies."

"Can fruit?" I was laughing harder.

"Mm-hmm, must be your peaches inspiring me."

I snorted. "Or my childbearing hips, perhaps?"

"Oh, yeah, those hips. Don't tease, love. My hand's starting to cramp and I need that sucker for typing."

Oh my God, he was killing me. "Okay, if you move to Seattle and buy a house, I'll move in with you, but I have conditions."

"Hit me."

"The house needs to be big enough to accommodate my growing harem."

"Growing? Who're you adding? You know Aithan and I have a say in new members, right?"

"Yes, and I already know he'll approve. I've got my eye on his best friend, Tobias."

"Oooh, interesting. That could lead to some seriously hot three-way action. So, yes, big house with a ginormous bed. What else?"

"Everyone pitches in with housework and cooking."

"I can't even boil eggs, but I'll scrub your pans until they sparkle. Anything else? Pool? Pool boy? Sex dungeon? I've always wanted one of those."

I couldn't stop laughing. "What? A pool boy or a sex dungeon?"

"Both in the same place at the same time, though the boy's for you. Not really my thing."

"You are such a dirty old man."

"Just like you like me."

When I stopped giggling, I added, "One more thing. We share the financial burden proportional to our incomes."

"Totally fair. It's a deal. Who's your realtor?"

Holy shit, he was really doing this. "Uh, hold on, I'll forward her info." I scrolled through my contacts. "I can't believe you're serious."

"As a motherfucking heart attack. I want to be with you every day, Zel. You inspire me. You make me fucking happy to be alive. You make me push my work to the next level. Babe, face it, you're good for me, my ego, and my income."

"Aww. You know that goes both ways, right? I'm so happy you came to Seattle and fucked the shit outta me."

"Yeah, me too. Let's do that again."

"And again?"

"Ad infinitum."

26

ME LOVING YOU

THE FIRST THING I noticed about Paulina Mazur was her figure. She was tall and curvaceous, just like me. The next thing was her personality. She was a force of nature swirling through Aithan's hospital room, opening the blinds, arranging flowers, moving chairs to his bedside.

I stood in the open doorway, wide-eyed and holding a vase of plum and white calla lilies, watching her twist and flow around the room.

Aithan spied me. "Hi, beautiful."

Paulina turned and smiled and, I swear, the room glowed from it. "How lovely!" She took the vase from me and added over her shoulder as she turned away, "And the flowers are beautiful too. You must be Zelda."

Aithan laughed, but it turned into a painful, shallow cough that made me wince.

"*Kurwa*," he gasped when he finally stopped coughing. Instead of being in bed, he sat in a chair beside it, dressed in gray sweats and a green tee shirt.

"Language." Paulina cuffed him gently.

I snorted and poured a glass of water. "What does that

mean?" The word sounded like *koorva*. I handed him the water and sat beside him.

"It's the F-word in Polish," Paulina replied.

My eyes widened. Aithan didn't curse. Ever.

As if reading my mind, she laughed. "Everyone thinks my brother is so sweet because he's never vulgar. They don't know he cusses like the devil in Polish." She held out her hand. "I'm Paulina."

I shook it. "Zelda." She had perfectly manicured, pale-pink nails. "Aithan said you were coming. I hope your flight wasn't too bad?"

She waved that away. "Too long when I knew my little brother was hurt." She leaned forward and kissed his forehead.

"Pauli ... stop fussing." He pulled in a labored breath. "I'm not dying."

"Could've fooled me. You're coughing like your lungs want out."

"The right one was stabbed by one of my ribs, you know. It's kinda mad right now."

She sat across from me. "Let's not talk about death. I need to update everyone at home. If it's not a positive report, Mama and Babcia will be on the next flight to Seattle."

He grunted. "Tell them to stay in L.A. Dr. Nathus swears I have the hardest skull she's ever seen. There's still no sign of brain bleeding and my concussion symptoms are already easing. As long as my lungs stay clear, I'll be out in a few days. Then it's just rest and breathing exercises for a few weeks. They don't even wrap broken ribs anymore."

"Rest? You?" She eyed him. "Right. Like you can stay away from Blue Water."

"No choice. But I talked to Juan this morning, and he's got everything covered. I might have to make him a partner after this. He's running the gym single-handedly."

She frowned. "Aithan, I know you. You suck at being still."

Wanting to convince her he was mending and could care for himself, I said, "Well, you're doing so much better today than you were yesterday."

He smiled gratefully. "See, Pauli? I'm healing just fine without you hovering around me like a dragonfly."

"The swelling around your eye has eased and your face is turning the most astonishing shade of green," I added and laughed at the sour look he gave me.

"Thanks, I think," he said.

Paulina persisted. "How will you manage without help at home?"

"I'll manage. I'm not a child and I don't need you to wipe my nose."

"No, but you're still my baby brother."

Her fussing reminded me so much of Greer, I almost snapped at her. Instead, I blurted out, "I'm here if he needs anything." I caught his hand. "You can even stay with me. There's room at my place, and Drew's coming back this week, so there'll be another person around to help."

"Thanks. I might take you up on that." He twined his fingers with mine. "Why's he returning so soon?"

"I told him what happened." I shrugged. "He wants to be here to help."

"Who's Drew?" Paulina asked.

"Zel's other boyfriend," he answered before I could open my mouth.

Other? Did that mean he considered himself my boyfriend, too?

Paulina's eyes widened. "You have two men?" She turned to Aithan before I could answer. "So are you gonna be Dieter or Jason?"

"Who?" I asked, confused by the whiplash curves of this conversation.

She answered, "Dieter the Donor is the biological father of all Mama's children. Jason is her husband and our dad."

I looked between them, trying not to laugh. "You call your biological father Dieter the Donor? Not a close relationship, I take it?"

Smirking, Paulina shook her head. "Actually, Dieter's great. He made us. Jason raised us. Mama also has two other lovers, Liam and Rustam."

I looked at Aithan. "So the whole idea of reverse harem isn't anything new to you?"

He grinned, looking a little lopsided. "Nope. Mama's unconventional. One husband and three lovers. It made school visits awkward when we were kids."

Paulina laughed. "Remember Mr. Sheever? He could never wrap his head around our mom and her men."

Aithan laughed, but it turned into coughing and wincing again. When he finally stopped, he shook his head and held his ribs. "That sucks."

I rubbed his arm. "It'll get better."

He smiled wearily. "Of course it will."

"The police better find the bastard who did this to you," Paulina snarled.

"They're trying." He sipped more water. "All we can do is wait."

Changing the subject, I asked, "How long are you in town?"

"Only until tomorrow. That's all the time I could afford off from work."

Aithan grimaced. "Let me know if you need money."

"That's sweet, but you have enough to worry about." She patted his knee. "I'm fine."

Two young nurses strode into the room. One smiled brightly for him. "Ready to take another walk, Mr. Mazur?"

The other frowned at us and the furniture rearrangement,

but the hard look Paulina gave her made the woman find something else to worry about.

"Sure." He slowly stood. The nurses arranged his IV on the stand so he could wheel it along and he offered me his arm. "Come with me?"

"Of course."

Paulina pulled her phone from her purse. "I'll call Babcia and Mama."

"You're definitely slower than usual," I remarked, "but you're standing straighter than I expected."

He smiled and kissed my temple. "I want out of here as soon as possible. Pauli is right, I suck at sitting still."

I nodded. "And I meant what I said. Come stay with me while you heal." I tightened my grip on his arm, suddenly wanting him to take me up on my offer. "It'll mean a lot less worry for me."

He looked at me side-long, a bemused smile on his lips. "You worry about me?"

"Since you got your senses knocked out? Yes. And I know you think you'll be a burden, but that's not true. I'm used to feeding another person and having you around won't interrupt my work." I peered up at him. I really liked that Aithan was so much taller than me. It was a nice change. "Please say yes. I want you to recover at my place. Besides, I offer home-cooked meals and therapy cats."

He chuckled and winced but managed not to trigger another coughing fit. "How can I say no to that?"

"You will?"

"You're sure about this, Zel?"

"One hundred ten percent sure."

We reached the end of the hall and turned to retrace our steps. "Then, yes, I'll stay with you."

Smiling wide enough to crack my face, I pressed my cheek to his shoulder. "Good. That's actually a relief."

He shook his head. "I didn't realize you were that worried. I'm sorry."

We passed his room and continued down to the next bisecting hallway. "Don't apologize." I stroked his cheek. "Aithan, you matter to me. Don't you know that?"

He stopped and cupped my jaw, tilted my head, and searched my face. "So soon?"

I bit my lip and nodded.

"I thought it was just me." He kissed me, and I wrapped my arms around him, forgetting about the nurses walking past, the hospital's murmuring machine noises, his IV and injuries. Until he winced.

"Sorry." I pulled back. "I'm sorry. Did I hurt you?"

He turned us back around. "No, that was my fault."

I exhaled relief. He wouldn't be alone in an apartment, and we mattered to each other. Was that love? Maybe not quite, but it was definitely on the spectrum.

After I left the hospital, I stopped at my local pharmacy for my thyroid medication. Halloween screamed from half the aisles — candy and fake tombstones, plastic pumpkins and creepy skulls that shrieked as I passed them. The thirty-first was just days away. How had October flown by so quickly? It seemed like only days ago that I was planning a sunny vacation and fighting with Tristan.

I'd invited Paulina to have dinner with me, but she wanted to spend all her limited time with Aithan; she had an early flight the next morning. So I picked up coconut milk and raspberries at the grocery store and headed home.

I pulled into the complex driveway and found my garage blocked by a sleek black Audi coupe. Drew got out, wearing a sexy grin. His emerald tee shirt made his green eyes gleam, and the tight fit of his jeans offered a helluva nice view; the man was packing heat and I don't mean a gun. His smile turned feral as he swaggered over. I rolled down my window, grabbed his face, and kissed him hard.

"Oh my God, I'm so fucking happy to see you," I said between kisses.

He chuckled. "I can tell. Want me to move the car?"

"No. Pull it into the garage. I'll park in the carport."

Once parked, I closed the garage door.

Drew was waiting. Mouth on mine, hands at my waist and in my hair, he walked me through the side door, into the first floor hallway, and pinned me to the wall. His lips drifted from my mouth, to my jaw, to my throat as his fingers made their way under my sweater. They danced across my skin, leaving gooseflesh behind, then found and unhooked my bra.

"You don't know how much I appreciate your easy-access lingerie, Brick." He lifted my sweater over my head. The bra joined it on the floor, and I moaned as his lips found my nipples. They tightened beneath his tongue as he nipped and sucked.

I squirmed against him. I'd worn a blue A-line skirt, and Drew made short work of its removal. Not to be outdone, I pulled his shirt up and over his head. God, I loved all his ink. My fingers found his belt and the button fly of his jeans. The hardness in his pants proved just how much he wanted me.

I slipped my fingers down them and giggled. "You flew commando?"

"Why bother with undies?" He hooked his thumbs into the loosened waistband and shoved his jeans off his hips.

His erection stood at attention between us. I took him in hand and slowly stroked his cock, watching his eyes close as he reveled in my touch. He groaned and his mouth found mine again, his tongue sweeping my lips then sliding between my teeth to stroke my tongue, the rhythm matching my hand's.

The press of his chest against my nipples sent bolts to my core. He maneuvered me away from the wall and into the office.

"I have a clean bill of health, babe," he whispered into my ear, his voice husky.

"Ooh," I exhaled and sat on the couch. He faced me, his thick cock still under my control. I slowly ran my tongue over its head, circled around, and licked my way down the shaft.

"Oh, shit."

His dick pulsed beneath my fingers. I smiled up at him. "I'm just getting started."

He gripped the back of my neck, leaned down, and kissed me fiercely. "Brick, I think I love you."

My smile became a smirk. "You will by the time I'm done." I pressed my lips to the head of his cock. Oh-so-slowly I moved my lips downward, taking my time to take him into my mouth and down my throat. All the way to the base.

The sounds coming from him were pure bliss as I came up off his cock, laved the head with my tongue, and slid back down, grazing the thin, sensitive skin with my teeth.

I relaxed my throat and pulled him as deep as possible into my mouth.

Then I swallowed.

"Oh, fuck." His body bucked and he caught my hair. But he didn't push or pull, he just held on for the ride and gave me complete control of his ecstasy. Drew was not a skull fucker. I didn't do this for those guys. If they wanted a top tier blowjob, they needed to trust me to run the show. Grabbing my head and fucking my mouth got them blue-balled real quick.

Time to increase the speed. I slid back slowly then went down hard and fast. I pulled back and, on the next descent, started caressing his balls. His entire body quaked. I gained speed and tightened my lips, fucking him with my mouth, letting my tongue add to the pleasure.

And I started humming. I couldn't say why, but a really good blowjob made me hum. It was such a joy to see a man lost in pure pleasure, not worrying about his performance or getting off. I loved the control it gave me. And I loved knowing all that bliss was my doing. I felt sexy and powerful, and incredibly happy to give Drew this gift.

He groaned as a slow tremor spread through his body. He touched my cheek. "Babe, stop or I'll blow my wad."

I paused just long enough to meet his gaze. "I want you to. Let me do this for you."

"But—"

Holding his gaze, I took his cock in my mouth again and slid back down to the base.

"Goddamn." He moaned and closed his eyes. His head fell back and he started to thrust into my mouth. I grabbed his ass and encouraged it. He still held my hair, but didn't tighten his grip. Relaxing my throat, I let him fuck my mouth until the tremors grew too great and his body convulsed. He groaned, long and low. Warmth filled my throat. I swallowed.

As his cock relaxed, I slowly eased him from my mouth.

Drew leaned over me, dragging in deep breaths, a fine sheen of sweat covering his chest and abs. He dropped to the couch then pulled me onto his lap and held me, his heart thudding under my ear. Contentment washed over me. I'd made him feel alive and amazing. He made me feel loved and appreciated.

And beautiful.

"You were right." With absolute tenderness, he brushed my hair off my face, then kissed me softly, slowly, deeply.

"About what?"

"Me loving you."

"Do you? Or do you just love my mouth, Drew Katterman?"

"I love you, Zelda Gordon. Your mouth is just a bonus I never expected and sure as fuck don't deserve."

I smiled and kissed him back. "I love you, too." I met his gaze. "And you totally deserved that."

27

PEACE OFFERINGS

FOUR DAYS later we moved Aithan into the townhouse's second bedroom.

While Drew wrote behind the closed door of the master bedroom and Aithan relaxed on the living room sofa, an icepack against his ribs, I went downstairs to get the mail.

The day was gray and rainy. Purple and orange Halloween lights still lit up the front window of the townhouse across from mine. My other neighbor had replaced her Halloween wreath with a Thanksgiving-themed one, a circle of orange and burgundy berries suspended from a dark-brown bow.

A box from Pure Lee Baking waited on the front doormat. I retrieved it and paused, enjoying the cool breeze on my face as fall leaves danced across the driveway. I inhaled. The air smelled fresh and sweet. Sighing contentedly, I went inside and carried the box upstairs to the kitchen.

Aithan pushed up from the couch with a pained grunt. "What's that?" he asked as he returned his icepack to the freezer.

"This is a bit of heaven from Pure Lee Baking. They're

local and specialize in allergen-free baked goods." I cut open the box and pulled out two dozen coconut sugar cookies shaped like ghosts and a dozen pumpkin muffins. "Ohh, she's feeling guilty."

"Who?"

"Greer. This is a peace offering, her way of apologizing."

He snorted. "Some things are universal among siblings, eh?" His voice sounded stronger every day.

I opened the package of cookies and passed him one. "Like never *saying* you're sorry?"

He raised it in salute to me. "Exactly." He took a bite. "Mmm, that's damn good," he said around a mouthful of cookie.

"I know, right? AIP compliant, too." I wasted no time stuffing one into my mouth.

Aithan helped himself to a second and we happily munched away. Gingerly, he put his arm around my shoulder and pulled me close. Every move knifed him as his ribs slowly knit back together. "It's good to be out of the hospital." He kissed my temple and rested his cheek against me. "You're the best, Zel."

I smiled. "I try." I kissed the hand he'd draped over my shoulder. "It's easy to be good to you."

He smiled back. "I try."

"I don't think you have to try hard," Drew said as he came off the stairs. "You're just a nice guy by nature, man."

Aithan shrugged, then winced and made a painful little noise in the back of his throat. "Does that mean I finish last?"

"You mean are you the loser?" Drew asked.

I shook my head. "Is there some game I don't know about?"

"Nope," Drew replied, "just a lame saying."

Aithan kissed my cheek. "If this is what nice-guy losers get, then I'm one hundred percent okay with dragging my broken butt across the finish line dead last."

Drew laughed. "Don't tell anyone, but I'm pretty sure we're the winners and Zel's on top."

Aithan grinned. "Right where I like her."

"Ohh, yeah." Drew leaned back against the kitchen counter and crossed his ankles.

Eyeing him, I said, "You look too smug." He had a suspiciously pleased air about him. "Like a cat that's eaten the canary *and* the goldfish."

He crossed his arms, and I recognized the purple fabric dangling from his fingers. "I found this in your lingerie drawer."

"Drew Katterman, why were you looking through my underwear?"

He smirked. "Planning for the future, of course." That smirk became a smile. "Like a trip to Mexico."

My eyes widened. "Yes! When Aithan is healed we should totally do that."

Aithan grinned. "That would be a helluva lotta fun."

"Oh, you know it." Drew draped the fatkini over his shoulder and pushed away from the counter to rummage in the box. "Cookies?"

"And muffins. From Greer," I said.

He barked a laugh. "Big sister finally admitted she stuck her nose too far up your business?"

"So it seems."

He shoved a cookie into his mouth. "Mmm-mm, I'm enjoying her guilt."

I savored another bite of cookie then frowned. The telltale scratchiness between my boobs told me I shouldn't've eaten something crumbly wearing a V-neck sweater. "Fuck."

"What's wrong?" Aithan filled a glass of water from the fridge filter.

I pulled my sweater forward and peered down my bra. "Crumbs."

"Snack bar's open!" Drew face-planted right between my tits.

I squealed and held onto him, laughing and squirming as he tried to capture the crumbs with his tongue.

"Stop! You're killing me." Aithan laughed and held his ribs. "*Kurwa*. It hurts to laugh."

"Almost got 'em," was Drew's muffled reply. He raised his head and kissed me. "You're delicious, Brick."

Grimacing in mock horror, I wiped drool from between my boobs. "You slobbered all over my cleavage."

Drew grinned. "Never heard you complain about that before."

"Pervert." I stuck the rest of the second cookie in my mouth and swatted him. The guys laughed while I closed the package of cookies.

Drew and Aithan talked while I started dinner. Donning an apron, I washed and chopped three pears and a big yellow onion. I sautéed them, added white wine to the mix and let it simmer while I sliced a pork tenderloin down the center. That got salted and I spooned the pear-onion mix down the length, added sprigs of rosemary, and tied the tenderloin closed with butcher's twine. The whole thing went into the oven under foil. In an hour, the house would smell like heaven.

My phone buzzed with a text from Tristan.

> Heard Aithan's out of the hospital.

> > Yeah. He's recovering @ my place. Drew is here too from NYC. Thought u should know.

> Thx. He doing OK?

> > Yes. Still can't move without pain, but the docs expect him to heal fast.

He sent the thumbs up emoji.

> So, thanks for talking to the cops. U saved my ass.

> Just told them the truth.

> U didn't have to. I've been pretty shitty to u. (Sorry again)

> Yeah, I did have to. I wouldn't let u go to jail for something u didn't do.

> I know. You're too good, Zel.

I shook my head.

> I'm just honest.

> Yeah. Thx. Tell Aith I'm glad he's doing better.

He really seemed to mean it.

> I will. Heard u went back to work early.

> They needed the extra hands with the boss laid up. Everyone's worried about him.

> Including u?

> Including me.

> OK. I will. Thx, Tris.

> NP

The doorbell rang and I ran downstairs to get the door knowing it was Tobias. He'd volunteered to pick up some of Aithan's things from his apartment.

"Hey, Zel. Can you grab this?" He held out a duffel bag.

"I can get that." Drew came down the stairs. He took the

bag and offered his hand. "Drew Katterman. Thanks for helping out."

Tobias returned the handshake. "Tobias Peters. And it's no problem. I'd do anything for my man."

"Shut up, you suck-up," Aithan rasped from the top of the stairs and we all laughed.

Tobias had a gray suitcase, too, and we returned to the main level "Think I got everything you needed." He and Aithan traded hugs.

"Thanks, brother." Aithan reached for the case, but Tobias headed up the stairs without letting him get a hand on it.

"Don't even try, man. I know you're not supposed to lift shit. Which room, Zel?"

"First one on the right."

Aithan shook his head. "I hate being useless."

I patted his cheek. "You're not. You look very pretty on my arm."

Drew cracked up, and Tobias chuckled as he trotted back down the stairs.

Aithan gave me the stink eye then laughed and winced and cursed in Polish under his breath. "*Gówno*."

"What's *goovno*?" I asked.

"It means shit." Tobias crouched to scratch Lulu between the ears.

"That," Aithan confirmed.

Tobias straightened. "You better call your roommates. They're picking out paint colors for your room."

Aithan nodded. "Shana's pregnant. I knew my days were numbered, just figured I had a few more months." He settled carefully onto the couch. "I'd planned to look at townhomes and condos, but my down payment's gonna go toward medical bills instead." Frank hopped up beside him, purring loud enough to be heard across the room.

"Sucks, man," Tobias said. "Wish I could help you."

Aithan waved that away. "You got Amara to worry

about. I'm good. Just means I need to find another room when Zel gets sick of me." He obliged Frank with chin scratches.

I shook my head. "Never gonna happen."

Tobias grinned. "Looks like you're stuck with her."

"Get out, fiend!" I threw a pillow at him.

Laughing, he caught it and tossed it back. "I'm going, I'm going!"

"Wait, do you really have to leave?" I asked. "I'm making pork tenderloin for dinner and there's plenty."

"Wish I could stay, but I gotta get Amara."

I nodded and walked him down to the front door. Once there, I caught his hand. "Hey. I know you're angry about me seeing Tristan and vouching for him. Are we cool?"

He stepped closer. "Yeah, Zel. We're cool." He brushed my hair over my shoulder.

"Good, 'cause I like you, Tobias. I don't want bullshit hanging between us."

He surprised me by leaning down and brushing a gentle kiss across my cheek. "Nah, girl, we're still A-okay."

When I got back upstairs, Drew and Aithan were sitting at the dining table with Drew's computer open before them.

"Whatcha doing?"

"House hunting," Drew replied. "Aithan's telling me which neighborhoods to check out. I want an ocean or lake view."

"You're looking to spend some big bucks then," I said, not thinking he was serious about that kinda cash.

"Six or seven million, I figure," he replied without looking up.

I gaped at him. "Are you serious?"

He laughed. "You keep asking me that, babe."

"Man's not messing around." Aithan turned the computer so I could see the kinds of mansions they were considering.

"Shit," I muttered. "I'm not cleaning all those bathrooms."

They cracked up, Aithan holding his ribs and panting. "Stop making me laugh."

"We'll hire a cleaning crew," Drew said. "Aithan knows a really good one." He turned the computer back around. "The question is, modern or historical?"

I pulled a bag of sweet potato chips from the pantry and poured them into a bowl. "Modern or down-to-the-studs renovated. Old homes are pretty but high maintenance and cold as fuck."

Aithan took a handful of chips. "That's what I said."

"Good. Then we're all in agreement. Okay, bedroom, bedroom, bedroom," Drew pointed to each of us, "bedroom for Tobias and one for his daughter, guest room. That's how many rooms?"

"Six," I said, amused by his pragmatism in the midst of wild speculation.

"Hmm, plus an office for you and one for me." He looked from me to Aithan. "What else?"

"Sex dungeon," Aithan said around a chip, straight-faced as ever.

"I like how you think!" Drew crowed. "And a home theater for watching porn on the big screen."

I stared at Aithan. "Do *not* encourage his madness, Mr. Mazur."

"What? I was just being practical."

"How is a sex dungeon practical?"

"He's thinking ahead," Drew answered. "Like going through your lingerie."

"Right." Aithan nodded, somehow managing to look innocent.

"Oh my God." I covered my face with my hands. "What have I done?"

They cracked up and Drew pulled me over to sit on his lap. "Okay, no sex dungeon, but a basement that can be converted if the need, ahem, *arises*. Good compromise?"

I sighed and slowly shook my head. "Fine." I met his gaze. "But I want a really nice kitchen."

"And a gym." Aithan sat back, making a face as the movement pulled bruised muscles and healing bones.

Drew added our suggestions to his growing list. "Yes to both." He opened his browser and brought up my realtor's site. "Now comes the fun part." He grinned at us and cracked his knuckles. "Let's go shopping."

Aithan shook his head, a bemused smile on his lips. "Those are pipe dreams for me, man. I'd be happy with a one-bedroom condo right now."

I went to the fridge and pulled out sweet potato biscuit dough.

"Because of your medical bills?" Drew said. "Already handled them, so you can dream away with the rest of us."

I stopped unwrapping the dough and turned to stare at him.

"What?" Aithan's blue eyes widened.

Drew sat back. "Look, don't make a big deal out of it. I can afford it. I'd rather spend my money on a worthy cause, like your medical bills, than watch it be wasted on the crap my ex-girlfriend bought. She's spent that much on handbags and fugly shoes. So, don't mention it and don't feel indebted to me. I fuckin' hate that."

"But—"

"Nope. You make Zel happy. I want to keep her that way. It's all part of my master plan to stay on that fine woman's good side so I can get in her pants as often as possible."

Stunned, Aithan shook his head and blinked rapidly, clearly trying to process what he'd just heard. "I don't understand. We hardly know each other. Why would you do that?"

I sucked in a deep breath. Drew's generosity was well known to those of us in the industry. I wiped my hands on a towel, then went and kissed him. "You're a good man, Drew Katterman. Don't let anyone tell you otherwise."

Next, I caught Aithan's chin and forced him to look at me. "Just accept the gift. Drew isn't foolish with his money, even if Livi was. He doesn't spend what he doesn't have."

He nodded. "Well, at least accept my gratitude and a lifetime of private training sessions."

Drew's face lit up. "Sweet! That's a great trade!"

Aithan shook his head, his expression equal parts baffled and amused. I kissed his cheek then returned to the biscuits. The guys went back to house hunting.

I smiled as I cut and rolled dough. I had a few worries — Greer, and Tristan, and whoever had jumped Aithan — but my joys far outweighed them.

I glanced at my lovers. It seemed crazy that we'd only been together for a month. At the beginning of October, I was stuck in a dead-end relationship. But here we were in November and I had the confidence to dream of a life with Aithan and Drew, and maybe even Tobias.

With my guys' encouragement I'd changed so much in such a short amount of time.

I felt strong and beautiful with Aithan.

I felt sexy and successful with Drew.

They shared my heart and took me, as I was, without reservation.

I got out a baking sheet and the parchment paper.

Someday maybe I'd have Tobias in my heart, too. I loved what a devoted dad he was. How he stood up for Amara and made her his priority. Knowing he was out there watching over her so carefully gave me hope. If I ever had a family, I'd want to start it with someone like him.

I put the biscuits in the oven, turned, and watched Drew and Aithan.

Yeah, life had taken some strange twists since the day Tristan turned his nose up at my fatkini. But that skimpy purple suit had opened the door for two incredible men who treasured me just the way I was. Where I saw flaws, they saw perfection.

Maybe if I spent enough time with them worshiping me, I'd learn to see myself that way, too.

I smiled as the two handsome men sitting at my dining table plotted our future together.

Yeah, I can get used to this life.

It definitely wasn't boring.

28

ONE LUCKY WOMAN

I STARTED the dishwasher then hung the orange dishtowel on the oven handle to dry.

The clock on the microwave read ten-thirty-four, and I yawned. But it became a surprised squeak as Drew's arms encircled my waist. I hadn't heard him approach.

He chuckled. "Did I surprise you?"

I nodded and let him pull me back against him. "You were in stealth mode."

He hugged me with his whole body and pressed a kiss to the back of my neck. Goosebumps pebbled my skin as his lips trailed more kisses up to my ear.

"Come to bed," he whispered.

I shivered and turned in his arms.

The hunger in his gaze was unmistakable. He pulled our bodies together and his kiss was even hungrier. His hands slipped under my shirt. They drifted up my back, past my bra line, and he smiled against my mouth when he realized I wore no bra. "Easiest access yet." He walked backwards toward the staircase, taking me with him.

At the top floor, even with Drew's hands and lips on me, I noticed the light leaking beneath the door to Aithan's room.

He'd gone up to lay down a few hours ago, still tiring quickly and getting headaches from the concussion, still knifed by pain in his chest and back with every breath.

"Wait." I knocked lightly on the door.

"I think he's asleep," Drew whispered.

But Aithan wasn't. "Come in." His voice sounded tight.

I opened the door. Shirtless, he sat grimacing in the middle of the bed, propped up by pillows.

"You hurting?" I asked.

He nodded. "Can't get comfortable. Can't relax. Can't sleep."

For the first time, I got a good look at the damage done by his attacker. The sight was a fucking shock. Bruises covered Aithan's muscular chest and back. When I'd told Drew someone had tap danced across his chest, I hadn't realized how close to true that was. Some of the bruises were green and yellow, but many remained black and purple. A round greenish-blue bruise surrounded the healing wound where the emergency room team had pushed a drainage tube between his ribs.

"Shit, man," Drew said, "you look like you lost a fight with an elephant."

"May have been one, for all I know," Aithan replied.

I sat on the edge of the bed. "What can I do to help you?"

He smiled weakly. "You've done more than enough, Zel. I have tramadol for the rest."

Drew grunted. "That shit's addictive."

"Yeah, which is why I'm taking less than the recommended dose. I just wanted ibuprofen, but Dr. Nathus won't let me take it with the concussion."

Drew nodded. "Yeah. It slows cognitive recovery and can prolong the headaches."

I peered up at him. "How do you know so much about concussions?"

He shrugged. "I'm an author. I know all kinds of weird shit."

I tilted my head in acknowledgment and turned back to Aithan. "You know this is gonna end up in one of his books."

"Probably." He took a cup from the bedside table, but frowned into it.

I reached out. "You need more water?"

"Thanks." He passed it to me and I went to refill it in the bathroom.

"What you need is a good screw, man," Drew said. "That'd help you sleep."

"I wish," Aithan replied as I returned and handed him the full glass. "But the doc said no strenuous activity for two weeks." He opened a prescription bottle and shook out an oval pill.

Drew grinned and pulled me against him. "And fucking Zel *must* be strenuous or you're not doing it right, eh?"

Aithan's smile was rueful. "Exactly." He snapped the pill in half and took one portion with the water, returning the other half to the bottle.

I bit my lip. "I don't suppose the hospital did STD testing?"

His pout was adorable as he shook his head.

Drew leaned his chin on my shoulder. "Nothing wrong with your eyes or your hands, man." He brushed my hair back from my ear and his breath made me shiver. "I owe him a show, babe."

Aithan's gaze flicked from Drew to me and hunger flared behind it. A slow smile curved his lips. "You know, Zel, those pajamas may be comfortable, but they've got to go." His eyes held mine. "Take them off."

Drew guided my hands to the hem of my shirt.

My breath caught. A little frisson of excitement skittered down my spine. I lifted the blue shirt up and over my head, baring my breasts to both men. They exhaled a collective breath.

"Bottoms, too," Aithan commanded.

Drew obliged, helping me step out of them even as I dropped my shirt on the floor. His sweatpants did nothing to hide his erection. It pressed against my ass, a promise of pleasures to come. He lifted my arms to wrap them around his neck and, like when Aithan had fucked me in front of him, my back arched and my breasts lifted. Drew's lips found my neck, his fingers found my nipples. I relaxed into him, sighing as his mouth raised gooseflesh all over my body and my tits tightened.

"How does that feel?" Aithan asked.

"So good," I murmured.

"Just good? What would feel even better, beautiful?"

I opened my eyes to find Aithan's cock straining against his own pajama pants.

"What should Drew do to make you feel even better? Tell him, Zel. Make him please you."

The way he demanded that I ask to be pleasured made my heart speed and my twat twitch. I licked my lips. Aithan muttered something in Polish as his gaze followed my tongue. His hand slipped into his pants.

"Tell me, babe." Drew's voice vibrated though me, making me shiver again.

"I want your mouth on me," I said, the breathy words coming in a rush.

"Where?" Aithan demanded. "Tell him where to put his mouth." He slowly stroked his cock and, god*damn*, I wished I could suck it. The thought of blowing Aithan while Drew fucked me shot bolts through my belly.

I swallowed. "I want your mouth on my clit, Drew."

He spun me to face him so suddenly I gasped, but the feral look in his eyes only heightened my excitement. "On the bed." He guided me to sit, then he went to his knees. But instead of scooting me back, he grabbed my hips, pulled my ass to the edge, and draped my legs over his broad shoulders. His tongue slid into my folds and flicked over my clit.

"Oh, fuck." I leaned back on my elbows and closed my eyes.

But Aithan said, "Open your eyes. Watch Drew. You like to watch him."

I opened my eyes but turned my head to see Aithan stroking his long cock. "I'd rather watch you."

He swallowed and reached his free hand to caress my face. I parted my lips. His finger slipped between them and I sucked it, tonguing the pad and holding his gaze until Drew's ministrations overwhelmed me and my eyes drifted shut. Aithan moved to stroking my breast, teasing the nipple with his damp finger.

I moaned and struggled not to clamp my legs around Drew's head as his tongue slipped down and teased my opening. My hips bucked in response. A tremor started in my legs and traveled up to my belly. The world fell away and Drew's amazing mouth became my only focus.

"Look at him, Zel," Aithan panted.

I opened my eyes to see Drew between my legs and my orgasm hit fast and hard. He grabbed my thighs and sucked my clit as I arched back, my head on Aithan's leg, my hands clawing the bedding. I cried out as pleasure surged through me, taking all sense with it and leaving only sensation behind. My muscles relaxed as fast as they'd clenched and I collapsed back onto the bed, dazed and breathing hard. "Holy fuck, you're good at that."

Drew chuckled and kissed his way up my body, from thighs to breasts. He captured my hips and turned me onto my stomach, pulling me up to my knees.

He hadn't come yet and neither had Aithan. Drew climbed onto the bed behind me, his thick cock against my ass. "I'm gonna fuck you from behind, Brick, and you're gonna kiss Aithan and let him suck your tits until he loses his mind and comes all over his hand."

"Fuck, yes." I crawled forward to capture Aithan's amazing lips with mine. He moaned and caught the nape of my neck, slipping his tongue between my teeth as he stroked his cock faster.

Drew positioned himself between my thighs and pushed into me, filling every inch as I groaned into Aithan's mouth. Drew grasped my hips and stroked hard, his rhythm matching Aithan's hand. I shifted positions to put my tits in Aithan's face. He obliged by sucking my nipples.

I moaned, already primed to explode. Every flick of Aithan's tongue zinged straight down to my crotch and my muscles clenched Drew's cock even harder.

But Drew wouldn't get me off that quickly. He slowed his strokes, pushed deeper, paused. "What do you want, Brick?"

"I want to cum. I want all of us to cum." I returned to kissing Aithan and reached between his legs to caress his balls.

"*Kurwa*," he panted, his voice hoarse and low.

Drew's fingers slipped between my legs and circled my clit as his cock stroked inside me. I gasped and pushed back, fucking him as much as he was fucking me.

Aithan's head arched back. I followed him and plunged my tongue into his mouth as he groaned and came. His muscles relaxed and, panting, he pressed his forehead to mine, eyes closed, pleasure and pain chasing each other across his face.

Drew didn't let my focus wander. He grasped my hips and shoulder and pushed into me harder, faster, deeper.

Down but not out, Aithan took over stroking my clit. "Look at me, Zel."

Our eyes met and I came hard again, lost in the intense, wonderful intimacy of his brilliant blue gaze, my body jerking and trembling, my muscles clamping down on Drew's dick.

Three more strokes pushed Drew over the cliff and he came inside me, his chest pressed to my back, his mouth on me, his breathing ragged.

We were a jumble of limbs, a sheen of sweat, panting and swearing. Smiling as the tremors of pleasure eased and we untangled our bodies.

I sighed and slowly stretched my back, content to lie between my lovers. Drew kissed my shoulder, shifted on the bed, and squawked, "Fuck!" as he tumbled off the edge.

I lost it completely and collapsed into the bedding, laughing my ass off. Aithan did too, holding his ribs and gasping, "Ow-ow-ow! *Gówno!*"

Drew lay on the floor laughing like a maniac. He tossed my shirt and pajama pants onto the bed. "Throw me a blanket, babe. I'll just sleep here."

"Go sleep in the master." Aithan grabbed a handful of tissues and cleaned himself up.

"You okay now?" I pulled on my pants.

He nodded and relaxed into the pillows. "Come here."

I donned my shirt and snuggled up to him. "What?"

"Thank you." He caressed my face. "You're amazing, Zelda Gordon."

I smiled. "So are you, Aithan Mazur."

Drew sat up. "And me."

I laughed. "Definitely, Drew Katterman. You're definitely amazing."

"Zel?" Aithan murmured in my ear. "I love you."

I turned to gaze into his eyes. "I love you, too," I whispered and kissed him gently. Then I faced Drew who was smiling like an idiot from the floor. "And you already know I love you."

He reached up and twined his fingers with mine. "Yeah, Zel, I know. And you know I love you back."

Aithan kissed my cheek with absolute tenderness. "Now, take your author to sleep in the master bedroom. There's not enough room in this little bed for the three of us, and I plan to sprawl across the whole mattress."

"Okay, okay, I get the hint." I slipped off the bed and pulled the bedding up around him. "Comfy?"

He smiled. "Very."

I kissed him, then Drew and I turned off the light and went to the master bedroom. Drew climbed into bed while I headed for the bathroom to get cleaned up. When I came out, he was sound asleep, his breathing slow and steady. Frank had curled up between his feet, eyes closed, motor buzzing.

I stepped into the hallway to turn off the light and spied Lulu slipping into Aithan's room. She jumped onto the bed and snuggled up to him, purring so loudly I could hear her in the hall.

I smiled. The cats had accepted their new daddies, and I felt as happy as they sounded. Hell, Drew had fucked the shit outta me in front of Aithan and not once had I worried about cellulite or pudge or jiggling. I'd only thought about giving and feeling pleasure. I ran my hand over my stomach then turned off the lights. "You're one lucky woman, Zaftig Zel," I whispered as I climbed into bed.

"Hmm?" Drew murmured sleepily.

"Nothing, Playboy. Go back to sleep."

He spooned against me and sighed. Frank remained undisturbed.

Good goddamn, I thought as my eyes closed. *Sex and life just got a helluva lot more wonderful.*

TO BE CONTINUED IN …
The Skinny

KEEP READING FOR A SNEAK PEEK OF ...
THE SKINNY

Ah, pipe dreams. Gotta love 'em.

Cold November rain pelted the bedroom windows. The room remained dark and I felt languid after an hour of early-morning nooky. Really, there was no better way to wake than between two horny men with the worst — and by that, I mean the best — intentions.

Goddamn, I loved these guys. They were so masculine, so alike yet so different. Drew was witty and brash, quick with an adorable, cocky grin and an arched brow. Aithan was quietly confident, neither seeking nor avoiding attention, rock solid and effortlessly sexy.

I loved them and they loved me and sometimes I even believed I was good enough for them. Sometimes when they looked at me, their gazes full of love or lust, I forgot my flaws and mistakes and regrets, and I kinda, sorta started to love myself. I kinda, sorta believed life had settled down and everything would fall into place from here on out.

Straddling Aithan, I arched and sighed as my muscles and ligaments popped deliciously.

He slapped my hip. "Stop that, beautiful. Or we'll shag you silly again."

Laughing, I rag-dolled onto my side, landing between him and Drew in the middle of the bed.

"Whatever she's doing, you shag her," Drew muttered. "I'm spent." He lay on his stomach, arms beneath his pillow, back slowly rising and sinking as he skirted the edge of sleep.

I scooted around to rest my head against his back and draped my legs over Aithan's impressive abs.

The guys had awakened me with fingers between my legs and lips on my breasts, both men working me over all at once and one at a time until I'd cum with a scream. Then they'd really gotten down to some serious fucking, and I'd gotten off twice more.

The three of us were naked as the day we were born — well, if we overlooked Drew's tats — and I was buzzing with pleasure. It still seemed equal parts marvelous and mysterious that Drew and Aithan were my lovers and neither was troubled by the intimacy of our shared bed. In fact, watching and being watched played a large part in turning all of us on. Another fact of this new relationship that still shocked me when I thought about it. Then again I was learning not to overthink things so much. Going with the flow was so much more fun.

Aithan drummed his fingers lightly on my knee, his touch like a butterfly dancing across my skin. He sang something beneath his breath, just a little too low for me to make out.

"What're you singing?"

"*I Walk the Line*," Drew replied sleepily. "Johnny Cash. Fucking great song." He yawned.

Aithan smiled, nodded, and kept singing.

I recognized it now that I knew the title. "I love Johnny Cash," I said and joined in, harmonizing around Aithan's bass voice and studying his face. Fuck, he was handsome. Sky-blue eyes and short, dark hair, full lips, chiseled jaw, and a body to make Adonis jealous — everything about Aithan made me wanna get naughty with him.

KEEP READING FOR A SNEAK PEEK OF ...

Drew's breathing slowed. I sat up and considered him. Green eyes closed, sexy lips parted, dirty blond hair mussed. I traced the lines of tattoos covering his back — knights, dragons, castles, and all manner of fantastical creatures and mythical symbols. Every tat held meaning for him — some referencing his books and characters, others reminders of his life and people he'd lost. I kissed his shoulder and he sighed sleepily.

Aithan shifted to sit on the edge of the bed. "I'm going running. You guys wanna come?"

"Pretty sure I just did. Three times," I replied and laughed when he tickled me.

Drew murmured something unintelligible.

"Was that a yes or a no?" Aithan asked.

"It's no. He's zonked out."

"Man, you can't avoid the gym forever." Aithan climbed out of bed and headed for the bathroom.

"Nice view," I remarked.

Aith glanced over his shoulder, a cute smirk lifting his lips. He turned around. "Better than this one?"

I arched my brows and matched his smirk. "Not better. Just different. I can appreciate both of them." I snaked out my hand and cupped Drew's bare ass, my palm covering the roaring bear tattooed there. He didn't even twitch.

Aithan laughed. "Well, that one isn't moving." He disappeared into the bathroom but called, "Run with me?" over the sound of water splashing into the sink.

"Definitely." I stood just as Frank charged into the bedroom and launched himself over Drew to land in the middle of the bed, cheeks and tail puffed up.

"Good morning, tuxedo cat," I said and scratched his noggin. He purred and made bread on the duvet cover, clearly pleased with himself. Lulu appeared in the doorway, calico tail flicking. "Okay, okay, I get the message," I said. Throwing on a robe, I followed the cats downstairs and split a can of shredded chicken between them. Purring and num-num noises ensued while I filled water bottles for Aithan and me. Lulu finished eating first and hopped up on the breakfast bar to bathe and rub her face on my hand.

"You're welcome, kitty-kitty." I scratched her chin then headed upstairs.

Drew slept soundly while Aithan shaved. I grabbed a washcloth and took a French whore's bath. Once dressed, we headed off to run around Green Lake.

"We're gonna get rained on," Aithan said as we walked the first few blocks to warm up.

I covered my mouth in mock horror. "What? In Seattle? In *November*? Surely not. Nooo."

He eyed me. "Thanks for the morning sarcasm."

I laughed. "Sorry. Native humor."

"You know, where I'm from, rain's a reason for celebration and sheer panic."

"People in Los Angeles get all crazy from a little rain?"

"Well, yeah, it's a desert. No one knows how to drive in it, so they all panic."

We crossed Phinney and started running as we headed into Woodland Park. A few intrepid fellow joggers nodded as they passed, and we dodged the usual happy dogs walking their bleary owners. Skirting the zoo and the rose garden, we headed downhill under Aurora Avenue, talking about Drew. Aithan had offered a number of different training approaches, but Drew had countered each with an excuse.

"Can't figure out how to motivate him," Aithan said, sounding a little frustrated and a little winded.

"Somehow you gotta make working out more interesting than writing."

"Ha! Not sure that's possible."

We cut back into the park, passed the tennis courts, and headed toward the soccer fields. A light drizzle began.

I glanced at him. Brow furrowed, he looked as annoyed as he sounded. "This is really bugging you, isn't it?"

"Yeah." He coughed and slowed to a walk. "*Kurde,*" he muttered in Polish.

"You okay?"

Aithan nodded. "Just pushed things a bit this morning." That came with a big, sweet smile that I couldn't help but match. "Worth it." He pulled his water bottle from his belt, drank, and offered it to me.

"Thanks."

"It bugs me because I don't like being indebted to him," he said.

Ohh. Ego. "Drew doesn't see it that way."

Aithan eyed me and annoyance underlay his frustration. "*I* do."

"Are you angry?"

"About him paying my hospital bills? No." He squinted at me then blinked rain from his eyes. "Maybe." Aithan sighed. "It's more that he did it without asking. He just made the choice for me, and I know he doesn't see anything wrong with that, but I'm not used to people making my decisions, and that's what my life has been for the last month. Suddenly I have a bunch of keepers."

We walked and he massaged his chest. I just listened 'cause I was pretty sure he wanted to vent, not get advice.

"I'm used to being in charge. I run my own business, have for almost a decade. I've been heading off problems and fixing other people since I bought Blue Water, but this blindsided me." That was Blue Water Fitness, the gym Aithan owned.

"The attack?"

"The attack. Drew's generosity. You."

"Me?" That jolted me and anxiety made my scalp tingle, my spine crawl. Was he saying he regretted our relationship?

"It's like the worst and the weirdest and the most wonderful things all landed in my lap at the same time."

Okay. No. We're good. I think. I took another sip of water to dissipate the rush of adrenaline his words had triggered. Fuck, I hated when anxiety hit like that. Lowering the water bottle, I said, "I'm sorry."

His brow furrowed. "Why are you apologizing?"

"Because I only thought about your physical recovery. I should've paid better attention to your emotions."

Aithan stopped and gripped my shoulders. "Zel, these are my problems. And despite what I said, you're not one of them. You're that 'most wonderful thing' I mentioned."

"But I want to help."

He kissed me. "You are. By listening and not judging."

"But—"

Aithan shook his head. "Not your worry, beautiful. *I* gotta get good with Drew's gift 'cause he's not gonna let me repay him. That problem is mine. Not yours. Not his." We started walking again. "You wanna help?" I nodded. "Then let's figure out how to engage him in a training program. I'll feel a lot better when I'm giving back to him."

"Okay. I can do that." We slowly picked up our pace to running again.

"You know him better than I do," Aithan remarked.

"Well, he runs pretty regularly, but you want to offer something more, right?"

"Yeah."

"Then look for something mentally challenging," I replied. "Something he'll see as beneficial to his writing. Like bouldering or mixed martial arts, something like that."

Aithan grimaced, cursed, and slowed to walking again, rubbing his chest.

"Hurting?"

"You think?" he snapped. "*Kurwa*! I hate this."

"Hate what?"

KEEP READING FOR A SNEAK PEEK OF …

He bared his teeth. "Being in pain, healing so damn slowly, jumping at shadows, people making decisions for me. Everything!"

I wasn't surprised to see him pissed off. Honestly, it was about fucking time he lost his patience.

He closed his eyes and sighed. When he opened them, he looked like a dog that'd bitten its owner and realized its mistake. "I'm sorry. You don't deserve to have your head torn off."

I laughed and wrapped my arm around his waist. "Aithan, you've met my sister, so you should know that what you just did was a little love nip. That woman can behead a bitch with her tongue at twenty paces and not break a sweat. You gotta bite a lot deeper than that, if you wanna hurt my feelings, lover."

"Oh, I can bite," he remarked, that little lopsided smile I loved so much returning to mingle with his regret in the cutest way.

"I know that's right." I said and glanced over my shoulder as if to see my back. "Pretty sure I've got the hickey to prove it."

"You do." He grabbed my hand and pulled me along as he headed down to the paved path encircling Green Lake. "And don't mention your sister's tongue. I find her and her mouth totally unappealing."

"Really? Most men think she's beautiful."

"She is, but beautiful doesn't automatically mean alluring. Greer is definitely not my type. Too scrawny."

"Scrawny?" I laughed. "Wow. I've never heard a man describe her that way."

He shrugged. "You're much more enticing."

"You mean I'm much *more*, in general."

At five-eleven and size twenty, I was not what you'd call petite. The world labeled me plus-sized. The guys said I was voluptuous. A Valkyrie. I could kinda, sorta see that…

sometimes. But my brain defaulted to *fat* and *ugly* way too easily.

Aithan slipped behind me, grabbed my hips, and pulled my ass against him. "I mean I want cushion when I'm pushin', Zelda Gordon."

I laughed and caught his hands. "Holy crap, that's a very Drew thing to say. I think he's a bad influence on you."

He pressed his lips to the nape of my neck. "'Cause I'm the wholesome one?"

"Yeah, nooo." I pulled him back to my side, twining my fingers with his. "You're so *not* wholesome."

He lifted my hand to his lips, "Not at all. That's just a lie I use to lure innocent maidens into my clutches."

"Then how'd you end up with me?"

"Damned lucky, I guess."

I looked down. Part of me wanted to believe he really found me more attractive than my beautiful, petite sister, but the damned bitchy Voice of Doubt that lurked in my head whispered lies.

He's too nice to tell the truth. He doesn't really think you're prettier than Greer. No way, Zaftig Zel.

"Zelda?" I looked up. He was watching me, brows furrowed and eyes filled with concern. "I'll never lie to you," he said quietly. "You know that, right?"

"I think so?" His expression fell and I grabbed his hand. "Aith, my doubt's not a reflection of you. It's my own insecurity. It's a lifetime of hearing I'm ugly. It's boyfriends telling me I'm too fat to love."

"*Pieprzone dupki,*" he muttered.

"Don't know what that means, but I'm sure I agree."

"It means I'd like to hurt the people who hurt you so much." He pulled me off the paved trail and onto the grassy slope surrounding the lake. "Zel, you're not ugly and you're not fat, and if I have to repeat that every damn day to drill through those layers of lies and the walls you put up to try to keep them out then that's what I'll do." He cupped my jaw. "You're beautiful and perfect, and I love you. Just. The way. You Are."

A noise to our left made us look over. A woman stood gawking at us while her dog sniffed the grass. "I'm sorry." She fluttered her hand at us. "I didn't mean to eavesdrop, but that was the sweetest thing I've ever heard a man say to a woman." We just stared. She awkwardly backed up. "Just, I mean, you gotta keep him." She turned and headed toward Green Lake Avenue, pulling her dog away from whatever smelled so intriguing.

"I know," I said then threw my arms around Aithan and kissed him hard.

Hand-in-hand, we walked the rest of the way around the lake and back home, kicking around ideas for Drew's training.

My phone buzzed in my pocket as we reached the townhouse. I glanced at it.

> How're you, honey?

"Text from Mom."

Aithan nodded. Inside, he toed off his shoes and took my running belt. He glanced at the hall clock. It read eight fifteen. "I'm gonna shower and head to Blue Water."

"You working all day?"

"No. Half-day. I overdid it this morning."

I smirked. "Yeah you did. You gonna be okay?"

He dropped the belt on the hall bench then trapped me between his body and the wall, his arms caging me in. "Why? Are you offering your services?"

His breath caressed my face. His chest and hips pressed against mine. I swear my heart rate doubled. I met his eyes and had to fight not to get lost in their beautiful blue depths. "No, but I know where you can take a cold shower."

Aithan snorted and kissed the tip of my nose. "Now I need it," he said and followed me upstairs. He continued up to the third floor while I went to the kitchen and started breakfast.

While turkey-apple-raisin hash heated in the microwave, I texted my mom.

> I'm good. Just got back from a run with Aithan, and Drew's almost finished with his next novel. They're both staying with me. Drew's house hunting in the coming weeks.

> The two boyfriends are permanent?

> Yes.

> Which means you're having sex with two men at the same time?

I groaned.

> Way to turn the convo awkward.

> Send me pics?

> Mom!

> Well, as long as you're happy and they're good to you and sticking around, I figure I should try to understand this whole thingy you've got going. It's more man than I could handle at once. I mean, how do you even do that?

> Mom!

> Don't get prissy now.

KEEP READING FOR A SNEAK PEEK OF ...

She posted the angel emoji.

> If you don't want to tell me, I'll go listen to that rich tattooed boy's audiobooks. He writes about threesomes and other racy stuff, right?

I couldn't believe I was discussing this with my mom.

> Yes. Ménage & more.

> Well, he must know what he's doing. Maybe I can pass on a few tips to your father.

She followed that with the smiling purple devil emoji.

> OMG! Mom! You're killing me.

> Hee-hee! Get used to questions. Your dad wants you to bring both guys here for Thanksgiving.

That surprised me. Dad usually kept out of my relationships. Then again, the last one with Tristan had turned into a train wreck. Maybe he thought he was heading off disaster by engaging early.

> He does?

> Yes, and so do I. We want to meet the men you've moved into your house so quickly.

> Part of it was convenience with Aithan being injured. And Drew still has his NYC apt.

> Uh-huh. So bring them. Greer may join us.

Huh? She never came up for Thanksgiving. *What the fuck?*

> She's coming home for Thanksgiving?

KEEP READING FOR A SNEAK PEEK OF ...

> Yes. I'll let you know when her plans are solid. I hope you'll still bring your guys, even if she is here.

> I'll discuss it with them. Thanks, Mom.

> Xoxoxo

Buy THE SKINNY

A NOTE ON POLISH SLANG

Wanna learn how to cuss in Polish like Aithan? Check out Reverso Context and LetsPolish online for usage and pronunciation.

THANK YOU

If you enjoyed this book, please consider recommending and reviewing it. Word of mouth is an indie author's best friend and much appreciated. And please take a moment to subscribe to my newsletter at monicarossromance.com. You'll be the first to hear about new releases, sales, and special events. Plus, all subscribers receive the *Fatkini* prequel, *Thick as a Brick*, for free.

Thanks!
Monica

ALSO BY MONICA ROSS

The Fatkini Chronicles

Thick as a Brick (prequel novella)

Fatkini

The Skinny

Thick and Thin

Thinly Veiled

Slim Fit

Thicker Than Water

Break

Speed Dating Series

Hot Lap

ABOUT THE AUTHOR

Like Zelda Gordon in the *Fatkini Chronicles*, I have Grave's disease (diagnosed in 1998) and I've struggled with my weight most of my life. Unlike Zelda, I don't have a harem of male friends and lovers. However, I do live in the Pacific Northwest with a teenager, three goofy cats, and a very supportive husband. When I'm not stirring up shit for my characters, I'm eating too many Autoimmune Protocol-compliant cookies and playing in the rain.

P.S. I also write romantic fantasy, fantasy romance, and (a little) romantic science fiction as Monica Enderle Pierce.

Printed in Dunstable, United Kingdom